The Beads of Lapis Lazuli

A Greek Mystery

The Beads Of Lapis Lazuli
A Greek Mystery

Outskirts Press, Inc.
http://www.outskirtspress.com

ISBN: 978-1-4327-6054-0

Library of Congress Control Number: 2010931361

Outskirts Press and the "OP" logo are trademarks belonging to Outskirts Press, Inc.

PRINTED IN THE UNITED STATES OF AMERICA

DEDICATION

To three remarkable women who lived
their lives embracing the principles of
loyalty, duty, honor, sacrifice, love,
and commitment as full-time
housewives and mothers.

Letha Burkhead Kenney
Emily South Burkhead
Florissa Young Kenney

ACKNOWLEDGEMENTS

Many interested family members and friends have waited so long for this little book to happen.

My dear friend Elisheva helped me plot, and enhanced my research with her knowledge of ancient religions and archeology. She taught me to rappel, made me Turkish coffee, and helped me find my way with laughter and empathy.

From the beginning, Kenneth encouraged me with kindness and love, and he and Patrick helped me win the battles with my computer as I learned a new way to write.

Joyce read for me, offered insightful suggestions and encouragement, and shared her knowledge of Greek history and mythology.

Karen, good friend, fellow sailor, and talented poet, read the manuscript with care and offered many valuable suggestions.

Although I can't thank them individually, I will never forget all the people who shared their life experiences with me and helped shape the characters in the story.

The best support of all, Edwin, the skipper of my life, my sailing companion through rough seas and calm waters, the person who has always believed I can do much more than I ever think I can, the person who encourages me to try to be the best that I can be,

Thank you

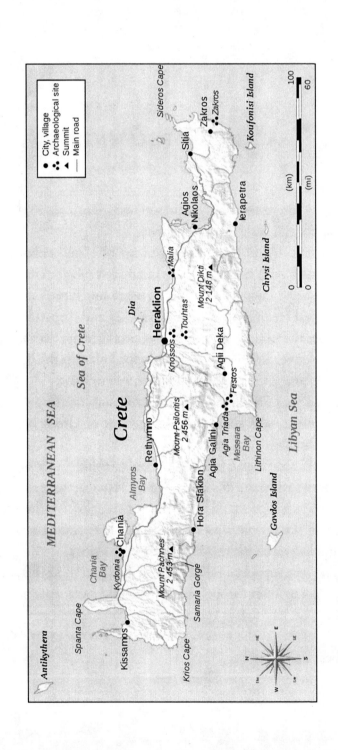

THE MYTH OF ARIADNE AND THESEUS
1435 BC

Princess Ariadne of Crete was a fair and holy maid.
Prince Theseus of Athens was handsome and brave.
He was one of nine hostages sent from Athens to Crete
to die in the Labyrinth as a sacrificial treat for the
Minotaur

Theseus swore to save the hostages if it cost him his life.
When Ariadne saw him, it was love at first sight.
A pact was made; Ariadne gave Theseus a token
to seal a bond that would never be broken.
Forever

Theseus escaped from the Labyrinth using Ariadne's thread.
He rescued the hostages and chopped off Minotaur's head.
The lovers sailed to Dia; Theseus sent Ariadne to shore.
He stayed with his ship to make all secure.
Trustworthy

The ship broke her moorings, swept away in a storm.
He never came back. Ariadne was lost and forlorn.
She waited and died all alone with her grief.
Brave Theseus died a hero, crowned King of the Greeks.
Justice?

How could Theseus desert Ariadne? She saved him his life.
He swore that he loved her, vowed to make her his wife.
Theseus was no hero. He was a liar and a cheat.
A man without honor, no better than a thief.
Retribution

CHAPTER ONE

THE PLAN

It was ten-fifteen Tuesday morning and I had a plan. I backed my station wagon out of the garage, made three right turns, and I would have pulled into my best friend Letty Marie's driveway, but it was blocked by a WanderWeed truck and a bare-chested body builder in skintight bib overalls.

The local WanderWeed man was treating Letty's lawn for the second time in less than a week. She mentioned something about an aggressive infestation of dandelions and wild violets which, in my opinion, are a gift from Mother Nature for enduring a long, drab winter without color.

I had to park half a block away, a minor irritation, but I was desperate for coffee, and Letty's kitchen was better than an upscale coffee house. No matter what time of day you walked through her door, the aroma of freshly brewed coffee wrapped around you like a warm hug…and I *really* needed a hug.

Huge mistake! I should have known better than to stop. Without even saying hello, Letty continued the argument that had begun over the phone earlier that morning.

"Why are you being so stubborn?" she asked without even looking at me.

"I need to finish my book and no matter what you say I won't force Dan to do something he clearly doesn't want to do."

"He'll come around if you handle him right."

"I don't want him to *come around*. There's no good reason

I can't go back to Crete, alone. I thought you of all people would understand. You're the most independent woman I've ever known."

It was becoming more and more difficult to accept Letty's lack of empathy. For years she had pushed me to be more assertive and now, suddenly, she was doing just the opposite.

"I've told you a thousand times, I need to see Dhia Island. I can't write about it until I walk the land."

"You're stalling. Who cares if it isn't absolutely accurate?"

"Thanks a lot for your support."

"Well, someone needs to be honest with you. You're just a housewife. You've been a stay-at-home mom for more years than I can count, and just because the newspaper printed a couple of your articles, you think publishers are going to erupt in a bidding frenzy over your first novel. I care about you, sweetie. You're setting yourself up for a big disappointment. You need to relax and enjoy your writing. It's a fine little hobby."

"It's not a hobby, and it's not about being published. It's about finding the truth."

I dumped a packet of sweetener in my mug and stirred so hard the coffee splashed over the rim onto the table.

Ignoring my obvious irritation, Letty leaned back in her chair and began to reorder my life.

"You're just bored. I think you should volunteer for something: join the Garden Club, play golf, play bridge, better still come to the Health Club and work out with me."

When she rambled on with half a dozen more suggestions, I tuned her out. I stared into the swirling brew in my mug, remembering how I used to relish all the brag stories she told about her victories in the high-stakes corporate world.

Interrupting her harangue I asked, "Do you ever think about our college days?"

"You mean how you quit school to marry Dan when you had only a year to go? It still ticks me off."

"No, I mean the women's lib marches, the sit-ins, the bra burnings. You used to drag me along to *make the act look big* you'd say when all I wanted was to marry Dan, have a home of my own, and make a family. You swore you'd never be wife to any man's house, but here you are...*Letty the Little Homemaker*. Whatever happened to all that propaganda you wrote canonizing the modern liberated woman?"

"Fed it to the garbage compactor."

"You compacted it? Why, that stuff was so caustic it could've eaten a hole right through the container. It was so abrasive you could've used it to remove the finish from your old hardwood floors." I expected an immediate reaction, but she didn't respond; she didn't laugh, or frown, or make some raunchy comeback like she normally would.

"Don't you miss your job?" I asked seriously. "Don't you miss the satisfaction of doing something really worthwhile? That must have been heady stuff. I'm surprised you could replace all that glory with pinch-pleated draperies, ringless toilets, and a dandelion-free, unnaturally perfect lawn. Speaking of lawns, what's with all the crabgrass control and lawn fertilizer? That Wander-Weed truck has been a permanent fixture on your front curb for the past two weeks."

Ignoring my lapse into nostalgia and dodging my question about weed control, she began loosening up for her Pilates class. With her face pressed against her outstretched leg she mumbled, "You need to wait for Dan."

Usually, I followed Letty's advice, easily convinced that

my opinions were worthless, but this time was different. With an unusual show of confidence, I leveled my eyes at Letty and said, "The main reason I stopped by is to tell you...since Dan can't interrupt his busy schedule I'm going back to Crete without him. I made a reservation at the Minoa Palace Hotel in Heraklion, I bought a plane ticket for the Island of Crete, I leave for Greece...three days from today."

Letty's chin dropped to her chest. Her shocked reaction was so out of character it took all the control I could muster to keep from laughing.

"What's the problem?" I asked solicitously, struggling to keep a serious tone. I reached over and gave the back of her hand a comforting pat. "It's just a business trip. It's not a big deal. You traveled all the time when you worked for DraCo. This is no different."

"What do you mean, it's no different? I wasn't married back then. Besides, I look like a business woman. When I wear my pinstriped suit and carry my black briefcase, I look intimidating. But you...my God, Kate, look at you! With your flippy brown hair, your healthy tanned cheeks, and those aw-ful buttoned-up little shirts you insist on wearing—you look like a kindergarten teacher."

"For your information, the way a person looks seldom re-veals who they really are, or what they're capable of doing. I'm strong enough to single-hand a nineteen-foot sailboat. I've sailed through storms that make strong men puke, yet, you're saying I can't travel alone unless I look like a Mafia Hit Mama. It's okay for a business woman to travel alone, but a housewife needs supervision. That's insulting."

"You know that's not what I mean. It's dangerous out there on your own. And to Greece? You've lost your perspective. You're blowing this whole writing thing out of proportion."

"Dammit, Letty, writing is not my *thing*. Writing is my work. Stop labeling me and trying to stick me into one of your designer shoe boxes."

Irked by Letty's selectively narrow attitude, I scooped up my mug, dumped the coffee down the drain, and looked for the dishwasher to stick it into.

"You moved it, again? Where's your dishwasher?" I had a real need to slam the door of Letty's new ultra quiet European dishwashing machine, but it was concealed somewhere behind a mass of new cabinet doors.

Setting the mug in the sink, I dropped back into the chair, stuck my legs out in front of me, crossed my arms, and nervously tapped the toes of my deck shoes together.

"Aren't we acting more than a little bitchy this morning?" Letty's snide remark was attached to a smirk, but the smirk instantly changed to a frown. "What's going on, Katie? You used to talk to me about everything, but lately you've become so…quiet."

"I talk to you all the time, but you're just like Dan. You never listen. What can't you understand? I have to go to Dhia Island and if Dan won't go with me then I'm going alone."

I reached for the strand of blue beads tucked inside the collar of my shirt and toyed with them, rolling them with my fingers, treating them as if they were a strand of Greek worry beads.

Letty raised one eyebrow, skepticism written on her face, and snapped, "And when was the last time you were on a deserted island, in a foreign country, alone? The answer is *never*. You've done a lot of traveling, but it's always been with

Dan. What if you get hurt? You don't speak the language and need I remind you that Greek men are the originators of machismo."

"That's not fair. The Greek men I've met have been courteous and respectful. Regardless, I won't be doing anything dangerous. I'll just be walking the island, looking for relics, pottery shards, something, anything that will help me solve the mystery surrounding the death of Princess Ariadne."

"You're not going to find a thing. The woman has been dead for thirty-five hundred years. Why can't you wait for Dan? You know it's his job to woo new clients for the firm."

"Sure it is. You want to know the real reason he cancelled the trip...again? He wants to go to Atlanta to play in a golf tournament. And that client he's supposed to be wooing? He's a sure thing. I've been waiting for over a year for him to find the time to go back to Crete. And, I'll still be waiting this time next year."

"You're being unreasonable. The firm needs new clients."

"Well, I need to finish my book. Dan thinks my life is about clean shirts, a neat house, meals, family, and crewing for him on his boats. You think my life should be about clubs and shopping. I'm disappointed in both of you. For your information, I don't need to be taken by the hand like some poor ignorant child to go on a lousy business trip. I can take care of myself. More to the point, I don't need a disinterested husband dragging along behind me when I'm trying to take care of business."

"You've never complained before."

"Jeezus, Letty! I'm not complaining. It's just...I'm finished waiting. I need to go back to Crete and it's not going to happen if I leave it up to Dan. Sooo...this morning I bought my plane ticket. I have my hotel reservation. I leave for Crete in three days."

I didn't need or want any more of Letty's advice and fortunately, before I could say something I might later regret, the alarm on my watch beeped.

"I need to go. I have an appointment at eleven. I just stopped for a quick cup of coffee."

"What kind of appointment?"

It was a simple question, but I wasn't sure I wanted to reveal any more of my plan.

It was okay when Letty was the audacious one, but for the first time since we became friends, I was the one moving outside my assigned role; I was disturbing the pecking order. At that moment I wondered what Letty's reaction would be if I told her exactly where I was going...so I did.

"If you must know, I'm going to Mt. Adams to talk to a psychic explorer."

"You're going to *what?*"

"Yesterday's paper had an article about a man who worked with a group of French archeologists on Crete; it said he helped them select a new place to excavate. The reporter referred to an article about psychic exploration in a Time-Life publication and I looked it up. Evidently, psychic exploration is an obscure, but legitimate, technique."

"You're going to consult a psychic. Are you crazy?"

"I'm trying to keep an open mind. I need help wherever I can find it."

"What do you know about this guy?"

"Do you remember Elisheva Tafal? She was in my archeology classes in college. Well, she's Dr. Tafal now, a forensic archeologist, and she's taking a sabbatical at Hebrew Union

College, doing research in their archives. I checked this guy out with her. She said he is legitimate and gave me his phone number. I called him this morning and he agreed to look at a chart of Dhia Island. He's going to select a place for me to begin my search. Hey, I gotta go. I'll call you later with all the juicy details."

"Kate…*KATIE!*"

"Later."

CHAPTER TWO
THE OLD ANTIQUE SHOP

D an said my writing was an obsession, but it would have been more accurate if he said I was *possessed* by an obsession.

For years, I had been writing in my spare time, mostly articles for the local newspapers: nothing anyone had ever gotten excited about, although I did have a byline once when I did an exposé about a gun show where vendors were selling pamphlets showing how to make incendiaries and explosive devices.

Writing articles kept me sane when my two kids were little, but it was always my dream to write something important, something that had real value. Then, unexpectedly, two years ago, I came up with an idea for a novel.

Dan and I had spent two weeks sailing a thirty-eight-foot Beneteau around the islands in the Greek Cyclades and I fell in love with Greece. At the end of our odyssey, I convinced Dan that we should squeeze in a land trip to the Greek island of Crete, and that's where I met a man, an old antique dealer, who sold me a very special strand of lapis lazuli beads. That's when the most unusual thing happened…the old man insisted that he knew me. He was positive we had met before, which was impossible. The whole encounter was so disturbing I couldn't forget it. Sometimes, I think that chance meeting may have changed my life.

Perhaps I should have begun my story with the old antique dealer, but I have always had great difficulty knowing at what point in time any story really begins. You would have to be clairvoyant to know which particular event had changed the course of your destiny,

As I said before, we arrived in Crete after spending two weeks living on a sailboat, continually faced with challenging situations. It felt really good to be on dry land, with a firm base under my feet instead of a rolling deck.

After we checked into the hotel, Dan wanted to relax and watch a soccer game on TV. However, watching television was the last thing I wanted to do. My goal was to buy tickets to visit as many Minoan archeological sites as we could manage during our short stay on the island. Archeology had been my major in college and would always be my second love. After wandering through the ruins on so many of the Greek islands, and seeing the stones of Mycenae on the Greek mainland, I was hungry for more ancient mysteries.

I took a taxi into the heart of Heraklion, the capital of Crete, bought a fistful of tour tickets, but instead of going back to the hotel to watch the soccer game with Dan, I wandered into a part of the city known as *Old Town*.

The burning Cretan sun had turned concrete and stone into a gigantic oven hot enough to bake *baklava* on the walkways. As in Spain, many of the Greek shops had closed for siesta and I needed a glass of something cool to drink. I saw a *taverna* across the square with several empty tables under a canopy of tall shade trees. It would be the perfect place to relax, slow down, and enjoy the easy island pace.

I turned to check the traffic before crossing the street, and caught a bright flash of light out of the corner of my eye. After spending two weeks navigating unfamiliar harbors, the flash reminded me of a channel marker showing safe pas-

sage through shallow water. I looked for the source; it was the sunlight bouncing off a diamond-shaped pane in a shop window at the far end of a narrow alleyway.

Many people would have ignored the incident, but since I'm a great believer in synchronicity, when the bony finger of fate beckons I'm usually willing to change course and investigate.

Using the last of my flagging energy, I walked down the lane to see if some rare and precious thing was calling me saying, "Come look in my window."

A weathered sign painted over the door read *Antiques and Souvenirs*, and I held my breath as I approached the display. I wanted with all my heart to see something more than the usual Minoan pottery and tarnished silver jewelry, and I was not disappointed.

A tiny statue of a bare-breasted Cretan Goddess of Snakes stood in the center of the display. Draped across her arms was the most amazing strand of lapis lazuli beads I had ever seen. The statue itself was an excellent reproduction, but the beads were exceptional. Worn smooth from wear, they were a shade of blue so deep, so vivid, they seemed to glow from within. The color was so intense, the stones could have been magically formed from a mixture of blue sea, blue flowers, and blue sky. To add to their beauty, they were flecked with tiny nuggets of gold and slender golden threads that looked like long-tailed comets streaking across a nighttime sky.

Dramatic jewelry doesn't usually interest me: I rarely wear more than earrings and a watch. However, the beads were such a vibrant shade of blue, even before I entered the shop, if I didn't have to mortgage my soul I knew that both the beads and the little Goddess of Snakes would soon be mine.

The resistant shop door needed a nudge with my foot. When it released its hold on the threshold I heard a bell tinkle somewhere in the distance.

Inside the dimly lit room, the air was pleasantly cool. I felt as if I had stepped into another age, one that smelled of dust, and anise, and twice-boiled coffee. I also felt the need to walk softly for fear a squeaking board might disturb an angry ghost who may not have willingly parted with his treasures.

The room was filled with long tables piled high with statues, tapestries and rugs, brass bowls, pots, and platters, and saddlebag covers woven in patterns of red and black and orange. Most things looked old, but a few things looked new. A rack of tired-looking Cretan costumes stood in one corner and religious icons, dark and austere, clung to the smoke-colored walls. Only one other person was in the shop; an elderly man sat on a tall stool behind a glass-topped counter.

Dressed in the traditional Cretan style, he wore a collarless white shirt with blousy sleeves, a black vest embroidered with heavy black braid, and a cap that was perched at a rakish angle on the side of his head. Heavy brows, grizzled hair, scruffy beard, and deep creases on his face revealed his advanced age. He greeted me with a nod of his head and a stiff sweep of his hand that offered the whole shop for sale.

"Do you speak English?" I asked hopefully.

"English? *YES!*"

He answered with amazing gusto. Considering his age, I was surprised by the strength in his gravelly voice. I was also puzzled by the sudden mischievous glow in his weak brown eyes.

"The blue beads in the window…are they for sale?" I asked.

"Yes! I have blue beads."

With slow deliberation, he pushed a rack of blue beads in front of me. To be polite I fingered them, lifting one strand, then another, testing their weight to see if they were made of plastic. They appeared to be stone, but they were not the same vibrant color as the ones in the display.

"Nice," I said, "but could I see the strand of blue beads in your front window?"

"You have been here before, I think." His English was excellent with only a slight accent, and he stared at me expectantly.

"No, this is my first visit to Crete. The blue beads…the ones in the window…are they for sale?"

"Of course." He gave an indifferent shrug and stood slowly. He took two steps, parted a wine-colored velvet curtain on a brass rod, lifted the tiny goddess with the blue beads still draped over her arms, and stood her on the counter between us.

Carefully, he removed the necklace from the statue's tiny arms and handed it to me curled like a blue garter snake on the palm of his hand. When I reached for the stones, the back of my finger lightly brushed his skin and a *snap* of electricity bit me like a bug. I jerked my hand away, but the old man ignored the sting and gently laid the strand of blue beads across my forearm.

"Pretty beads," he whispered. "Very, very old. Genuine lapis lazuli."

Although we were barely two feet apart, he leaned forward slightly, tilted his head, and stared at me with an intensity that would have been rude back in the States. However, I was not offended. After visiting some of the remote islands scattered around the Aegean Sea, I had learned from experience that Greek men often stare boldly at foreign-looking women. It was obvious that I was not a native: I couldn't speak the language, the timbre of my voice was much lower than most of the Greek women I heard in the market place, and my brown hair and green eyes and casual dress were an additional confirmation.

An obstinate look of disbelief tightened the muscles in the old man's jaw. He shook his head, sat back down on his stool, and declared firmly, "I know you. You have been here before. Many years ago, I think. Maybe with your mother… or your grandmother."

"I wish that were true, but no one in my family has ever been to the island of Crete, or anywhere else in Greece."

"Strange," he muttered.

Although his face softened a bit, I knew he still didn't believe me. Instead of arguing, he turned his head and growled over his shoulder, "Nikko!"

A young boy carrying a short-handled broom walked out of the shadows.

"Make coffee. We must drink coffee while madam considers the beauty of these rare blue stones."

It was clear that he would not discuss selling the beads until after we drank the coffee, so I sipped the thick, sweet elixir in its doll-sized cup while he spoke about the age of the beads. He rambled on about ancient Crete, Kriti as it was pronounced in Greece, when the island was known as Kaphtor, and his people were called the Kephti.

I enjoyed listening to him talk about Crete's history. He was obviously an historian, actually a pre-historian considering the Minoan time-frame. When he confirmed my own belief that the Minoan society had been a matriarchy, I felt a warm flush of satisfaction.

"Where did you learn to speak English so well, if I may ask?"

"I learned your language from a trader who stayed with my family when I was a boy. Then, for a short time, I taught Greek mythology at a small school just outside of London."

That's when I knew it wasn't just the beads that had drawn me to the shop; it was the old man and his knowledge of the ancient Minoans. He could probably answer my questions about Theseus and Ariadne. He might know things about the legends surrounding the lost Minoan civilization that no one else knew. And, odd as it seemed, he had just reaffirmed my belief in the mystical laws of fortunate coincidence.

"I, too, am interested in mythology," I said, "especially the myth of Theseus and Ariadne. I'm searching for more information about the story, especially the ending. Do you know anything about her: about Ariadne? Other than the myth, as famous as she was, her life is shrouded in mystery. The main reason I wanted to visit Crete was to see where she lived. I felt the need to walk through the ruins of Knossos Palace."

"Ahhhh, the little golden princess. Many come to Kriti to search for her."

"I've tried to learn more about her, but she is an enigma. She was one of the world's great heroines. Except for the myth about her love affair with Theseus, everything else about her has been forgotten, or erased. The whole world knows Theseus. Even today, he is honored as a Greek hero but I think he was a coward. No decent man would ever abandon a remarkable woman like Ariadne, especially when she sacrificed everything she held dear to save his life."

From the surprised look on the old man's face, I realized that I had just insulted him, every citizen on Crete, plus the whole nation of Greece.

"Please. *Please,* forgive me. I am so sorry. Sometimes, I speak without thinking. I intended no disrespect to you or your people."

"No need to apologize to me. Theseus was no relation of mine. I'm no God-damned Greek. I'm a true son of Kriti."

"Thank you. Truly, I meant no offense."

"Obviously, the story of Ariadne fills you with intense emotion…and I know why. The myth is a factual account of events that happened many thousands of years ago. Some of the myths have been passed down to remember the exploits of extraordinary human beings who were not gods or goddesses. The myth of Ariadne and Theseus is a true story of love that reaches out and touches the heart of every person who hears it. Anyone who loves another human being and suffers the pain of abandonment can relate to Ariadne's story; it transcends time and place."

The old man had used his hands to emphasize his words… broad gestures, pointing fingers, and sweeping arms.

"Hundreds of writers and composers have been inspired to retell Ariadne's story because each character in the tale represents a basic human emotion. They loved…they bled… they suffered." When he finished his passionate speech, he leaned forward, looked deep into my eyes, and his voice dropped to a sultry growl. "Just like you…just like me."

Although I was extremely uncomfortable with the probing intimacy in his gaze, I felt compelled to disagree.

"The myth can't be a true story. What about the bull-headed monster, Minotaur? He had to be a mythical creature. No woman could mate with a bull and live, and no child could have been born with the head of a bull and the body of a man."

"True. Minotaur may have behaved like a monster, but he was an ordinary man, an evil man, who wore the head of a bull to frighten the people."

"Do you know what destroyed the old culture on Crete? I know there were earthquakes and there was that massive volcanic explosion on Santorini, but was there something else? And even more important, were Crete and Santorini the source of the Atlantis legend? Does the myth of Ariadne and Theseus tell the truth about the Minoan people, or is it a lie?"

"Truth? Whose truth? Yours? Mine? It would take a magician to find the path through the labyrinth that conceals the true story of our little golden princess and her handsome Athenian prince. As for tales of Atlantis, I think only the gods and goddesses know the answer to that question."

The old man's hands were shaking so hard, he had to use two hands to steady his cup. His shoulders were still arrow straight, but most of the intensity had left his eyes. I felt I had pressed him too much with my questions.

We bargained over the price of the beads and the statue, and he seemed well pleased when we reached an agreement. While I tied the blue stones strung on a thin leather thong around my neck, he wrapped the statue of the Snake Goddess in a sheet of pretty flowered paper.

We shook hands when we parted and his skin felt as thin and brittle as parchment. He seemed extremely frail...and yet...for one brief moment that mischievous glow returned to his eyes and his voice once again dropped to a throaty whisper.

"The old ones say that the last woman to wear these precious blue beads of lapis lazuli was High Priestess to the Holy Earth Mother when Kriti was Kaphtor and my people were the Kephti. If these blue stones could speak, they would tell you unbelievable stories about the ancient mysteries. Perhaps, if you wear them next to your skin, your dreams will bring you the truth that you seek."

CHAPTER THREE

A PSYCHIC EXPLORER

After we returned home from Greece, I spent the next two years doing research, finding every scrap of information I could about Ariadne and the mysterious lost Minoan civilization. It was like assembling the shards of a broken jug to form a whole, and now all of the disparate bits of information were in place. My novel was finished, except for one vital piece of information that would plug the last hole in the story. However. If I could not find that one missing piece, I would be left with two choices: I could end the story the same way most writers, composers, and poets had done for four thousand years, or I could make up a different, more plausible, ending that I could never prove. I felt that both solutions were lazy lies of convenience. Neither one was acceptable to me. My only other option was to find the truth.

Although every other version of Ariadne's story said she died on Dia Island (modern-day Naxos), I felt in my bones that it was a lie. I believed the answer to this conundrum was hidden on Dhia Island, a tiny chunk of rock and sand just off the northern coast of Crete. During the first year of my research, I confused Dhia Island with the Dia Island in the Ariadne myth. Even today, on some charts and maps, cartographers identify Dhia Island as Dia; it's no wonder I made the mistake. Although Dhia off the coast of Crete was not the place where most mythologists say Ariadne died, I was convinced that it was the place where I should search for the truth. And no matter what anyone said, I was going back to Crete to pursue my ethical responsibilities as a serious writer.

For two long years, I had been tormented by an unrelenting need to find out what really happened to Ariadne. Letty said I was crazy for consulting a man who claimed to be psychic, but if he could help me choose a place to begin my search, I was willing to listen to whatever he had to say.

ψ

It took less than thirty minutes to reach Mt. Adams: one of the seven hills in greater Cincinnati. The Mount, as it's fondly called, is an old and artsy neighborhood filled with condos, restaurants, boutiques, art galleries, and office buildings.

Driving slowly through the narrow streets, I passed a row of renovated storefronts, a neighborhood bar, a boutique, and a single-wide shotgun house covered with new cedar shakes. When I finally found the house number Deupree had given me over the phone, I nearly drove past without stopping.

I had wrongly assumed that Deupree's office would be in one of the old office buildings, however, the number he'd given me over the phone was nailed to a down-and-out derelict, a faded old Victorian that had once been an elegant lady. Now, except for new windows of mirrored glass, the place looked one day short of being condemned.

Thoroughly disheartened, I pulled to the curb and sat for several minutes, deciding if I should climb those sagging steps, or turn around and go home. It was not an easy decision to make. One thing I knew for sure…if I could not find the courage to face this simple unknown, my search for the truth surrounding the myth of Ariadne and Theseus would end in failure. Like it or not, with his knowledge of Crete and his alleged ability to select archeological sites, Psychic Explorer Jake Deupree was the only navigator in sight.

As I walked up the steps, I was thankful that Letty wasn't with me. I could imagine what her reaction would be to a house that could be a haunted mansion dressed for Halloween.

The only reason I was here was because I was desperate. Without this man's help, I could walk for days on the island and never learn a thing. Deupree might be a charlatan, but I had nowhere else to go for directions. If I had any other option, I would never have turned to a stranger with such unorthodox credentials for help. But when I used Google Earth to look at Dhia Island, it added an additional challenge to my search. It showed a place that was bleak and so littered with stones it would be difficult to walk the land; it would be nearly impossible to find something of importance.

Pushing my uneasiness aside, I followed Deupree's directions and turned the car into the vacant lot on the west side of the house. Rolling over weed-clogged gravel, I pulled in next to a black, Corvette Z06 convertible. Parked beside the low-slung sports car, my ancient station wagon, a relic of my carpool days, looked dowdy and old.

Nothing moved around the house—no bird, no cat, no dog and I wondered if the absence of life was an omen foretelling dire things to come. My apprehension was largely the result of seeing way too many horror movies.

A tarnished brass sign nailed over the door read,

FORTUNES UNLIMITED, and a water-stained card taped beneath the doorbell said, *One Ring is Enough*. So, obedient person that I am, I gave the dirty ivory button one firm push and listened.

There was no ring-a-ding, no cascading ripple of chimes and I fidgeted, listening for the sound of footsteps, waiting for the doorknob to turn. Barely breathing, thinking, *God, I need to pee*, I wiped my sweaty palms on my jeans and realized that I had forgotten to change my clothes.

I had been in such a hurry to leave, I was still wearing yesterday's jeans. There was a stain on my right knee where I knelt to pull a few weeds from the flowerbeds that morning.

"Who cares?" I muttered. But I did scratch at a dirty streak with my fingernail, and flicked a small clod of mud off the toe of my deck shoe.

"I didn't come here to impress anyone."

I said the words loud enough to be heard by anyone who might be listening on the other side of the door. At that moment, if my friend Elisheva hadn't praised Deupree's abilities, mentioning a few of his more important discoveries, I would have turned around and walked back to my car.

Finally, the knob began a slow-motion turn and it took as much courage to stand before that battered door as it took to sail toward a great black squall. It would have helped if I had someone to go with me into this frightful place, but there was no one. This was a passage I had to make, alone.

The door opened and when I saw the pleasant face of a fairly ordinary-looking man, I felt an immediate sense of relief.

"Hi. I'm Jake Deupree," he stuck out his hand, firm and callused, and gave me a vigorous handshake. "You must be

Kathryn Marshall. Come on in."

Like a magician opening a cape, he pulled the door wide and released the most delectable fragrance of fresh baked bread I had ever smelled. Also, wafting along on that deliciously scented air I could hear the faint sound of panpipes playing somewhere in the distance. Oddly enough, it reminded me of the tinkling bell in the old antique store on Crete.

Feeling slightly disoriented, I stumbled as I stepped over the sill. I had expected to be greeted by the stale odor of damp-rot and mold, but there was only that delicious aroma of fresh baked bread. I was a little less apprehensive, although I was still cautiously alert.

Concerned about what might be waiting inside, I stole a curious peek past Deupree and once again I was taken by surprise.

White couches and white chairs, overstuffed and casual, were scattered around a large room to the right of the entry. Clusters of paintings created rich splashes of color against dark paneled walls. The pegged wood floors were covered with oriental rugs so luxurious I knew that if I could dig my bare toes into them they would feel soft and warm. The whole room was a kaleidoscope of colors, shapes, and textures that created a beautifully complex design.

Before Deupree closed the door behind me, I looked back at the rotting boards on the porch, the unkempt yard, the flaking paint on the siding. It was obvious that the outside of the house was a ruse intended to deceive. I probably should have felt duped, but instead of feeling like a victim of subterfuge, I smiled. It was like seeing a beautiful butterfly emerge from an ugly gray cocoon, and the experience made me feel more optimistic than I had in days.

Deupree graciously invited me to follow him to his office in the rear of his home. I managed to push my nervousness aside and I walked a few paces behind him. However, my senses were still alert to the slightest hint of danger.

When we entered the next room, my eyes were immediately drawn up to a ballroom-sized chandelier suspended from the center of a skylight two stories above my head.

Radiant with light, the lamp was ablaze with a thousand sparkling crystals, each facet reflecting rainbows of color. The glittering creation illuminated the most unusual room I had ever seen. Asymmetrical in shape, the ceiling and the floor of the space above had been whittled away until only a narrow balcony rimmed the upper level of the room. Accessed by a spidery flight of steps, the loft was completely lined with shelves that were crammed full of books, books, and more books. An incredible library crowned the room like a multicolored tiara.

I turned, and turned again, taking in the wonder of so much knowledge stored in such an unlikely place.

"Please, come this way. My office is just off the kitchen."

Still sedated by the fragrance of the bread and mesmerized by the power and beauty of the room, I followed Deupree's voice. From the pleased expression on his face he appeared to be enjoying my candid appreciation of his treasures as if seeing them again for the first time through my eyes.

A wall of windows at the far end of the library offered a sweeping view of the Ohio River and the rolling Kentucky hills beyond. A black marble fireplace anchored one corner, and in the center, directly beneath the chandelier, an enormous amethyst geode was displayed on a clear glass pedestal. It could have been a giant dinosaur egg with half the shell broken away. Inside, a miniature grotto bristled with crystalline spikes of purple and lavender, each one juxtaposed at odd angles that flashed like swords frozen in a battle with time.

In another corner, a grand piano sat on a raised platform surrounded by stacks of audio equipment and towers filled with CDs. The rest of the room was tastefully furnished with antique clocks, candles, and flowers. A pile of floor pillows covered in exotic Indian prints brought a touch of softness to the room.

"Please, excuse my messy kitchen. This is baking day."

The source of the homey aroma that greeted me at the door was rising from four perfect loaves of crusty French bread that had been set to cool on top of a masculine-looking gas range, all black and chrome.

Deupree removed his striped apron, tossed it on a coat rack outside the office door, and motioned for me to take a seat in a gently used, brown leather Morris chair. For the moment, he busied himself behind his desk, which was good since it gave me time to take a closer look at Mr. Deupree.

With a title like *Psychic Explorer*, I had come prepared to meet a hollow-cheeked Dracula, or maybe a wild-eyed voodoo priest carrying a skull on a stick. However, Deupree was neither of those things. Plainly dressed in tan chinos and a faded blue short-sleeved shirt, instead of carrying a skull on a stick, he held a stack of papers he had just removed from his fax machine.

However, Deupree would never be considered ordinary.

He was a head taller than me. His black hair was long, very long, and touched with gray at the temples. He had pulled it straight back from his face and it ended in a ponytail wrapped with a narrow leather band which made it look like a big, fat Cuban cigar hanging down the center of his back.

There was a sizable hole in his left earlobe, the skin on his arms and face looked naturally tanned, and I could see just the bottom part of a tattoo on his left bicep that looked like the claws of a bird.

Considering his dark skin, he could be Mexican, or Native American, or maybe he was a Romanian Gypsy who read Tarot cards for a living. My eyes moved back to his face and his mouth was spread in a big, wide grin. He looked as if he knew everything I had been thinking about him and found me amusing.

My temper instantly flared. The one thing I could never stand was being laughed at and his *attitude* hit a raw spot in my ego which lately had become hyper-sensitive to even the slightest hint of ridicule.

Stay cool, I cautioned myself, and from habit I reached inside the open neck of my shirt, my little buttoned-up shirt that Letty had mocked, and fingered my strand of blue lapis beads, rubbing them like a talisman. I thought, *Can't leave yet. Not until I have what I came for,* and the calming words of reason smothered the childish flames of indignation well enough for me to meet Deupree's wide, toothy grin with a small, tight smile.

Never before had I felt such immediate hostility toward anyone. But, at the same time I also felt an unexpected sense of relief that Deupree was not handsome. He wasn't ugly— his nose and chin were strong and his face looked used by sun, or worry, or laughter—but it never occurred to me until that moment that a handsome man would have been very difficult to deal with when I felt so painfully insecure.

Returning to the business at hand, Deupree continued to make me wait while he shuffled through his papers, which was fine with me. It gave me additional time to look at my surroundings. I hoped to see something to confirm his legitimacy, anything that might validate the integrity of the man.

Unlike the rest of the house, his office was small and unimpressive: a windowless room with plain white walls and bare wood floors littered with piles of geological survey maps, charts, pictures of drilling rigs, drawings and layouts of excavation sites. His L-shaped desk held a year's worth of clutter, two computer monitors, a printer, *three* telephones, and of course one of them was red.

The long wall behind me was lined with museum-style glass cases filled with Indian Kachina dolls, wands, and masks, and dozens of sinister-looking artifacts. Hanging behind his desk, dominating the room, was a poster-sized sepia photograph of a group of Australian Aborigines dressed in nothing but feathers, paint, and bones. The middle-man in the portrait was a clearly recognizable, fiercely painted, and sparsely feathered Jake Deupree. A large bone sticking through his left earlobe explained the oversized hole.

"Coffee?"

Without waiting for my answer, he reached for a pot on a cart beside his desk, poured the steaming brew into two mugs, and added a generous slosh of cream.

"Now. Let's have a look at that chart you're holding so close to your chest."

Just as he pulled the roll of heavy paper from the tube, the red telephone rang. He picked it up and snapped, "Deupree."

Holding the receiver between his shoulder and chin, he continued to unroll the chart and then exploded with, "The *HELL* you say!" and the chart flew back into a tube.

He poked it into my hands and shouted, "I told you to sell, yesterday." He yelled something more with a few expletives added, dropped down into his desk chair, and brought up a computer display that looked like stock market quotations.

"You are one lucky son of a bitch. You can still triple your investment, unless you want the write-off. Well? What did I tell you? Do it right this time! Yeah...later."

He reached again for my chart, but this time, even before he could take it from my hand, one of the black phones rang. After listening for only a few seconds he growled, "No, madam, I do not read tea leaves."

He rammed the phone back into the charger and cursed the being who would suggest he do such a despicable thing and I had to look away. I couldn't keep from grinning, and from the scowl he threw me it was evident that he, too, had a low tolerance for ridicule.

"These phones won't leave me alone. We'd better go down to the workroom."

He stood up, pushed several buttons on the consoles, and motioned for me to follow him toward an ornately carved oak door that until we crossed the room had been concealed behind a row of tall file cabinets.

I rolled my eyes in disbelief and braced myself for the monstrous door to creak and groan, but it didn't...the heavy hinges were well oiled and silent. Once again, I followed Deupree at a distance as he led the way down a long, dark flight of stairs.

Keeping a firm grip on the railing, I slid my free hand down the opposing cellar wall for additional support. Feeling rough stones, instead of smooth concrete, told me that the house was as old as it looked: one of the originals built back in the 1800s.

"I haven't lived here long," he said. "I recently inherited the house from my great grandfather. He was a gold prospector—a stingy ol' coot who never felt the need to install wall switches in this part of the house. Wait there while I go down and turn on a light."

The suggestion was totally unnecessary. Nothing could have persuaded me to take one more step toward that black pool of darkness waiting at the foot of the stairs.

CHAPTER FOUR

THE BEADS OF LAPIS LAZULI

Standing on a step halfway down the stairs, cool air laced with the scent of incense and warm candle wax brushed across my face and swirled around my bare arms. Feeling more than a little apprehensive, I turned and looked back up the steps toward the open door. As long as I could see a way out, I would hold my course.

When Deupree switched on a green shaded lamp hanging over a round table set with four captain's chairs, the atmosphere changed; it felt much less foreboding. The light would be perfect for looking at the chart but the rest of the room was still concealed in shadows.

"Hand me a couple of those jars sitting on top of the chest. I'll use them as weights to keep the chart from curling back into a tube."

Always good crew, I was used to taking orders. I found the jars setting on a chest with dozens of small drawers labeled with Aramaic symbols and Latinate words. More jars were stacked behind an apothecary scale piled high with twigs and dried herbs.

Seeing the scales, mortar and pestle, odd bottles and herbs conjured images of Merlin preparing gaseous magic potions in a dark laboratory hidden deep in the bowels of the earth.

Stop it! I put a lock on my imagination, and without comment passed Deupree several of the glass containers filled with shriveled black things. However, I couldn't keep from wiping my fingers on my jeans.

"Lizard tongues, or maybe bat's wings...it's hard to tell 'em apart." Deupree's voice was serious, but there was a suspicious glint in his eyes. He was mocking me and I deserved it. My overactive imagination had hooked me again, and it took a stern jerk to pull my thoughts back to the problem that had led me to seek the advice of this unusual man.

"That's mainland Greece," I said, leaning over the chart. "There's Crete. And that's Dhia Island just off the northern coast. *That's* the place I need to see," and I tapped the island with my finger. "I'm going to Crete the end of this week especially to see the Island. I need to walk the land. The problem is...although Dhia is small, there's no way I can search the whole thing in the short amount of time that I'll be there. It would really help if I knew where to begin. I was hoping you might have been there, since the article in the paper said you worked on Crete with both American and French archeologists."

"Nope. Never been there. Never had any reason."

Deupree motioned for me to sit down opposite him. He bent over the chart and inspected the dot of land with a magnifying glass. Then he covered the tiny island with his bare palm, hovering over the image, slowly passing his hand back and forth as if he was trying to sense it through his skin.

"Something *is* there," he said with a slight nod of his head.

Slowly, he eased down into his chair and pushed the air from his lungs in a long, soft whistle. With closed eyes, he seemed to will his body to relax, and as I watched, the color faded from his face, leaving his skin as pale as ash.

He sat motionless for a very long minute, and when he

opened his eyes they were no longer light gray. The irises had been reduced to thin silver rings and his pupils looked like deep holes filled with black oil they were so dilated. The dramatic change was unsettling, but the most disturbing thing of all…those great black orbs were focused on my chest as if he could penetrate cloth, flesh, and bone and see my rapidly beating heart.

Then, without warning, and with the dexterity of a jewel thief, Deupree lifted my strand of blue beads from where they lay partially exposed inside the open neck of my shirt. He lifted the stones possessively, rolling them slowly over his fingers, focusing on them as if they were specimens under a microscope.

I swallowed hard and tried not to move, but it was impossible. I had to resist the man and his hand, but the beads held me like a yoke, and the more I pulled away from him the more the tension between us increased.

Ignoring my obvious distress, Deupree rubbed one of the stones between his thumb and forefinger, turned it to the light, and again reached for his magnifying glass. He examined the blue bead with great care. The whole time he was evaluating the stones, the crudely polished edges of the beads were digging holes in the back of my neck, and the more I resisted his pull the greater the pain.

At that point, we were sitting nose to nose, so close I could smell garlic on his breath.

"Where did you get these blue beads?" he demanded, giving the necklace a slight tug as if to force me to speak.

"Greece…two years ago…in an antique shop on Crete. The old man who sold them to me said they were thousands of years old. He swore they were genuine lapis lazuli, but they couldn't be…they were too cheap."

"The stones are real lapis and they are very, *very* old."

Fed up with his strong-arm approach, I twisted painfully.

"Let go! You're hurting me!" Just as I reached up to pull the stones from his hand, he released them. His eyes had returned to normal, but a deep frown seemed to crease his whole face.

"How can you tolerate those stones against your bare skin? Don't you feel their energy?"

I massaged the back of my neck and tried to calm my racing heart. At this point, I was more annoyed with the man than afraid. As eccentric as he seemed, I still needed his help for without it I was no better off than before I came to this spooky place.

"Forget about my beads!" I said. "I came here to find out about Dhia Island."

"Don't you know the two are inseparable?"

"You don't know that. How do you know that?"

"If you're going to doubt what I say, then maybe you should find someone who can read tea leaves."

Now, he was being as rude as he had been over the phone when he tried to brush me off by telling me he would charge me a hundred dollars to do a reading of the island. Since I had taken him up on his offer, it was time for him to do his *thing*, whatever his *thing* might be. Like a poker player placing a bet, I pulled a rumpled wad of bills from my pocket and slapped them down in the middle of the chart.

Dan was going to be upset when I told him I spent grocery money to get a psychic reading of Dhia, but I had paid Deupree's price, now it was his turn to play the game.

Grimacing slightly, he once again willed his body to relax.

This time, instead of looking at the chart, he focused on a spot in the middle of my forehead...a place just above and between my eyes.

"*The beads...tell the tale.*" He spoke softly, but his deep voice resonated with such a prophetic timbre a platoon of goose bumps marched up my arms and across my shoulders.

"*Treasure is not all you seek...that...for which you have searched so long...will soon be within your reach.*"

Deupree fell back against his chair, coughed slightly, and passed his hand over his face.

Now...I was afraid.

He looked exhausted, completely drained of energy, and he spoke in a hoarse whisper, "You may as well tell me all of it."

"Why can't you just do what I ask? Tell me where to begin my search on Dhia Island."

Instead of answering, he looked at me with a mulish stare. He would use silence to force me to speak.

"All right. What haven't you already guessed? I'm a middle-aged housewife. My children have left the nest. I'm pre-menopausal and I'm bored. I'm trying to add a little excitement to my life."

I watched him with the cold eyes of a tiger, and from the uncomfortable look on his face I knew I had accurately described his view of me. Only minutes before, he had guessed what I was thinking about him; now I had correctly guessed what he was thinking about me. I knew he would label me the second he heard my inane babbling over the phone that morning.

I should get up and leave, I thought. *But if I do, where will I go? There is no one else I can turn to for help.*

My children, bless them, encouraged me to explore, but no one else in my circle of friends and relations understood my obsession with finding the truth and finishing my book… not my husband, not my best friend, certainly not my mother. None of them understood my reason for wanting to go to Dhia Island and I was tired. I was tired of defending my passion for finding the secret locked inside the myth of Theseus and Ariadne. I couldn't control the awful, driving need to know the true ending to one of the world's oldest love stories. The feeling that I must find the truth had become so intense it was a physical torment, always there, just beneath the surface, unrelenting, never giving me any peace.

Sensing the pain behind my eyes, Deupree lowered his steepled fingers, and this time his voice was more sincere.

"Look. If you want me to help you, I need to know your real reason for going to Dhia Island. I must know everything, every detail."

"It's a long story. You wouldn't be interested." Past experiences with my critics made me doubt that he seriously wanted more information.

Deupree smiled a crooked smile that seemed genuinely warm and encouraging and said, "I like a good story. I'll get us some more coffee. I have plenty of time to listen. Nothing else scheduled for today."

While he went back up the stairs, I sat with my eyes closed, hanging on to my blue beads with both hands. Unless I told Deupree the whole story surrounding my quest, I might as well roll up my chart and go home. I sighed. The telling would not be easy.

CHAPTER FIVE

REINCARNATION

Deupree returned with the two mugs of coffee. I cradled the hot cup between my hands and wondered how many times a warm cup of coffee was the only real comfort I could depend on in my ordinary, everyday life.

"Do you know anything about Greek mythology?" I asked.

"Geology is my specialty, but I know some of the Greek legends. I'm aware of most of the myths that mention Crete. It's a fascinating subject."

"Two years ago, before my husband and I went to Greece for a sailing holiday, I read Greek history and mythology. I was intrigued by the myth of Theseus and Ariadne, especially the stories about Ariadne and her people. Hoping to satisfy my curiosity, on our way home we took a brief side-trip to Crete. As we toured the island, I felt even more drawn to the remains of the old culture that once flourished there with such elegance and grace."

"You're talking about the ancient Minoans?"

"Yes. I came home from our holiday determined to raise the dead. I wanted to write a novel that would bring Princess Ariadne, the Minoan people, and their exotic culture back to life. Now, after two years of research, I've solved many of the mysteries surrounding that lost civilization. My book is finished except for the last chapter, and unless I can solve the four-thousand-year-old mystery surrounding Ariadne's death, I may as well throw the whole thing in the trash."

"How does Dhia Island fit into the picture?"

"The traditional telling of the myth says that Ariadne was abandoned by Theseus and she died, betrayed and alone."

"I know that part of the myth. It reads like a soap opera: a typical love 'em and leave 'em saga if you ask me."

"Right. The problem is that if you look at it logically, it doesn't make sense. Why would a hero, a man honored for his courage and compassion, break a sacred vow to the woman who gave up everything to save his life? What would make him behave like a cowardly thief? And why would the proud Greeks still honor him as a hero, the savior of the weak and downtrodden?"

"You believe the answers are somewhere on Dhia Island?"

"Yes. My biggest problem is that I'm drawn to the wrong island. The legend says that Ariadne was stranded on Dia, not *Dhia*. However, it's Dhia Island that haunts me, and this driving need to go there and search has become so demanding it's a physical pain. I haven't said anything to anyone else, but the feeling has become so intense I can't concentrate. I haven't been able to write any new material for weeks. I can only rewrite: going over the same words again and again and this need to know is with me day and night. I can't rest. I can't sleep. I must find some kind of peace."

One of my hands was pressed over my aching heart, and the other twisted my ever-present beads of lapis lazuli.

"One last thing." I paused and drew a ragged breath. "I'm not a mythologist. I'm not even a legitimate archeologist, but I *know* things about the Minoan people…people who have been dead for thousands of years. And I knew intimate details of their daily lives even before I began the research.

Now that's crazy."

"Hogwash! Insights stranger than that happen to writers and artists all the time. It also happens to research scientists, although they don't always admit it."

"Well, I don't like it."

"Could be a flashback. Reincarnation. Have you ever been led through a past life regression?"

"No!"

My eyes instantly filled with distrust. My whole body grew taut as a sprung willow tree. I had been lulled by Deupree's seeming sincerity. I had forgotten that he was a professional mind-bender and, like a gullible fool, I had been confiding in him as if he were an old and trusted friend.

"Your beads could be acting as a touchstone to the past. They may be helping you recall a life you once lived."

"Beads! BEADS! I didn't come here about my beads!"

Deupree shrugged his shoulders and said, "Perhaps you will allow me to regress you . . . when the time is right."

I slid out onto the edge of my chair and looked back over my shoulder toward the light at the top of the stairs. Unwilling to listen to any more reincarnation mumbo jumbo, I would wait only a moment more for his response.

Before he spoke again, he reached out one last time and with only the tip of his finger he lightly brushed the roughly shaped blue stones that could be the source of every blue in the whole world.

Finished with his reading, he stuck a yellow pencil over his ear, leaned back in his chair, and folded his hands on top of his chest.

"I'll use a pendulum to mark a place for you to begin your exploration, but only if you agree to share with me one-third of whatever you find on the island. And I want to go with you to help with the search."

"You've got to be kidding. *You* want to go to Crete with *me*? You want to go to Dhia Island?"

"That's the deal."

"But why?"

"Curiosity. Actually, I have friends who own a villa on Crete. I didn't have time to visit them the last time I was there. Now…the timing is right. I'm between projects. Not to worry. I won't get in your way."

What could I say? Sharing whatever I might find on the island presented no problem. If I discovered any antiquities—pots, broken tablets, seal stones—I would obey Greek law and turn them over to the authorities.

However, accepting a psychic explorer as a partner was a concession that would very likely create some very large personal problems for me. I could already hear the objections from my husband and my mother, not to mention Letty Marie who would never trust any man who might be able to read her mind.

As for Dan, he denounced any and all psychic phenomena, believing that those who claimed to have extrasensory abilities were nothing more than charlatans whose true interest was in swindling fools like me out of their money. And my mother, bless her heart, believed that anything to do with ESP was the work of the devil.

Half an hour later, I backed out of the parking lot next to Deupree's house, took a firm grip on the steering wheel and said, "Well! I'm going back to Crete, but it looks like I may not be going alone."

Before I left Deupree's office, he asked me to wait while

he sent an email to his villa-owning friends who lived and worked in Italy, but vacationed in Crete. He hoped to catch them, time difference and all, while they were still at work. He spoke the words as he wrote:

KORIATOS IMPORTS AND EXPORTS, MILAN ITALY OFFICE

HEY THEO,

ARRIVING HERAKLION, CRETE, LATE FRIDAY NIGHT. NEED A PLACE TO STAY. MAY ALSO NEED THE USE OF YOUR BOAT. POSSIBLE CODE GREEN AFOOT. CONFIRM ASAP. JAKE

"That should do it," and he hit the SEND key.

"What kind of boat? What's Code Green?"

"Theo has a sailing yacht of some kind or other, and Code Green is a running joke between old war buddies. The two of us worked for the government a long time ago, and Code Green was our catchword for gathering information... hunting treasure...eh, finding artifacts. You know. That sort of thing."

"Right."

I drove away wondering which government they had worked for, and what the true meaning of Code Green might be.

CHAPTER SIX

GOOD-BYE...SO LONG

That night, I made Dan's favorite comfort food, hoping to put him in a good mood. I tried to work up the nerve to tell him my decision to go back to Crete without him during dinner, but it didn't happen. After I finished the kitchen cleanup, I joined him in the den in front of the television where he was reading the newspaper and watching the six o'clock news.

The familiarity of the room offered me some support. Most of the furniture had once belonged to Dan's mother, or my grandmother. Being surrounded by our family's heirlooms, heavy pieces of furniture built of dark wood that was aged from years of diligent polishing, gave me a modicum of comfort.

Memories filled the room.

Tall bookcases held the family's favorite books, all of our sailing and soccer trophies. Dan's old guitar stood in the corner still wearing a flowered neck strap with a *Make Love Not War* sticker on its belly. My grandmother's silver tea service sat on a Shaker breakfront, the only piece of furniture, besides the couch and lounge chairs, I had actually bought myself. The rest of the room was overloaded with other people's odds and ends. Perhaps one day I would replace it all with furniture of my own choosing, but for the moment I sat in my grandfather's Windsor chair, fingering my blue beads, running the worn stones back and forth across my teeth.

Three days. Three more days and I'll be on a plane to Crete.

I kept saying the words over and over, hoping to fortify my intention to stick to my plan. I was determined to stand up to Dan's criticism. I knew he would try to guilt me into staying home. He would try to persuade me to wait so he could go with me, which was something we both knew was never going to happen.

Closing my eyes, I tried to remember the feel of the hot Cretan sun against my skin, the fragrance of the clean sea air, the rugged hillsides dotted with whitewashed houses, blue-domed churches, tiny villages, donkeys, and goats, and flowers, lots and lots of flowers.

My stomach was filled with a delicious flutter of excitement that vied with waves of queasiness. Thoughts of finding the true ending to a story about Ariadne and her people battled with the dread I felt over facing the consequences of my actions.

I would tell Dan about my meeting with Deupree, but I decided it was best not to tell him about the partnership. I may have been *just a housewife*, but I was no fool. I knew what his reaction would be. He would disparage my claim that any *real* professional of any persuasion would take my research seriously; then he would declare that Deupree was a charlatan and a thief, something he would believe no matter what I might say.

I had no reason to trust, or distrust, Deupree. For all I knew, he probably had no intention of going to Crete. He could have been leading me on out of some perverse need for amusement.

"Dan?"

Silence. A recap of the Cincinnati Reds baseball game flashed across the screen.

"DAN? Would you listen for a minute? I have something important to tell you. Since you're going to Atlanta to play in the tournament with Ferguson, I have decided to go ahead with the trip to Crete on my own. I leave Friday morning. Letty can take me to the airport. I'll be staying at the Minoa Palace Hotel, just like we did before."

"You're what?"

And the fight was on. It hit the fan and splattered all over the walls. Normally, when I argued with Lawyer Dan it was rarely worth the effort it took to win. But not this time. After years of being Dan's adversary, I was wise to his courtroom antics. I expertly cut off his attacks, refused to put up a defense, and merely stated the facts.

"I've told you a thousand times that I need to go back to Crete. I must see Dhia Island in order to write the last chapter of the Ariadne story. Until I do, I can't finish my book."

"What's gotten into you? You've let this fixation with Ariadne and those degenerate Minoans run your life. You can't just up and leave home. Who's going to cut the grass and water the flowers while you're gone? Who's going to do my shirts? Who's going to pick me up at the airport when I get back from Atlanta?"

"I'm sure the neighbor boy will take care of the lawn, the cleaners can do your shirts, and if you can't get a limo, Letty or your executive assistant can pick you up at the airport. All my duties as wife of the house can be delegated to others and, whether you believe it or not, I'm the only one who can finish my book...and that's what I'm going to try to do."

"This is the most irresponsible thing you've ever done."

"I don't think so. Since you can't or won't make room on your schedule, I have no choice but to go back to Crete alone. It's no different than when you go out of town to get a deposition for one of your clients. You do everything you can to find the facts in a case, and that's what I need to do. You don't quit until you learn the whole truth, and I can't quit either. I believe there's something on Dhia Island that will explain why Theseus abandoned Ariadne. There *is* an explanation and until I find it, I can't write the end of the story."

My best efforts to have a calm and reasonable discussion were wasted. Dan raged off and on until four in the morning, repeating each of his arguments over, and over: that I was being irresponsible, I was putting the family at risk, that I would get myself into trouble and he would have to come and rescue me. He would lose business, and it would cost him a bundle of money.

"All for what?" he shouted. "All for some irrational, female fling."

Frustrated and out of control, he pointed toward the door and yelled, "Fine! GO! If you're so determined to go to Crete without me, maybe you shouldn't bother coming back home."

We were in the same bed, but we had never been farther apart. Normally, I fell asleep on Dan's shoulder and during the night we would turn in tandem and sleep spoon fashion with his arm over me, holding me close. That night, neither of us slept, angry back turned to angry back.

He had never hurt me more. How could you tell someone you love to go away, especially when all they wanted was to see a deserted island that was probably nothing more than rocks and dirt and weeds? All I wanted was to satisfy my need to know. What was so God-awful wrong with that?

The most bewildering thing of all was that our marriage

was very comfortable, very safe, very secure. I loved and admired Dan. He was more handsome now than when we first married. We rarely argued, mainly because I felt it was a useless waste of energy. Dan was the skipper and I was the crew, but for the first time, it was my turn to make the final call. This time, my honor was at stake.

No matter what Dan or anyone else said, I was going to Crete. Even if the doors were locked when I returned home, I was going to Dhia Island. I would go to Dhia, even if it meant a major break in our marriage.

ψ

Next morning, the kitchen phone rang. I picked up and listened for a full minute without saying more than, "Hello."

Letty Marie continued to lecture me about the dangers of women traveling alone. Saturated with good advice I yelled, "You're right! I'm still going."

I threw the phone back in the charger. For the first time in my life, I had hung up on my best friend.

The phone rang again…and again.

"Hello!"

I expected it to be Letty Marie calling back with another version of the same speech, but it wasn't.

"Yes, Mother, it's true."

Dan, or Letty, must have called my mother with my *big news*.

"No, I really don't want to talk about it."

But my mother wanted to talk about it, so I dutifully listened, although I felt so nauseous I thought I might throw up, or smother to death.

"I know you wanted me to go with you to look at retirement condos, but we both know you'll make up your own mind, which is good. You can do just as well going with one of your friends."

However, that was only one of the many reasons my mother thought I should not go to Crete without Dan.

"Explain something to me, Mom. Why is it that Dan can travel alone and no one says a blessed thing? I'm perfectly capable of looking out for myself. Tell me, what's so wrong with me traveling on my own?"

The voice on the other end of the line knew the answer to that question, too, and it droned on and on and my nausea worsened.

"You are most definitely right. I should count my blessings, and I do. I know you never went anywhere without my father, and it's true that Dan works very hard. I have lots of beautiful clothes, and jewelry, and a nice house. I should stay home and clean. You're right…what more could any woman want?"

Pause.

"You think that since Dan can't take me to Greece that God is telling me I shouldn't be a writer. Yes, I'll pray about it. I have to go."

This time I left the phone line open. Hands clenched, I raised my arms over my head to protect myself from the battering fists of an invisible foe and shouted, "I am *not* my mother. I can never *be* like my mother!"

The intense emotion triggered Dan's angry face and his hurtful words: "Don't come home. If you go to Greece alone, don't come home."

Do as Dan says or what? The consequences of failing to do as expected were too painful to even consider. I wondered what it would feel like to have just a little support.

I fumbled for a tissue, blew my nose, and that simple act cued the old familiar, internal, unstoppable chorus of whimpering voices. *Go ahead. Wallow in it. Poor thing, nobody understands her. Nothing but a coward she is. Go ahead. Give up. Stay home and sulk. Too chicken to take a stand. It's pee or get off the pot time, sweetie.*

I rolled off the bed, dropped to my knees, and dragged a suitcase out from under the frame.

"No more analyzing. I AM GOING TO CRETE."

Determined to mute the inner chorus of voices, I pushed a CD of lively Greek music into the player, and accompanied by the brash sound of a *bouzouki* and drums, I piled all the stuff I would take with me on top of the bed. Soon the intensity of the beat led me into a Bedouin belly dance routine I had learned in order to write the rituals for the Snake Goddess ceremonies.

When my blue beads bounced hard against my chest, I immediately stopped dancing and walked over to the window. Taking the beads in both hands, I looked at them in the strong sunlight.

Deupree was right about one thing: the beads were my link to Greece and the island of Crete. I bought the beads in a funny little antique shop in Heraklion just before I began really delving into the story of Ariadne and Theseus; before I began recreating the old culture on Crete. I could never touch the beads without thinking of the island, the antique shop, and the old antique dealer who sold me the strand of pretty blue stones.

The old man said they were once worn by a Cretan High Priestess and if they could speak they would reveal secrets about the ancient Minoans. Could they really be a connector to the past?

Odd and peculiar things began to happen after I bought the beads. Specific information about the strange Minoan way of life came to me in ways I could never explain. When I needed information about the Minoan bull-dancing ceremony, I met Barnaby Conrad at the Santa Barbara Writer's Conference. He had actually fought the bulls. I was able to talk to an honest-to-God bullfighter, a man who had been gored by a bull and showed me the bloody cape to prove it. How odd was that? There had been other fortunate coincidences, so many I lost count—far too many to be ignored.

I rubbed the beads and frowned.

Maybe it's a mistake to accept Deupree as a partner. What if I find something really valuable on the island? Twice, Deupree called it a search for treasure.

So far, no one knew a psychic explorer was going with me to Crete, not Dan, not Mother, not Letty Marie.

For the first time in my life, I had a secret…I had made my very first business deal. I wasn't sure how it was going to turn out, but as my hero Joseph Campbell said, "Follow your bliss," and that was what I was determined to do.

Now, only the gods and goddesses knew what the outcome would be.

CHAPTER SEVEN

BON VOYAGE

The day of departure finally arrived. I sat next to Letty
Marie in the Delta terminal at the Greater Cincinnati
Airport and prayed that she would stop preaching. My prayer
went unanswered, so once again I tuned her out and thought
about my children.

For the past few months our daughter, Suzie, had worked
the evening shift in the ICU at Christ Hospital, and when I
told her I was going to Greece she seemed almost too enthusiastic. Jim's family had been pushing them to set a date for
their big church wedding, but with me out of the country they
couldn't possibly make plans. My trip would give them a little
breathing room and Suzie seemed enormously relieved.

"Don't worry about us," she insisted. "We'll keep an eye
on Dad and make sure he's okay. He can have dinner with
Jim when they play racquetball mid-week."

Steve, our high-energy son, shared an apartment with
his fraternity brother, and when I told him my plans to go
to Crete, his first remark was, "Go for it, Ma," and without
taking a breath asked, "Can I use your wheels while you're
away?"

Love for my children warmed my heart. From the beginning, they both had encouraged me to write, and I valued
their loving support. It felt good. However, their support was
not the support I needed the most.

Letty's insistent voice broke into my thoughts. "It's such
a shame Dan had to work. I'm sure, although the two of you

are at odds, he would go with you to Crete if he could. You both have always shown such love for each other. He just wants to protect you."

"It doesn't feel that way. He has never taken my writing seriously. He thinks it's a hobby, like knitting, or gourmet cooking. For him, it's not really important."

"I hate watching you hurt each other. I know he would come around if you asserted yourself. Show him the couch and he'll beg to go with you. That's what I do to Pete when he decides to display his manly assertiveness. Regardless, I still think you should wait a little while longer."

"How long do you think I should wait, Letty? How many years?"

Arguing with Letty was as pointless as beating a sponge.

At least she approved of the way I looked. Forsaking the comfort of a skirt and blouse, I wore khaki slacks, my safari vest, and a jade green shirt that complimented my eyes. I could be a reporter, or a photographer, traveling to some exotic country to cover a human interest story about the War on Terror. I could be going to a place where a friendly face and understanding eyes would be an asset and not an invitation to commit mayhem.

Silently thanking God that it was finally time to go through security, I bent over to zip my carry-on and was immediately confronted by a pair of shoes, shiny black men's shoes: shoes that stopped directly in front of me.

Before I could straighten up in my seat, a large male hand sporting a barbaric diamond pinky ring appeared directly beneath my nose. A friendly male voice said, "Why, hello there, Kate."

I slowly raised my eyes and followed the dark-suited arm

upward until I reached the happy, smiling face of Psychic Explorer, Jake Deupree.

"HELLO, KATE," he said again in a voice so loud I wanted to shush him.

He shook my hand vigorously.

"I didn't expect to see you again until we arrived on Crete. Looks like we're on the same flight to New York. I finally connected with my friends and I'll be staying with them at their villa. I can't remember the name of the place, just that it's east of Heraklion. I'll give you the address on the plane. By the time we get through security, I think they should be ready to board. Are you in first class?"

"No. I'm not in first class." I responded meekly and silently cursed fate for putting us on the same flight. I should have foreseen such a meeting. I should have been prepared to respond with some finesse; instead, I felt like a naughty child with pirated jam on my face. I didn't even think to introduce him to Letty Marie.

"You're staying at the Minoa Palace Hotel. Right? Well. See you on the plane."

Deupree had held my hand during the whole conversation, and Letty Marie's brown eyes were big as chocolate bonbons, ogling his paisley tie, creamy silk shirt, gold Rolex watch, and elegant leather attaché case. She shamelessly appraised his Italian-cut business suit and flashy diamond ring.

After Deupree released my limp hand, he politely dipped his head to Letty Marie and continued on his way. Our eyes followed him as he walked with a slight swagger toward security. He greeted three flight attendants by name, joking with them as they walked together like best buddies.

"Who…was that?" Letty asked breathlessly.

I scratched my nose, covered my mouth, and mumbled, "Jake Deupree."

"Jake Deupree! That psychic is going with you to Crete? Is he married? Does Dan know he's going with you?"

"Damnit, Letty Marie. That is absolutely the last straw. Were you listening to the conversation at all? No, you were not listening. You never listen to anything that concerns me. You were too busy checking the label in his suit and using a jeweler's loop on his diamond ring. He said he was staying with friends on Crete, yet you have the *gall* to ask me in that insinuating tone, *Is he going with you...is he married?* God! I knew that's how you would react."

I had never been so angry and Letty still didn't understand. She seemed bewildered by my explosive response and looked at me with big sad eyes, however I wasn't falling for any of her puppy dog looks. Not today.

"You, all of you, treat me like I'm nothing more than a naive schoolgirl who has to be protected from the big bad temptations of a world gone mad. I am an adult, Letty. I am the mother of two grown children, and I'm taking a lousy business trip."

I lowered my voice to a controlled, but steamy, whisper.

"Have you forgotten that this is the age when millions of respectable women travel alone? Tell me one thing. Would it be okay for Dan to travel alone with a female colleague? We both know it would because he's done it before, and so has your Pete; and so has just about every other businessman we know."

I couldn't sustain my anger any longer. I was about to leave on the first real adventure I had had in a whole lifetime of sensible living. And, for some peculiar reason, only my

children seemed willing to accept the fact that I, Kathryn
Ann Marshall, had the right to go on a quest.

A great surge of love filled my heart and my eyes.

"Have faith in me, Letty. My feet are firmly planted on
the ground."

I hugged my best friend and squeezed her hard.

"Stop worrying. Even if I get hurt, at least I'll know that I
tried to do something I can be proud of. And, who knows…
maybe I'll make a discovery that will leave my shaky thumb-
print forever on this dusty old world of ours."

Letty Marie couldn't think of anything more to say.

I turned to go, but then I stopped one last time.

"You know. If this were one of our kids, or Dan, or anyone
else we know, you would be cheering them on and wishing
them well. Don't hold me so tight, dear friend. I'll phone you
from Crete."

"But…but…what should I tell Dan?" Letty yelled after
me.

I shouted over my shoulder, "Tell him anything you
want."

What more could Letty say except, "Good-bye…have a
safe trip…*Bon Voyage.*"

THE MONSTERS BEHIND THE DOOR

A garbled voice announced our arrival at Kennedy International Airport.

Deupree hadn't put in an appearance and that was a great relief. This was not only the first leg of my journey; this was the point of no return. From here, I could continue on to Athens, or I could change my ticket and return home in defeat.

Go? Not to go? I knew that there were monsters waiting behind each of those mythical doors. Either path would most certainly lead to a life-altering conclusion. In the end, I would still have to do battle with my nemesis, my Fear of Failure. That old fire-breathing dragon had lived for as long as I could remember in a slimy green puddle of self-doubt in the darkest corner of my heart.

But even if I failed, maybe I could find a magic sword that would slay the beast, or at least give her a smack hard enough to make her stay in her place. If I could find the courage...if I could pass all the tests.

I missed Dan. I knew before I ever left home that I would miss him, and with all the gloomy predictions from my mother and Letty Marie, I was afraid that I would feel so lost without him I wouldn't be able to function.

So far, I had managed just fine. What I wasn't prepared for were the new and unfamiliar feelings that for the first time in my adult life, I was not accountable to, or responsible for, another human being. I had always had someone to worry over, someone else's well-being to consider: whether it was my parents, my husband, or my children. Even in college, I clucked over Letty's wild escapades, trying to tuck her under my wing to keep her safe.

Now, I was too far away to rescue any of the people I loved. My total focus was on myself and it felt strange. For a full three hundred and sixty degrees, nothing blocked the wind, or filtered the light. I felt exposed, but at the same time I felt strong and in control.

Most important of all, there was no timer on my wrist: that maniacal little invention with its beeping alarm that pulled my strings and programmed my life. It was fun to picture my digital watch as a tired old man sitting on the hearth back home, dejected and all alone, covered nose deep in a never-ending list of things to do to keep home and family running smooth and problem-free.

ψ

The flight to New York was uneventful. There was still no sign of Deupree which was fine with me; not when we landed in Newark and not when I boarded the plane to Athens. Maybe he missed the flight; maybe he changed his mind and decided to stay in New York and take in a play.

When the seat next to me remained empty, it felt like a good omen. I could stretch out and fly in comfort all the way to Greece.

After the dinner service was cleared away, I gazed wistfully at the rising moon and made a wish on the first twinkling star. Thinking of other wishing stars and other moonlit nights, the aura around me changed. I sensed that someone was standing in the aisle beside me and without looking up,

I knew it was Deupree.

"I've come to drink a toast to our partnership. I thought we should celebrate our joint venture." There he stood, solidly balanced, holding a bubbling flute of champagne in each hand.

I managed a stiff smile, offered him the empty seat next to me while trying my best to subdue the urge to run away and hide. Letty's scornful overreaction to him as a traveling companion was still fresh in my mind.

To avoid the possibility of another long handshake, I moved closer to the window, straightened my shirt collar, adjusted my blue beads, and smoothed my hair—which still felt strange. Letty had talked me into getting a wedge cut and adding more blond highlights to my already sun-streaked brown hair. She assured me that her hairdresser had succeeded in adding some degree of sophistication to my usual careless look.

Deupree was completely at ease, having changed into a wine-colored western shirt, gray twill pants, and a comfortable-looking pair of low-heeled boots.

Sitting there together, we looked like a twosome, which made me even more acutely aware of him as a man. Stalling, to compose my thoughts, I took a sip of champagne and frantically searched for a topic of conversation that would sound both businesslike and neutral. Feeling totally inept, I knew that if I were Letty, I would know exactly what to say and instantly I thought of the perfect lead.

"I want to apologize for not introducing you to my friend back at the Cincinnati Terminal. I didn't expect to see you before we arrived on Crete."

"No problem. I'm the one who needs to apologize. I promised to give you the address of the villa where I'll be staying, but I stuck my notes in the side-pocket of my suitcase instead of putting them in my carry-on. The best I can do for now is to write my friend's name on the back of my business card. I'll give you the phone number and address later."

It came as no surprise that Deupree's handwriting was bold and confident. I held the card carefully between my thumb and forefinger. The paper felt smooth and substantial. The text was simple, but the lettering was surprisingly ornate.

"*FORTUNES UNLIMITED.* That's the sign over your front door. The name of your company certainly promises a lot."

"I wouldn't exactly describe myself as a company. I'm more of a one-man show. I sell my services, offering my clients a variety of psychic tools, and a few other special abilities, to aid them in their search for things that are lost, or things that need to be found. Of course, there are plenty of skeptics who say I'm nothing but a charlatan, a freak, a sideshow illusionist. Then there are a few gullible souls who pay a lot of money for what I have to offer. Several of my clients have so much faith in my abilities I'm beginning to think I should try a little water-walking."

I felt a rush of heat and knew my face had turned a revealing shade of pink. Deupree had repeated much of what Dan had said when I told him I had spent a hundred dollars for Deupree to perform a psychic reading of Dhia Island.

Once again, I wondered if he could read my mind, but I immediately knew the answer to my own question. The man could not read my mind. He was baiting me, testing me, trying to see just how naive I might be.

"Is that the way skeptics usually describe what you do?" I asked.

"How'd you guess? But, as I always say, I don't care what they call me just as long as I get paid." He made the comment with a half-laugh.

Although there was a smile on his face, there was also a strained look around his mouth, as if the disparaging description caused him pain. The look was difficult to interpret. Was he telling the truth when he said he didn't care what people thought about him and his alleged abilities, or was he lying? Maybe he was doing a little of both. Maybe he was one of those amoral individuals who have the ability to lie even when they are lying, which was a thought more convoluted than a snake swallowing its own tail.

The incident was a timely reminder to be cautious. Whatever his abilities may or may not be, I must never forget that Deupree was a professional adventurer, a man who made his living by using his extraordinary mental and intuitive abilities to his own best advantage.

"Can I ask you a question?"

"Sure." He grinned and added, "Sock it to me."

"That article in the newspaper said you not only work with archeologists; it said that you also find oil and mineral deposits for mining companies. I've been wondering if you've ever dowsed for water. When I was a little girl, I saw a man use a forked stick to look for water on my grandpa's farm. Everyone was amazed when he found an underground spring of pure, sweet water after two different drilling companies hit nothing but dry holes."

"It's been years since I used a water witch. New technology has taken a lot of the guesswork out of prospecting, but there are times when the old ways still seem to work best."

"It was amazing to see. I don't think I'll ever forget it."

As we spoke, Deupree's eyes fastened on my necklace, but this time he made no move to touch.

"I see you're wearing your blue beads."

"I rarely take them off," and to remove them from the conversation, I tucked the necklace inside my blouse, where it lay solid and cool against my bare skin.

"You could use the beads to do a past life regression, you know—to satisfy your curiosity, of course."

"You mean to satisfy *your* curiosity," and I pointed my finger at his chest.

"Whichever way you want to say it, the beads are very powerful. I could read them myself, but they would most likely have more meaning for you. Why don't you let me regress you? It might be a good thing to do before you get to Crete."

"Here? In the middle of a plane full of people?"

"Couldn't be a safer place."

"I don't know. I'm not sure. I have a couple of friends who boast about their regressions, but I don't like mind games."

"Neither do I. The mind is a sophisticated tool. It's not a toy. It's one of the least understood and most underused organs in the body. As for the regression, you only need to enter a light trance. You will be aware of your surroundings and you can pull out at any time."

I was usually cautious and conservative, and it would not be easy for me to entrust my mind to a stranger. The truth was that I was afraid I might be allowing him access to my soul.

"Believe me. No one can hypnotize you unless you allow it to happen. There are many techniques for regression, but I've had the most success with one in particular. When you're ready, take a few deep breaths. Feel the beads against your skin. Close your eyes. Relax. Listen to my voice and we'll see what happens."

I fluttered my eyelids tentatively, allowed them to close naturally, and relaxed my hands in my lap.

"Good. Now. Picture a beach, somewhere in the sun. Don't watch yourself from the outside. Go inside and imagine yourself looking out. Feel the golden light of the sun as it warms your skin. See a long, sweeping beach. Smell the sea. Hear the sound of the waves rushing toward land. Listen to the gentle sounds filled with the colors of the sea, deep green, and deeper blue. Rest. Relax. After a time, slowly walk across the sand and feel the warm grains squeezing up between your toes and then…"

Soon, Deupree's soothing voice brought me to a place of calm and peace. "Go back. And back. Where are you now?" Jake asked softly. "What do you see?"

"Water. An ocean, and a black ship with crimson markings. I've seen pictures. It looks like an ancient Athenian ship and it's sailing toward an island."

"What island? Is it Dhia Island?"

"I don't know. No. Not Dhia. The silhouette is wrong."

"Tell me what you see."

"Oarsmen dozing, lying across their rowing poles. I think I can smell pitch. And warm wood. I hear beams creaking. A white sail flogs in the wind."

"What else do you see?"

"A man. A helmsman. He's naked and he's leaning against a long steering oar. Powerful body. Thick-muscled legs braced against the roll of the deck. His eyes are fixed on the island as if he wills the boat toward it, as if he hungers for it."

"Look at his face."

"A thin scar crosses one cheek. Full beard. Dark curly hair streaked with strands of silver. Black eyes. Haunted eyes filled with grief."

"Slowly look around you. What else do you see?"

"A bay. Whitecaps. They're driving the boat onto the beach. The helmsman says, *Must meet Lycomedes.* I see something dangling from the helmsman's wrist. It's a small strand of blue beads. Beads of lapis…"

I shot upright in the seat, my eyes stretched wide.

"My beads!"

I slapped my chest with my hand, frantically searching for the blue stones beneath my blouse. The panic I felt didn't ease until I held the blue beads in my hand and I clutched them as if to shield them from harm.

"Whoa there, partner. Lie back. You came out much too fast. Go back to the sunny beach in your thoughts. Relax there a few minutes so you can come out more slowly."

Jake's mellow voice tried to calm me. He attempted to lead me back to the comforting warmth of the sun so I could make a gentle reentry back into normal reality.

"Feel relaxed and refreshed."

Bright-eyed with excitement, I was far from relaxed. I sat on the edge of my seat, straining against my loosely fastened seat belt.

"The helmsman. It was Theseus. I'm sure it was Theseus."

"You should know. He's your hero."

"He looked just like I pictured him. I can't believe it. But the island wasn't Dhia. Wait! Lycomedes. I know that name. Lycomedes was the king of Skyros Island. Skyros Island…oh, my God!"

I fell back against the seat as if I had been shoved by a ghostly hand. Afraid to speak the words out loud, I covered my mouth with my hand and whispered, "That's where Theseus fell from the cliffs. Skyros is the island where the storytellers say Theseus died."

My throat ached with a powerful surge of emotion that pushed up from my chest. I covered my eyes, pressed them hard, and tried to re-penetrate the shadowy veil. But it was useless. The moment was lost.

After such a disturbing experience, casual conversation was impossible. I wasn't sure what had happened, but I didn't want to talk to Deupree about it. I was much too upset. What I wanted most was to be left alone to try and capture some kind of meaning from the experience.

After a few failed attempts at conversation, Deupree said, "Well, *adios*, partner. See you when we get to Crete."

By the time the plane landed in Athens, I had pushed the incident aside, rationalizing the whole experience as nothing more than a predictable response. I had worked so long with the characters in the myth, it was obvious that the scenario was nothing more than visual association. It was like creating images out of cloud formations and ink blots.

I didn't see Deupree again until I was standing in the immigration line in the Athens airport. Scanning the faces in the crowd, admiring people of different nationalities in their native dress, I saw him standing barely fifty feet away, talking to a smartly uniformed Greek customs officer. From the effusive touch-and-pat going on, he appeared to be well acquainted with the dark-eyed, vivaciously attractive blonde.

Sensing my stare, Deupree turned toward me and raised his hand in greeting. I smiled and waved back, then busied myself with passport and papers.

Changing money and collecting luggage without a strong male arm to help was a new experience, but I managed reasonably well. I found a taxi, drove to the domestic airport, deciphered the Greek-English signs, and boarded the plane to Heraklion with five heart-stopping minutes to spare.

The last I saw of Deupree, he was walking toward the exit with the adoring customs officer hanging on his arm. He was not on the plane to Crete. Perhaps he would take a later flight. Evidently, he had more pressing personal business to take care of in Athens.

CHAPTER NINE

WELCOME TO CRETE

W hen we landed in Crete, a red carpet connected the plane to the terminal: a dignitary must have recently arrived. Three military men dressed in camouflage, each holding an automatic weapon, stood either side of the crimson ribbon leading to the entry.

One soldier's stance was particularly aggressive and I gave him a look that must have expressed my displeasure. I was shocked when he immediately lowered both his weapon and his eyes, a response you would expect to be given to a superior officer. No one had ever shown me such deference. Crete was certainly an unusual place. First, an antique dealer insists he knows me, and now a Cretan soldier treats me like his superior. Letty would really be impressed.

I was pleased to see that the Minoa Palace Hotel had not changed.

Colorful banners showing Heraklion's nightlife were still draped across the façade. The vibrant pictures brought life to the gray stone walls. It was a feeble attempt to imitate the lively fresco paintings that had once decorated the walls of Knossos Palace thousands of years ago.

The inside of the hotel also hadn't changed. The same welcoming sofas and chairs were still in place, flowers everywhere, simple and understated. As before, the hotel check-in seemed to take forever. As soon as the bellman left me in my room, I dropped my things on the bed, threw open the sliding door, and walked out onto the balcony.

The sensation was like walking into the sea.

Two stories below my feet, white-laced combers persistently pushed a long curl of foam onto the beach. Boulders haphazardly piled along the shore resisted the battering force of a stormy Cretan sea, and happy children were still making castles in the sand.

Nothing had changed. Everything was just as it had been two years ago…just as it would have been four thousand years ago. I felt the intensity of the hot Cretan sun burning my skin, but I didn't mind. The sea air smelled just like I remembered it, fresh and clean.

Holding my breath in anticipation, I raised my eyes to the horizon, turned slightly to the east and saw Dhia Island in the distance. Nine miles off shore, she looked like a sleeping dragon barely visible beneath a blanket of smoky blue haze.

With a smile I whispered, "You're hiding now, but tomorrow I'm going to lift your veil and find the secret you conceal."

Too excited to rest, I splashed water on my face and changed my slacks for a loose fitting skirt. I walked down the broad staircase, out the front entrance, and took a taxi into downtown Heraklion.

The hotel had been built in the traditional Minoan style: the rooms were arranged around an open light well that provided natural circulation. Combined with a steady sea breeze and high ceilings there was no need for air conditioning. I had not felt the full power of the Cretan sun until I stepped out of the air-conditioned cab in the middle of town. The blistering heat from the paving stones quickly penetrated the soles of my sandals.

After only a dozen steps my skirt dragged against my

damp legs and I wiped perspiration from my upper lip, passing the tissue across my brow, over the back of my neck, and
under my chin. The wise Cretans were taking their afternoon
siesta, either sitting quietly in the shade, or resting on a pallet
discreetly placed in the back of their shop. Later in the day,
when the heat was not so fierce, the stores would reopen and
business would resume its leisurely pace.

In a shady corner of a *taverna*, a group of men sat on
straight-backed chairs, sipping coffee, or drinking tall, milky-
looking glasses of ouzo and water. Huddled around a gaming
board, their arguing erupted into shouts of excitement when
an old man wearing a black skullcap gave a whoop and a
holler—evidently he made his point.

As I strolled along the uneven stone sidewalk, I stepped
into a pocket of air touched with the fragrance of garlic sim-
mering in olive oil. The satisfying aroma gave me a giddy,
pit-of-the-stomach feeling like coming home after a long
voyage.

I stopped to admire an open courtyard in front of a two-
story white stucco house with green shutters and green
window boxes filled with red geranium that spilled over the
sides in a vivid splash of scarlet.

An old woman wearing an ankle-length apron over
a black widow's dress came to the door of the house and
broomed a cat from the middle of the sill. When she saw me
admiring her flowers, she bobbed her head in greeting. I wondered if she was the one making the moussaka and baking
the crème caramel that would be eaten late in the evening
when the family would gather at a table beneath the shade of
the lacy plane tree in the side garden.

Although the surroundings seemed oddly familiar, I was

acutely aware that I was a stranger in a foreign land, a wanderer and a seeker listening to conversations in a language I could not understand.

It was almost two years to the day since I browsed alone through the antique shops in the old section of the city. I passed the tourist's office where I had bought our tickets to the Minoan archeological sites at Knossos, Mallia, and Phaistos. The tours had also taken us to the ruins at Agia Triada and the troglodyte caves near the town of Matala on the southern coast. We had visited the Heraklion Museum early morning or late afternoon, and by the time we left for home, I felt I had been properly introduced to the world of the ancient Minoans.

Enjoying the memory of my first experience on Crete, I realized that I was near the place where those brilliant flashes of light had led me to the antique shop where I bought my blue beads, the place where I met the old antique dealer. It had been a casual encounter, but I had come away from that shop with more than a pretty strand of blue beads. The conversation with the old man had inspired me to search in earnest for the missing pieces of the Ariadne puzzle. I'm not sure I would have attempted anything so grand as writing a novel, if it had not been for him.

Many things had changed since that day two years ago, but the change that disturbed me most was that now, whenever I thought about Crete, I thought about Deupree. Could all that mystical nonsense he said about my blue beads be true? Could they actually be a psychic connector to the past?

Okay. I'm here. Now, what do I do? And the answer came to me as clearly as if a soft voice was speaking in my ear.

Return to the place where you found the beads.
Of course. That made good sense.

I remembered that the shop was at the end of a narrow lane opposite a *taverna* with red-checkered tablecloths. On a chance that it had not changed its colors, I turned the corner and saw the restaurant in the distance, still gaily dressed in its distinctive red and white. As I entered the narrow lane and walked toward the antique shop, once again, sunlight was bouncing off the diamond-shaped windowpanes, flashing like harbor beacons showing hazardous passage.

The store should have been closed for afternoon siesta, but a dark-haired man stood outside the shop slowly turning a long-handled crank, lowering a faded, peach-colored awning over the window to protect the display from the strong light.

A new gold-lettered sign, *ANTIQUES AND OBJECTS De ART,* was freshly painted on the glass; however, everything else in the window looked much the same: amber bowls, tarnished silver hand mirrors, carved jade and rose quartz. Even the same gold colored Minoan double ax lay beside a tiny statue of a bare-breasted Cretan Goddess of Snakes.

The only difference in the display was my strand of lapis lazuli beads. At that moment, I could feel the stones warm against my skin, beneath my blouse, next to my heart.

I turned the knob, gave the door the requisite nudge with my foot as it dragged over the sill, and once again I heard the tinkle of a bell in the distance.

The name may have changed, but the aroma was still the same: a dusty mix of age, and anise, and strong Greek coffee. The room also looked the same: filled with copper pots, faded oriental rugs, saddle bag covers, antiques, and oddments.

The sameness was there, but it somehow felt different. Perhaps it was the absence of any special feeling of excitement—nothing that drew me with the passion to possess like my strand of blue beads had from the moment I saw them.

The quiet of the shop was broken by the clacking made by a curtain of wooden beads as an attractive young woman pushed them aside and walked toward me. Smiling pleasantly, she stood at a distance, politely waiting to serve.

The woman's hair was black like Letty's, but instead of looking like a spiky wig, this woman wore her hair pulled straight back from her face. The sleek strands were taut as black enameled filament and carefully twisted into a heavy bun at the nape of her neck. She looked to be in her midthirties, which seemed a young age to be dressed in widow's weeds. Looking chic and not the least dowdy, her dress was made of cleverly cut black silk.

Her deep brown eyes were skillfully lined with kohl, her cheeks brushed with a hint of rouge, and she had one of those rare olive complexions that have the translucence of fine porcelain.

Although the woman's beauty was striking, her jewelry was extraordinary. She wore a gold signet ring on her left forefinger, a gold cuff on her forearm, and a matching gold band around her neck. Any one of the three pieces could have been lifted from a case in the Heraklion Museum. They were impressive enough to have been worn by Princess Ariadne, or her mother, the great whore, Queen Pasiphae.

"Do you speak English?"

"Of course, madam."

"May I see the Snake Goddess in the window?"

"Certainly. You will find it a flawless reproduction."

The woman's voice was mellow and low with a refined British accent.

While I waited for the woman to take the statue from the window, I recalled my first visit to the shop. From the authority in the old antique dealer's demeanor, and from the things he left unsaid, I felt that he might know the truth about what happened between Theseus and Ariadne. It might be very helpful if I could meet him again, although his manner had been very intimidating. Even now, I felt a bit apprehensive at the prospect of seeing him again, mainly because he had insisted that he knew me even after I assured him that we had never met. His persistence had been very unsettling.

The woman quickly returned and placed the Snake Goddess on the counter for my inspection. Although I had a statue just like it back home, it was so inexpensive I decided to buy it anyway. Maybe the brazen little goddess would bring me the good luck I would most surely need.

Before I could ask her about the old shopkeeper, she reached below the counter and brought out a clay disk standing on a wire; both sides marked with pictographs.

"Since you are interested in the little goddess, you might also like a replica of the Phaistos Disk. The symbols have never been interpreted, but many find it fascinating to study."

"I have never seen the disc up close. If it isn't too expensive, I would like to buy it, too."

We agreed on a price and she wrapped them both in flowered paper and set them on the counter.

I wasn't sure how to properly ask about the old man, so I just plunged in and hoped I wouldn't say something inappropriate.

"Several years ago I was in your shop and a very pleasant older gentleman sold me a strand of beads. Does he still work here? He seemed very knowledgeable about the ancient Minoan culture, and I have some questions he might be able to answer."

"What kind of beads? Were they blue beads? Are you an American?"

I was startled and slightly alarmed by the woman's direct manner. I was also relieved that my blue beads were tucked safely out of sight beneath my blouse. I had to resist the urge to touch them, not wanting to call attention to their hiding place.

"Yes," I answered cautiously. "I am an American, and the beads he sold me were blue. That's why I bought them. I was drawn to them by their intense color. Why do you ask?"

Seeing my frown, the woman realized she had been far too intense.

"Please, forgive my inquisitiveness. My name is Elana Demopolis. I am the new owner of this shop. You are, undoubtedly, speaking of my grandfather. He became very, how do you say, ah, old in the mind before he died. You must have met him during his last days. It will soon be two years since he passed from this earth."

"I am so sorry. He seemed a very kind and gentle man. He spoke with great authority about the ancient Minoan culture."

"We will have coffee. I must speak with you about... about my grandfather. He would be very pleased that you remember him with such kind words."

Without waiting for me to reply, the woman brushed back through the beaded curtain and called, "Demetri! Make coffee. We have a guest." Then she said something more, very high pitched in rapid Greek.

Feeling a little uncertain as to what I should do next, I continued to browse through the shop, pausing before a mirrored case of antique silver jewelry.

I was thinking about buying gifts for Letty Marie, Suzie, and my mother, when a man suddenly appeared behind me—a dark reflection in the rippled glass. Tall and angular, his black hair tipped with auburn, the man had a full black mustache and eyes that were stark white with pupils carved from ebony. His grim face could have been cut from stone.

Disturbed by the man's aggressive stance, I was unsure whether to turn around and confront him, or keep him at my back.

"Do you come for more lapis beads?" the man asked gruffly.

Thankfully, the smaller image of Elana entered the reflection. I turned quickly and moved closer to the young woman.

Elana gave the man what sounded like a scolding in Greek, then switched back to English and sent him away to finish the coffee.

"Please, pay no attention to Demetri. He is an artist, a distant relation, a companion to my brother. He sometimes helps me with the restorations here in the shop. Please, come. My office opens onto a shaded courtyard. Usually, there is a small afternoon breeze that is very refreshing."

How could I refuse such an invitation? This was an unexpected opportunity to speak to a real Cretan. Since the woman was the granddaughter of the knowledgeable old man, and an antique dealer, she might also be an expert on the ancient Minoans. I followed her through the workroom into a comfortable outdoor patio enclosed within a high stone wall. It was shaded by several tall trees that filtered the light.

We sat down at a small table set with two small crystal glasses filled with a gold-colored liqueur, two goblets of cool water, and a cut-glass dish piled high with candied fruit. I was being treated to the traditional Greek offering served to an honored guest.

I touched the liqueur to my lips, enough to be properly polite, and slowly sipped the cool water. I ate a piece of candied fruit and praised the beauty and serenity of the delightful little garden. Its charm was enhanced by the sound of water trickling from a crevice in a wall of solid stone. The setting was so natural, the greenery so uncontrived, it could have been transplanted from some wild and secret wood.

Demetri served the coffee, and then busied himself at an adjacent workbench, where he slowly polished a large brass urn. Without pretense, he watched and listened, his black eyes fierce and darkly alert, his ears straining to hear every word.

While we sipped the tiny cups of coffee, thick and sweet, the conversation easily turned to the Minoans. I told Elana about my plan to visit Dhia Island and I explained that it was a curiosity I hoped to explore.

"I think there are no tours to the island," she said with a frown. "There are no restored ruins, you know, nothing of real interest for tourists to see. In ancient times, there was a settlement there, but very little remains."

Demetri cleared the gravel from his throat and said, "If you want to go to Dhia, go to Venetian Harbor and hire a boat." Having made his pronouncement, he carried his chair over to the table and sat down.

"Ask her about the beads."

Elana twisted her gold bracelet nervously. The facade of polished sophistication lifted for a moment and she gave me a timid smile.

"I must explain. Several years ago, Demetri saved my brother's life in a climbing accident. We are greatly in his debt, although my dear husband lost his life I am…"

"Ask her!" Demetri demanded.

Elana's nervousness instantly vanished. Her dark eyes flashed Demetri a warning and she made a vicious, cutting motion with her hand and pointed her ringed forefinger at his nose. He compressed his lips in an obvious effort to keep silent.

Elana spoke slowly, choosing her words with great care.

"Through an involved set of circumstances, Demetri was entitled to inherit a valuable strand of lapis lazuli beads that had been given to my grandfather for safekeeping. When the time came for Demetri to claim the beads, my grandfather said he sold them to an American woman and…"

"And he had no right." Demetri brought his fist down on the table, rattling the tiny cups in their saucers. "Those beads were mine and that old man robbed me of them. He acted no better than a sheep stealer. An enemy would have been treated with more honesty."

This time Demetri's insulting accusation brought Elana to her feet.

"Watch your tongue, cousin. No matter the debt we owe you for my brother's life, you will *not* speak such words against the dead, especially in front of a stranger."

Elana's beautiful face was twisted with outrage and indignation.

Demetri looked slightly intimidated, but he did not back down. He did not recant what he had said. He just glared at Elana with the stubbornness of a donkey.

Elana said something venomous to Demetri in Greek. This time his eyes wavered and his expression changed from anger to sullen resentment. Satisfied that he understood her words, she sat down, returned to English, and included me in the conversation.

"Demetri is obsessed with the blue beads. Not so much for their value. I am afraid that he thinks, like my grandfather, and my dear departed husband, that the beads have the power to recall the past."

Elana flipped her hand at Demetri, dismissing him and his ridiculous beliefs. "The beads are nothing. Nothing more than old blue stones."

"I want what is mine."

Although he said the words with stubborn determination, his body language changed and he looked meek and apologetic. When he spoke his voice was husky with emotion and his black eyes looked sad.

"If I had the beads, I might sell them and use the money to open an art gallery in the Plaka in Athens."

"If you have such a great need for money, stop trying to sell your paintings to tourists. Sell in New York and Paris. Paint modern. Stop painting the past. Who wants to buy pictures of Snake Goddesses and half-naked women dancing with bulls?"

"What do you know of my art, woman? You know nothing! NOTHING!"

Demetri stood abruptly, sending his chair crashing to the floor. This time he turned on me and shook his fist in my face.

"Those beads are mine. That old man had no right to sell them. You do not know their power."

He turned to Elana and poked her on the shoulder with one stiff finger.

"You do not frighten *me*, Elana Demopolis, with your woman's curses. Those beads are *MINE!*"

Growling with anger, he kicked the leg of the table, once again rattling the fragile cups in their saucers, sending them teetering dangerously close to the edge.

Having had his say, Demetri stalked across the courtyard and left the garden through a small gate in the far wall. For the first time I noticed that he walked with a limp, dragging one stiff leg with difficulty.

Elana was mortified by the unpleasantness of the scene.

"Please, *please*, forgive. Both Demetri and my grandfather are to be pitied. I have seen it before. Something happens when the *Old Ones* take you by the hand. You become possessed. It is as if you lose control of your destiny. I believe this enchantment may have cost my dear husband his life."

The infamous strand of lapis lazuli beads felt like forty ingots of lead hanging around my neck, and I could swear they were radiating heat. It was as if they had absorbed all of the passion in Demetri's angry words.

Frightened by the confrontation, I neither confirmed nor denied that I was in fact the buyer of the notorious beads. Although I was bursting with questions, I was too afraid to ask them. After a few polite words of thanks, I left the shop more puzzled and confused than when I came.

Who were the *Old Ones?* Were they the ancient Minoans? Were they the mysterious Kephti? And what was it the *Old Ones* were supposed to lead a person to do? Out of habit, I reached for the blue beads and rubbed them as I hailed a taxi for a ride back to the hotel.

I reproached myself for becoming distracted from my true purpose. I must forget about the beads and concentrate on my mission. Tomorrow, I would go to Dhia Island and learn why I felt so compelled to walk the land.

CHAPTER TEN
TAKING CHARGE

By the time I arrived back at the hotel, I was totally exhausted.

Elana's disturbing words about the mystical power of the beads and Demetri's demand for their return played over and over in my head. The more I tried to sort through the ethics of rightful ownership, the more confused I became.

"Key, please. Room 201."

"Ahhh, yes, Ms. Marshall. A gentleman requests that you join him in the Seaside Lounge."

"Oh?"

I looked out from behind the reception desk, down the long hallway, past the dining room, over to the far side of the hotel, and saw Deupree sprawled in a club chair, laughing and talking to a young woman dressed in a brightly flowered beach sarong.

"Great. Just what I need: a conversation with a wandering psychic."

I forced my tired body to walk. Jet lag was finally taking its toll. It took a major amount of effort to make the long trek across the hotel, but it did allow me time to take another, unobtrusive, look at Mr. Deupree.

He wasn't old, but he certainly wasn't young. He looked tanned and virile, but his features were too irregular to be considered handsome. During the past few days, I had seen him with a variety of women, and each time his attentions seemed well received. Evidently there were females who found an arrogant, know-it-all man an irresistible challenge. When Deupree stood and offered me a chair, the pretty young thing fluttered her eyes and gracefully drifted away. I ordered a lemonade and briefly described my afternoon encounter at the antique shop.

"I told you the beads have great power. I knew it the first time I saw them." Learning that his opinion had been corroborated, Deupree looked obnoxiously smug.

Unwilling to believe any more supernatural nonsense about the beads, I untied the stones and carefully coiled them into a circle on the table. I was always charmed by the intensity of their color. I inspected the stones carefully, touching them, turning them possessively. They were just a pretty strand of roughly shaped blue stone and I stroked them lovingly. There was nothing malevolent about them.

Without warning, Deupree clamped his hand on top of mine and pressed it down onto the beads, grinding my flesh onto the stones, and a sudden burst of energy shot through my palm. Reacting instinctively, I ripped my hand out from under Deupree's. Inspecting my skin, I expected to see scorch marks although I was not in any real pain. My flesh tingled as if it had been singed, but the skin was unblemished, a normal shade of pink.

"You are unbelievable," I said, massaging my palm with my thumb.

Determined to expose his dime-store magic trick, I grabbed Deupree's hand and flipped it over expecting to see a concealed gadget of some kind, something that would explain the buzzing burst of energy that had shot through my palm.

I found nothing—nothing but a few calluses. He wasn't

even wearing his diamond pinky ring. And from the told-you-so grin on his face I knew it would be a waste of words to ask him for an honest explanation. I knew that he would insist that the charge had been generated by some mystical power in the beads.

I threw Deupree's hand aside, refusing to give any credence to his pitiful attempt at psychic prestidigitation. I also refused to act as if anything unusual had happened. I willed my body to relax, curved my lips into a smile, and took a lazy sip of lemonade.

"Are you going to give the beads back to the shopkeeper?" Deupree asked sharply.

"Would you?"

"Hell, no! That's what tradin's all about. You paid the price. The beads are yours, but if I were you I wouldn't leave them carelessly lying around."

I was too tired for any more talk. Too much was happening, too fast. At this point, I knew only one thing for sure. *Nothing* was going to divert me from my primary goal, not Elana, not Demetri, certainly not Deupree and his amateurish legerdemain that turned my blue beads into some kind of psychic amplifier.

As I retied the strand of blue stones around my neck, I wished I had never taken them off. They felt fine. They felt perfectly normal—satiny smooth—maybe a trifle cool.

"I have to get some rest," I said. "Tomorrow, I'm going to Dhia Island."

"I've never known anyone more obstinate," Jake said with a curl of disdain on his lips. "*You* are the one who's unbelievable. You felt the power in those beads with your own flesh and still you refuse to acknowledge it. On one hand, you're determined to explore an uninhabited island when you don't have any concrete evidence, no scientific proof, that anything is there. You have nothing more to go on than some gut-generated compulsion. You think your hunch is valid, yet you refuse to give mine any consideration. You are inconsistent, and you are illogical. You women are all alike."

I responded to Deupree's emotional outburst with silence and what I hoped was an enigmatic stare.

Deupree shook his head in exasperation. It seemed that from his experiences with women, he knew it would be useless to pursue the discussion any further. Since we were both heading in the same direction, we walked together to the foot of the stairs.

"I've rented a car," he said. "Here's the address and phone number of my friends—that's why I stopped to see you. I wasn't able to talk to them directly when I telephoned from the airport, but the maid said Theo had his boat brought over from Italy by a professional crew last month. I'm sure they will be happy to take us over to Dhia Island. If you come with me now, we can talk to them together. They could put you up for the night."

The nerve of the man! After such a show of chicanery, how could he possibly think I would accept his casual offer to spend the night with his so-called friends? And to cap it all, he had the audacity to say that women are illogical. Men!

Too tired to challenge his ludicrous proposition, I yawned and said, "No, thanks. I have a bed of my own for tonight."

He shrugged his shoulders as if to say, Suit yourself, stuffed his hands in his pockets, and turned toward the lobby door to leave.

"Oh, by the way." I spoke to Deupree's back. "Don't bother your friends about going to Dhia Island on my account. I intend to go to Venetian Harbor tomorrow and charter a boat. If you want to go to Dhia with me, you'll need to be here by eight in the morning. Otherwise, I'll go alone."

Deupree turned slowly. His *I'm-so-cool* facade was replaced with a look just short of open-mouthed surprise. He obviously did not think I was the type of woman to take the initiative and make arrangements on my own.

Since I had nothing more to say, I turned my back on him and slowly walked up the stairs to my room. Although I was tired to the point of pain, I felt a giddy flush of satisfaction. I was experiencing the most delicious feeling…as if I had won a victory, as if somehow I had taken coup. I felt certain that in some inadvertent way I had outmaneuvered the amazing Mr. Deupree.

Before I went to bed, I made the promised call home. No one answered, so I left a message on the answering machine.

"I arrived safely. You don't have to call back. I'm exhausted. I haven't had any real sleep since I left home and tomorrow is going to be a very busy day."

CHAPTER ELEVEN

VENETIAN HARBOR

J ake arrived promptly at eight the next morning.
The streets into downtown Heraklion were jammed with
tourists in rented cars; hundreds more were packed onto
bumper-to-bumper buses lined up waiting to leave on early-
morning excursions through wild mountain gorges, past the
snow-covered pinnacles of Mount Idha, or Mount Dhikti
(the legendary birthplace of the great god Zeus). Each tourist
was a seeker, traveling to any of a thousand mystical places
all across the island.

Some of the more athletic explorers would plumb the
bowels of Crete. They were eager to crawl through subterra-
nean caverns filled with stories about the bull-headed monster
Minotaur, and the Cretan Goddess of Snakes. Others were
intent upon visiting the tiny blue-domed churches decorated
with famous religious icons.

Whatever their special interest might be, nearly all of the
sightseers would make at least one pilgrimage to the evoca-
tive ruins of Knossos Palace. Many were hoping to experience
some sense of recognition, wondering if the puzzling remains
of the lost Minoan civilization would trigger a memory of a
life they once lived in another time and another place. Every
person who came to the palace marveled at the ingenuity
of a race of people who celebrated the joys and mysteries of
nature, and practiced a lifestyle difficult to surpass even in
modern times.

We felt extremely fortunate to find a parking place close

to the inner harbor. Although Jake had worn a bored look ever since we left the hotel, he stopped midway down the hill to the port, spread his arms in a wide embrace, and said, "What a centerfold."

The panoramic view was so grand it would surely satisfy the most romantic yachtsman's dream of perfection.

The harbor entrance was guarded by a stone fortress called the *Koules*. A simple fort built by Venetian invaders, it stood like a formidable castle with crenellated stone walls, solid and impregnable. Ocean-going cruise ships and ferries were banished to the outer harbor, and the picturesque inner harbor was reserved for sailing yachts and the small fishing *caciques* worked by men who could be the first cousins of Zorba the Greek.

The harbor smelled of fish, wet hemp, and tar, and a light onshore breeze carried the sounds of bells and birds and the soothing splash of water lapping against the weathered rocks on the outer part of the mole. A long breakwater protected the anchorage from the ravages of a raging Cretan sea.

I stopped at the few boats advertised for hire only to find that each one had been chartered months in advance.

I tried to talk to the fishermen about renting a *cacique*, but they would have nothing to do with a pesky foreign woman who could not speak Greek. Even when I pointed longingly toward the deserted island of Dhia, the men did not understand. They evidently thought that no tourist would be fool enough to want to go to such a desolate place.

An hour passed, and Dhia was still tantalizingly out of reach.

"I can't believe this. They won't even talk to me."

I leaned despondently against the sea wall at the end of

the mole and watched a young boy doggedly beat a dangle-legged squid against a large boulder. He was tenderizing the long, suction-cupped tentacles the way it had been done since the first human decided the nasty looking creatures were good to eat.

The lad's slim build reminded me of my son Steve when he was a boy, and I waved and yelled, "Hello."

The youth surprised me when he responded politely in perfect, schoolboy English.

"Good morning, madam. Welcome to Kriti."

Jake and I looked at each other and in unison said, "An interpreter."

Despite the bad mood he had been in all day, Jake seemed pleased with our developing rapport, but I was not at all impressed.

I persuaded the youth to take a few coins, and he shyly agreed to help me with my search. In a matter of minutes, we learned that only two boats were for hire in the whole harbor: one of them smelled so much like diesel I suspected her bilge was full of leaking fuel; the other was in a similar state of disrepair, sitting in a rainbow ring of oil.

"I've been around boats all my life and these are nothing but bait buckets. They don't look seaworthy to me."

"Why don't you quit this nonsense? I'm telling you, my friends will sail us over to Dhia."

Before I could seriously consider Deupree's suggestion, a beautiful white yacht sped into the harbor, cut her engines to a purr, and settled into the water like a giant nesting seabird.

As the boat slowly passed us by, I read the name *Sheitan* painted on her transom and her homeport was *Miami, Florida.*

The boat flew an American flag and also sported a sign saying, BOAT FOR HIRE.

I shouted a loud and ecstatic, "*YES!*" and gave the heavens an exuberant high-five. I felt certain that this was a gift
sent straight from the gods or goddesses…perhaps they had
decided to bless my mission.

Without a word to Deupree, I took off at a brisk trot, trail-
ing the boat across the wide harbor to its mooring. Waving
my arms as I jogged along; I tried to attract the attention
of the two crewmen dressed in immaculate white pants and
shirts who stood at the ready on the foredeck.

"Hey! You guys! I would like to charter your boat!"

At first, I thought they were too far away to hear me over
the engine noise, but when they continued to ignore me after
they turned off their engine, dropped the anchor off the bow,
and had the stern of the boat securely tied to the mole, I realized that my words had no more substance to them than a
gnatty wind blowing across their ears.

I motioned to the boy for assistance.

"Maybe they don't speak English. You talk to them."

The lad tried, but the men ignored him, too.

Deupree finally arrived on the scene. He had followed
me at his own leisurely pace and was wearing the same scowl
he had worn all morning.

"What *are* you doing?" he asked irritably.

"Obviously, I'm trying to find out if I can charter this
boat. *You* speak to them! Please."

Reluctantly, Deupree ambled over to one of the crewmen
whose eyes were hidden behind dark mirrored sunglasses.

"Do you speak English? The lady wants some information."

"I speak English." The cigarette hanging between the

crewman's moist red lips waggled as he spoke. Without looking up or stopping what he was doing he added in a gruff voice, "I do no business with women...or boys."

"Is that so? Well, the last time I took a piss, *Bucko*, it was obvious that I am not a woman, and only a fool would mistake me for a boy."

The crewman raised his head and slowly looked Jake up and down. He must have decided that he looked either too old, or too mean, to take the matter any further. He just shrugged his shoulders, took a long drag off his cigarette, and flicked the butt into the water.

Like a performer doing a card trick, a five euro note appeared between Jake's fingers. He held the money out to the man and asked, "If your captain is on board, tell him I want to talk to him about hiring his boat."

Without hesitation, the crewman deftly slipped the bill from between Deupree's fingertips, looked at it carefully, ran his tongue over his lips as if thinking about the cheap bottle of *Raki* the money would buy.

"Where you wanna go?"

"To *that* island."

Jake pointed toward Dhia Island with another euro sticking between his thumb and forefinger.

"For what reason?"

"Curiosity. Take a few pictures. Maybe do some exploring."

"Would cost extra if we take you ashore. When you wanna go?"

"Today."

"Not possible. We have other business today."

The crewman dropped his half-coiled line, stuffed the

second bill in his shirt pocket, stepped to the doorway to the salon, and spoke a few words in Greek to someone in the cabin that I could not see.

"We take you tomorrow morning, if you come early."

I had never before witnessed machismo in action, but I was forced, just because I was a woman, to stand there and listen in silence. Oh, how I wished there was some other decent-looking boat for hire.

"We furnish water. You bring your own food if you wanna eat. Where can we reach you if wind turns bad? We had small Meltemi late yesterday. Could be another tomorrow."

"What's a Meltemi?" Jake asked.

The man sneered with contempt, and made what was probably a crude gesture with his left hand.

"Even child knows Meltemi. Meltemi is big north wind. Meltemi blows forty knots or more. When Meltemi is very bad, port police close the harbor. Nothing leaves the mole."

After a minor discussion, it was decided that a message could be left with the desk clerk at my hotel. Deupree wrote the name of the hotel and my room number on the back of his business card and gave it to the man. They agreed that we would meet at seven the next morning.

It was barely ten o'clock and my business for the day was done. We slowly walked up the hill toward the car.

"Last time I was here with my husband, we spent most of our days walking the ruins of Knossos Palace and visiting many of the other archeological sites scattered all across the island. The rest of our time we spent in the museum. I think I would like to see the old Venetian fort. My visitor's book is old, but it says there are some self-guided tours."

"I saw a sign that said it's closed. Something about re-pairs or cleaning."

"Well, then, I guess I'll revisit the museum after all. Thanks for the ride, and thanks for your help chartering the boat. You don't have to come tomorrow. You can go to Dhia with your friends. I can manage perfectly well on my own."

Even as I said the words, I knew I was lying. Thoughts of the long trip out to a deserted island, spending the day alone with those rough-looking crewmen was growing more frightening by the second. Although the arrangements were made, I doubted that I had the courage to board the *Sheitan* alone, no matter how virginal she might look.

Jake frowned and looked as if he could see the disturbing scenes that flitted across my mind.

"That's okay," he said. "I'll tag along. After all, we're partners, don't cha know."

My eyes softened and for the first time since we met, I smiled at Jake. I would never have believed it, but I was glad he had insisted on coming along. If it weren't for him, I would probably have given up at that point, forced by the lack of safe transportation to return home in defeat.

"Forget about the museum," he said. "How about driving over to Aghios Nikolaos for lunch?"

Faced with an afternoon of walking around a museum full of relics that were as familiar to me as the pots and pans in my own kitchen, I hesitated only a moment before open-ing the door and easing into the seat.

CHAPTER TWELVE

AGHIOS NIKOLAOS

The island could not have been more beautiful.

We drove past secluded bays and blue pools of quiet water at the base of steep cliffs where more than a few solitary swimmers bathed naked in the sun. We drove past olive trees and vineyards, past one-room farmhouses sheltered by a single tree and a woman working outside in the shade while an old man watched her, sitting in his straight-back chair, fingering his worry beads, and contemplating the vagaries of life.

We saw donkeys penned up with nanny goats whose distended udders were filled with milk. Basic food and basic transportation were kept next to houses with TV antennas and solar panels mounted on their roofs. The wise Cretans combined modern technology with antique practicality.

On the eastern end of the island, the little town of Aghios Nikolaos slept in the afternoon sun. It was much too early in the day for the townspeople to dress in their best clothes and join the tourists for an evening promenade around the inland lake that nourished the center of town.

We found a shady sidewalk *taverna* where we could sit and watch tourists buying their souvenirs. Skipping small talk, we relaxed and enjoyed the slow-paced ambiance.

Spearing the last satiny black olive from my Greek *salada*, I sighed.

"This has been a perfect day except, perhaps..." and I let the words trickle away.

"Perhaps what?" Jake asked quizzically.

"I guess I don't have a very good feeling about the boat trip tomorrow."

"Glad to hear you say it. Did you see that sleazy-looking character inside the cabin? He was wearing one of those micro-sized male bikinis; the kind that leaves the pubic hair exposed; not my idea of an all-day companion. I've been sitting here hoping you would reconsider asking my friends to sail us over to the island."

"I don't want to impose." What I didn't have the nerve to say was that I didn't want to feel obligated to him or his friends.

Jake oozed sincerity when he said, "I'm telling you it won't be an imposition. I didn't mention it to them last night, since you had already made other plans, but we can stop and talk to them on the way back to Heraklion."

Anxious to avoid spending the day with the crew of the *Sheitan*, we left immediately for Hersonissos and a villa Jake called Sea Cliffs.

In no time at all, he pulled the car into a circular drive in front of a large home with a red-tiled roof. Built in the typical Cretan fashion with white stucco generously slathered over large rectangles and squares, the design was severely simple in the popular Greek style. True to its name, the house was built on the edge of the cliff, spread out along the rim so that every room had a view of the sea.

A stone walkway led to a green copper-covered door and continued on to the edge of the cliffs where a wrought-iron railing with a locked gate barred the entrance to an open stairway cut into the living rock. The narrow steps plummeted down the face of the cliff to a tiny half-moon beach.

Flowers grew everywhere: artfully espaliered against gleaming white stucco, planted along the walkways, and flowing from enormous, man-sized clay urns. I was deeply moved by the beauty of the place and, once again, had that peculiar sensation of coming home.

The crescent-shaped living room was open to light, and wind, and the sound of breakers dashing themselves against the base of the rock-faced cliff far below. Paddle fans slowly stirred the air, creating a potpourri of light and sound.

Jake introduced his friends, Tina and Theodore Koriatos. They were a mismatched couple. He was tall, dark, and thin and she was short, petite, and blonde, but I had never met a couple who so obviously adored each other. Theo vigorously shook my hand and they both welcomed me with great warmth and charm.

"Don't let the Greek name fool you," Jake said. "These guys are one hundred percent made in the USA."

"Jake is correct." Theo smiled broadly. "We are genuine Americans, although both of our families came from a small village near Thessaloniki on the Greek mainland. One might say we are also Italian, since we find it more convenient to live and manage our business enterprises from Milan."

After the usual polite exchange of information, the subject of sailing to Dhia was quickly and easily broached.

"Dhia," Tina said and her clear blue eyes glowed with remembered pleasure. "There is one special anchorage, an ancient Minoan site at St. George's Bay that I find particularly intriguing. I love to snorkel over the rubble. I know that one day I will discover something wonderfully important."

Flexing his slim, eloquent hands, Theo revealed his own grand passion for finding some antiquity of great value.

"I must confess that I am enormously jealous of those who know the excitement of finding the artifacts that pass so quickly through my hands."

I was charmed by Theo's soft, expressive voice. He spoke with an international accent that marked him a speaker of many languages.

"So, you deal in antiques?"

"Sometimes," Jake answered for his friends. "Theo and Tina are in exports and imports. In fact that's how we first met."

The two men laughed like school chums enjoying a very old and very private joke. My curiosity was piqued, but I hesitated to ask probing questions, although I had an uneasy feeling that later I might wish I had been more assertive.

Instead I asked Tina, "Do you spend much time in Crete?"

"We usually spend several months each year. We have a few weeks of holiday left before we return to Milan for the rest of the summer. At the end of this week, we will send the *Crystina* back to Italy since the time for Meltemi approaches. This sail to Dhia will be our farewell cruise."

"Speaking of farewells," I said, "we should cancel our charter with the boat we hired today in Venetian Harbor."

"Call the port police," Theo said. "They can usually be relied upon to deliver a message of importance."

Jake made the call and returned with the universal answer, "No problem."

"Theo, let's invite these two to join us this evening." Tina's pretty eyes were warm and her smile seemed genuinely sincere. "We're having a small party on board the *Crystina*. Afterward, we'll spend the night on the boat."

"I can't," I said with a feeling of honest regret. "I must return to the hotel. I'm expecting a call from home."

"You'll miss all the fun! Well, at least stay long enough for a swim. And please eat. This morning our housekeeper brought us some of those delicious little Greek eggplants from her garden and insisted on making *moussaka*. Please, stay. Make yourselves at home."

"How about swimsuits?" Jake asked.

"Suits and robes are in the bathrooms. Towels and sea-water showers are in the cabana. I am so sorry, but we really must leave. See you tomorrow morning at the harbor. Theo will write down the directions so you can find us. Enjoy your swim."

Bathing suits with matching robes were neatly folded in individual cubbyholes inside the bathroom. I changed and met Jake down on the beach.

The water was cold, but not icy, and I swam out far enough to float, rising and falling, suspended inside an undulating blue globe of sea and sky. Adrift, lost in the sameness of the sun, the daytime moon, and the sea, a sudden spinning sensation distorted my sense of direction. Fighting panic, I flipped onto my stomach and frantically searched for shore. Thankfully, I had not drifted far, but I swam hard, suddenly afraid of an undertow.

I reached the beach and tried to stand, but a breaking wave knocked me down and my bathing suit took a gulp of sand. When I finally gained my footing and pushed the hair out of my eyes, I saw Jake standing on the beach waiting for me. A hot rush of fear, much greater than the one I had just experienced, grabbed me by the throat.

This was an almost perfect reenactment of a scene from

my novel, a scene that no one else had read, a scene where Ariadne walked from the sea to find Theseus waiting for her. This was a time when they first made love.

I walked past Deupree without looking at him. "I'm cold," I said and ran up the steps to the cabana. I stood under the shower, washing away the sand. I let the seawater spray beat against my forehead until it turned my skin bright red and my lips ash gray.

Later, properly showered and dressed and feeling more in control of my pesky imagination, I stood at the edge of the stone-walled patio and watched the sun lose its hold on the horizon. In a flaming crimson blaze, it slipped over the rim of the earth, and the strong north wind sent a shiver up my spine.

"You're still cold," Jake said, coming up behind me with one of Tina's shawls. Sensing his intention to wrap the soft warmth around me, I immediately moved away.

"Thanks," I said. "I do feel a little chilly."

I took the shawl from his hand and gratefully snuggled into its fuzzy warmth. The gesture was thoughtful, but I was still feeling apprehensive. The unpleasant experience on the beach was nothing more than coincidence, but it did reinforce my determination to keep the relationship with Deupree businesslike and casual.

I could still hear Letty's warning about the dangers of women traveling alone. It was better to appear remote and unfriendly than to send the wrong signal and later cry foul.

"I'm hungry." Jake rubbed his hands together greedily. "Salads are great, but they don't last all day. Let's eat."

He opened a bottle of Cretan wine, and I found some nice dinner music on the stereo. We carried our plates out to the patio, where we could enjoy the sea view, a three-quarter moon, and a sky full of stars.

Responding to the food and the wine, I relaxed and told Jake about my family and my best friend Letty Marie. For a little while, I forgot where I was and who I was with. I forgot until I looked at my watch, and that small gesture caused the old puppet-master to remind me that he was still on the job. Although my watch was analog without alarms, it didn't matter. My old taskmaster had only been temporarily banished and he was back on the job.

"I really must get back to the hotel. My husband should call between twelve and one Greek time."

On the drive back, we didn't talk and it felt nice.

"I think I'll come in with you and get some coffee in the bar. I need a slug of caffeine before driving back to the villa."

We walked into the hotel together, but instead of leaving me at the foot of the stairs, Jake insisted on walking me to my room.

"It's a gentleman's duty to see a lady to her door."

Another woman might have invited Jake inside. Instead, I opened the door and gave him the only thing I had to offer, my hand in friendship.

"Thank you for a perfect day."

It truly had been an exceptional day mainly because tomorrow I would go to Dhia Island.

"Good night," I said.

I opened the door, switched on the light, stepped partway into the room and swung my arm to pitch my purse on the bed but my arm froze mid-swing.

Every drawer open. Clothes thrown around the room like

discarded rags. Suitcase gaping, empty. Sheets ripped from the bed. Mattress askew, hanging halfway off the frame onto the floor.

Clutching my purse to my chest, I backed out of the door and nearly collapsed with fright when I bumped into Jake standing exactly where I had left him.

"Your room's been ransacked," he said even before I shrieked, "*I've been robbed!*"

Terrified, I expected at any moment to see someone come leaping through the door.

"They've gone," Deupree said with calm certainty, but just to be safe he pulled me away and moved me down the hallway toward the stairs and the hotel manager's office.

"You don't know they're gone," I resisted stubbornly. "Stop pushing me!"

With a flash of temper, I pulled free of his hand. I was dangerously close to hysteria.

"No," I said firmly, holding up my hands to physically stop the adrenaline surge. "You're right. There was no one in the room when I turned on the light. But my things...oh, God." I moaned and pressed my hand over my racing heart. "I can't believe what they did to my room."

By the time the police and the hotel security finished their investigation, two hours had passed. As far as I could see, nothing had been taken. The hotel manager was extremely solicitous. He assigned a bellman to sit in the hallway as a night watchman. He sent coffee. He even offered a maid to straighten the room.

"Coffee sounds wonderful. But I prefer to put my things away myself."

I scrubbed my hands over my arms. The intruders left

behind a presence that crawled like roaches over my skin.

"Can I help?" Jake asked.

"It feels like they urinated on everything. Maybe if I lay my clothes outside on the balcony, the night air will make them feel clean again."

"I really think you should come back to the villa with me. You shouldn't stay here alone."

"There's no logical reason for them to return. The only things I have of any value are my tape recorder and my camera. If I hadn't taken them with me, they would surely be gone. No one would be foolish enough to risk coming back for things so common and ordinary."

"You're right…I'm sure you're right."

"At least they didn't break the statue of the Snake Goddess or the Phaistos Disk. They must be superstitious. Look. They unwrapped the little goddess and stood her there on the dresser to watch while they vandalized my room."

"It's odd that they didn't take anything."

Deupree looked very serious. He started to say something more, but appeared to think better of it. Since I was determined to stay, he gave me an encouraging pat on the shoulder and said a second good night.

A half hour later, Dan called. He asked a few disinterested questions about the flight, about the hotel, and about Deupree. When I told him I would be sailing to Dhia on a private yacht, he was clearly impressed. He was more than impressed when I told him I would be sailing on a fifty-one foot Hinckley, a cruising sailor's dream. He sounded so envious I felt an unpleasant twinge of guilt.

"You should have come," I said defensively.

I wanted to tell him about the break-in, but my nerves

were too fragile to deal with an inevitable I-told-you-so scolding. Withholding the information made the conversation awkward and stilted. By the time we said good-bye, the guilt I felt earlier had changed into resentment.

I slept very little that night, tormented by bouts of terror when the wind moved the draperies and the moonlight sent flickering shadows across the ceiling and the walls of the room. Thinking about the painfully inadequate conversation with Dan made sleep nearly impossible.

CHAPTER THIRTEEN

THE *CRYSTINA*

Although I didn't get much sleep, the next morning I felt much better. I refused to let the break-in ruin my anticipation. Today was the day I would accomplish my goal. Today, I was going to Dhia.

It was aggravating to have to spend time on my clothes, but when the vandals trashed my room they treated what few things I brought like rags. I would be living in shorts when I explored the island, but my blouses and skirts were a mess. Since I was up early, I took the time to give them a press before I went down to the dining room for breakfast. I wore a skirt and blouse over my bathing suit for the trip into town, and put my sunshirt, vest, hiking shorts, and boots in a small sea bag.

The dining room was crowded. Most of the guests seemed to be speaking German

With a choice of American, which meant eggs, bacon and toast, or Greek, I chose Greek. I could never understand why some people missed the experience of sampling foreign cuisine when traveling. Greek meant a cup of coffee or tea, cheese and olives and bread, but I personally preferred sesame puffs, and honey, which were a hotel specialty. As for Greek coffee, for me it was an experience best kept to a minimum. To start the day, I wanted the diluted version that the Greeks and Turks called Nescafe.

ψ

Deupree was exactly on time, which was a minor relief.

Venetian Harbor was even noisier than the day before: honking automobiles, birds squabbling over discarded bait, boat horns, church bells, boisterous children at play. The combined activity of city and harbor created a concerto of discordant sounds.

Directions in hand, we walked along the mole looking for the *Crystina*. The trek was made more difficult since Theo's handwriting was worse than a poorly written prescription.

"Ayee-e-e. Look who comes. *Misss-ter Fortunes Unlimited.*"

The loud greeting was obviously meant for Jake.

"Here comes the big man who bargains like a woman."

The coarse speaker was the crewman from the *Sheitan*. Once again, he was dressed in white and wearing his mirrored sunglasses like a mask. Despite the early morning hour, he and his inebriated friend were drinking from a flat brown bottle that they passed between them.

They were leaning against a stone wall only a few feet from where we had to pass.

Without stopping or slowing his pace Jake said, "I canceled the charter with you, yesterday. Our plans changed."

"No excuses! A real man keeps to his bargain."

The sailor punctuated his remark by spitting on the ground a scant inch from the toe of my white deck shoe. Then he flipped his glowing cigarette butt across our path, barely missing Jake's arm.

"Hey, Misss-ter Fortunes Unlimited, what fortunes you lookin' for on Dhia Island?"

Jake showed no reaction, but he didn't like the direction the man's questions were taking.

"My fortunes come from investment banking. I'm an

amateur botanist looking for unusual plants." Jake threw the words over his shoulder, never changing his pace, continuing to walk naturally.

I counted boats, deciphering Theo's directions, hoping we were on the right side of the harbor, praying we would not have to retrace our steps and pass the men again.

"Over here!" a cheery voice called. Tina yelled and waved. She was only a few boats away.

"Thank God!" I stole a look back and saw the men pointing at us, laughing and posturing like hoodlums on a city street corner. "Do you think they're the ones who trashed my room?"

"I doubt it, but hindsight says I should never have given them my card, and most certainly I should never have given them your hotel name and room number."

Pushing the incident aside, we boarded the *Crystina*, stowed our gear in the salon as the deckhand released the last docking line. Theo immediately eased the boat away from the mole and motored toward the harbor entrance.

I squeezed my arms around my stomach to quiet that pit-of-the-stomach sense of expectancy that always filled me every time I went to sea. I couldn't keep from wishing that Dan had come with me. He would have loved Theo's boat. It had been built by a master builder, and I looked around me, appreciating every detail.

Comfortable padded benches lined the cockpit and the table in the center was fitted with holders for drinks. The deck was formed from strips of hand-rubbed teak, and to imitate sailing ships of old, the spars were faux painted to look like wood. In the salon, the paneling was also dark wood enhanced by the gleam of polished brass fittings. A chart table at the bottom the stairs held charts, dividers, plotter, and a handheld compass. The galley, off to the left, had a stainless refrigerator and matching freezer. An oversized table, flanked by cushioned benches, could easily seat eight.

The *Crystina* was a lady of first quality. Although she had all the modern conveniences, she had an old world appeal that held the romance of the sea when ships with topsails flying set sail for adventures in the new world.

Jake flashed me an understanding smile and nodded his head as if I had spoken my words of admiration out loud. The uncomfortable feeling that he could read my mind was becoming more and more disturbing.

Once we were in open water, Theo brought the boat into the wind. The deckhand raised the mainsail, I unfurled the genoa and then, ever so gently, Theo put the *Crystina* on an easy reach. This time, the feeling of coming home was more than I could bear and I couldn't stop the tears. Embarrassed, I turned my back and thought, *I wish I could be alone.*

"Theo. Is it okay if Kate goes up front to watch for dolphins?"

Jake asked the question with my back turned to him; there was no way he could see my wet cheeks.

"The front of the boat is called the bow, my friend, and yes, Kate may go forward."

Bless you, I thought, and this time I hoped Jake really could read my mind.

While Theo checked the sails and tinkered with the trim, Jake poked his head down the open hatch and yelled, "Hey, Tina, do you have anything cold to drink on this here yacht?"

Carefully, I made my way forward, walking along the

slanted deck, holding to guard rails and shrouds. I was seek-ing that small space before the mast where metal, line, and cloth come together to harness the wind. I felt that the heart of every ship was in that special place just before the mast, a mystical site of soul, if ever a ship had such a thing. There was just enough room to stretch out on the warm teak deck, fitting myself around hardware and hatches, lying with my cheek flat against the smooth sun-bleached wood.

Feeling at peace, breathing in the faintest odor of warm linseed oil, I turned off the world and for those few moments in time, yesterday, today, and tomorrow were one. There was no island, no book, no truth to find, no home to return to. Only the wind, the sun, and the sea.

CHAPTER FOURTEEN

OLD FRIENDS

Theo held the wheel with one hand, allowing the boat to reach off at an easy angle to the wind. When he looked at Jake, his lean face softened, and his pale brown eyes warmed with the affection he felt for the man at his side.

"It has been far too long, my friend. It truly is marvelous to see you again."

"The feeling is mutual, *amigo*."

The two men had formed a lasting bond of friendship when they were young men serving together in a Marine Special Forces unit in Vietnam. They met a few years after the war that wasn't a war came to an end.

"I am truly sorry that I've been so busy since you arrived. We haven't been able to speak more than a few words, and I must say, I'm hellishly curious to know what this expedition is all about. First you send a message saying you need a place to stay and the use of my boat. You also say you are looking for a Green something or other, and I can't remember what the old code words mean anymore. Then you arrive with a woman who seems very pleasant, but," Theo paused, tilted his head, and looked at Jake knowingly, "a woman unlike those you usually select as a traveling companion."

"You read that one right. And you claim you're not psychic."

Jake laughed weakly. Then he gave a tired sigh, which was completely out of character. Jake never let anything get him down.

"I should have scared her out of coming. I should have made the trip alone. I guess I'm getting soft, but it seemed so blasted important to her. Well, here's the gig. Less than a week ago, she came to me insisting that there's something special on that island out there."

Jake sighted down his finger and pointed toward Dhia Island.

"As you know, people are continually coming to me with nutty hunches, so I didn't think much of it at first. I told her I would do a reading, and I was about to do the old pendulum and map bit when my palm began to itch, which means there *is* something, maybe some kind of treasure, out there on that island."

"Treasure?" Theo spoke the word with reverence. His heavy eyebrows lifted and his whole body came to attention.

"Yes. And she's wearing the damndest strand of beads I've ever touched. The things actually jumped in my hand. There's more energy in those stones than in any of the shaman tools in my whole collection. I don't yet know their significance, but something tells me they've been used in one of the old Cretan mystery cults."

"You did say treasure? Why, Jake, that's the nicest word I've heard in a very long time."

Theo was so excited he all but levitated with delight. "A treasure hunt!" He said the words with the exuberance of a boy. "I've always wanted to go on a *real* treasure hunt."

"Whoa, Long John!"

Jake held up his hand in warning.

"Don't go cocking your pistols just yet. Kate doesn't know what she's looking for. She's thinking relics and broken pots, and I'm getting nothing specific. Just a hunch. Well, maybe something more than a hunch. She's been writing a novel about the old culture on Crete, the ancient Minoans, and it's possible that when she was in deepest contact with the artifacts, her beads cued some past-life impressions. That can happen when you get caught up in the flow of lives as powerful as the archetypes she's tapped into."

"Fine. That explains why Kate is here," Theo said. "But I know it would take more than a flashback to interest a hard-nosed prospector like you."

Theo was one of the few people in the world Jake trusted, but even so he hesitated. He steepled his fingers, appearing to weigh the cost of adding Theo to the play, deciding just how much he wanted to reveal.

"Okay. I'll tell you what I suspect. As you well know, several major, I mean *major*, discoveries of Greek treasure have been found by foreigners just because their intuition led them to it. Hell! She could be another Heinrich Schliemann. He used common knowledge and gut instinct to find the ruins of Troy and God only knows how much gold. The same thing happened here on Crete when Sir Arthur Evans found the Palace of Knossos."

Jake was about to compare the inspiration of these two pioneer archeologists with Kate's urge to explore Dhia, but felt that the theory was too preposterous to be true.

"Actually," Jake backed off a bit, "I knew the time had finally come for me to pay you two a visit. I've lost count of the times you've asked me to vacation with you here on Crete. I came to finally take a sail on your precious floating palace."

Theo ignored Jake's attempt to change the subject. He was not going to be put off the treasure scent so easily.

"I knew it was something special when you said you were

coming. Where on Dhia Island?" Theo asked softly.

In Vietnam, Theo had worked with Jake doing readings on fuzzy reconnaissance photos, and between the two of them they had come up with some unbelievably accurate information. However, Jake always felt that Theo was afraid of his own extrasensory abilities. He never acknowledged his natural talent, always blaming his accurate analysis on dumb luck, so Jake decided to stay away from the subject as much as possible, not wishing to test the limits of his friend's skepticism.

"The chart she brought me was too small to pinpoint an exact spot. I felt something with my hand, and I got a few pulls with the pendulum, nothing specific. I must walk the land. As I said before, Kate doesn't really know what's drawing her to the island, or even where to look. For her, this whole thing may be her time of life: one last menopausal fling."

Tina had been sunbathing on the aft deck, listening to the conversation between the two men without comment. However, Jake's obnoxious remark was too sexist to go unchallenged.

Streaks of blue lightning flashed from her eyes, and her tightly wound blond curls seemed to rise like hackles on the back of a polar bear. She came up on one arm and boldly looked Jake up and down.

"Perhaps, Jake, it is you who are having one last hormonal fling. You must be about the age for male crisis."

"Tina! Where are your manners?" Theo scolded.

"Manners? Don't talk to me about manners. We have barely said two words to Kate, and I doubt that Jake has bothered to find out any real thing about her, but he's labeling her and evaluating her by the condition of her hormones."

"Well, my sweet, if she were a he," Jake whipped, "we'd

probably be discussing balls, or something else equally intimate and coarse, and you probably wouldn't object to those remarks in the least."

"That's not the same thing."

"Oh, but it is." Jake's face was red and it wasn't from sunburn. Tina's words pierced his armor, nicked his skin, and drew blood. "We're talking hunches here. Gut feelings. And if you don't think gonads have something to do with that then you've never played poker, or made any high-stakes business deals."

Theo knew from past experience what was going to happen next. His wife took too much pride in her trading skills to allow such a jab to pass unchecked. Although Tina and Jake had been friends for years, they could never be together more than ten minutes before Theo had to hide the cutlery. They had an uncanny knack for baiting each other. And they both loved a good brawl.

"Well, you just let me tell you about the load of shit Emery tried to sell me last month." Tina was furious. "He was touting his fabulous hoard of paintings, saying they were from a private collector on Long Island, hinting that there were some Picassos and Chagalls which I knew had..."

"Enough!" Theo said sharply. "I hereby grant Tina balls, and I agree that you, Jake, are a bitch. *Now!* I want to talk treasure. And since I'm the captain of this ship, I will be obeyed."

The two adversaries laughingly eased their stance.

"Another day," Tina said with a polite nod of her stylishly coifed head, and Jake bowed to his hostess with mock gallantry.

CHAPTER FIFTEEN
THE SEARCH BEGINS

The wind was perfect for relaxing, and since I had managed very little sleep the night before, I dozed off for a few much-needed minutes. Loud voices coming from the cockpit sounded an alert. Concerned, I made my way back along the deck and joined the others.

"Is something wrong? Can I help?"

"No," Theo answered quickly. "Only a minor foray between two old fencing partners. And don't ask what it was about, or it will start all over again."

I smiled with relief and said, "The *Crystina* is the most beautiful boat I've ever seen." Admiration filled my eyes. Dan used to say my eyes looked like green fire opals whenever I was emoting.

Theo seemed pleased by my appreciation for his beloved boat, and it made me feel warm inside. I couldn't put it into words, but there was something about him that seemed so familiar. Something I recognized, but could not name. The feeling was too tenuous, too ephemeral to grasp. Perhaps when I knew him better I would know what it was about him that touched me.

"Would you like to take the wheel?" he asked.

"It's been a long time. My husband usually takes the helm. Are you sure?"

"Yes. Jake told me earlier that you're a blue-water sailor, and I watched you help my deckhand without instruction. I think the *Crystina* will be safe in your hands."

"Do you have a compass heading, or may I take her up?"

"She's all yours."

"Then…bring in the sails, please."

Theo cranked in the main, then the jenny, and the *Crystina* gave up her easy reaching angle to the wind. She leaned into a nice heel, and the spray flew high in the air over the pulpit and splashed onto the foredeck.

Tina looked at Theo with surprise. She leaned over and whispered in Jake's ear, "Did you put a spell on him or something? He never lets anyone steer his precious boat."

"Not me," Jake said.

Theo relaxed, sitting on the edge of the cockpit, and I stood with my feet braced, the wind whipping my loosely buttoned sun-shirt as I diligently watched the luff of the sails. A feeling of contented pleasure filled my squinty sailor's eyes, and Theo smiled at me like a compatriot admiring an old friend.

Theo said I was the first person he'd ever had on board his boat who felt the same way he did about the *Crystina*. He knew how I felt, not by what I said, but by the way I touched and admired the things that other people pass over as ordinary.

Holding the *Crystina* close to the wind, I teased her, bringing her up nearly to luff, then falling away. I hoped my lack of experience at the helm did not show to my three companions. Thank goodness they could not feel the tremble in my knees.

This was a glorious day for me. It was my *Day of Days*. I was sailing the most beautiful boat in the world, and I was returning to Dhia Island. I knew I was returning. I felt it with unshakable certainty. I felt in my bones that I had sailed to

Dhia Island on another day such as today. I also felt that it had been in a life I had lived many years before.

ψ

We dropped the anchor near a place Theo called Aginara Bay on the southeast coast of the island. The rocky bottom lay clearly visible beneath nine meters of clear blue water. Looking at the rough terrain on shore, we decided it would be wise to change from bathing suits to shorts and hiking boots. I wore my vest of many pockets and carried my camera.

Jake looked like he just stepped out of an L.L. Bean catalog. Always well dressed, not in a foppish way, his well-worn clothes seemed to be very carefully chosen for each particular occasion.

The dinghy made its noisy way toward the beach, and when Theo raised the outboard motor Jake jumped into the surf and dragged the boat inshore far enough so that the rest of us could disembark with dry feet.

I was immediately filled with despair. I knew Dhia was barren, but it was still a big disappointment. I had heard a rumor about a resort opening up on the western part of the island, but at this point there was nothing but rocks and weeds, sand and gravel. In a few years all of it could change if some farsighted entrepreneur decided to take a chance on developing it.

"It's so scrubby. Walking is going to be very difficult. It's absolutely desolate."

The island lay parched and hot in the noonday sun. The bleached landscape was strewn with small stones, boulders, and brittle clumps of dry weeds.

"I had hoped for something more."

"Don't get discouraged yet, partner," Jake said. "Perseverance is the name of the prospecting game. Since each of us has a water bottle, why don't we fan out and cover as much terrain as possible. We'll meet back here in an hour."

"What are we looking for?" Tina asked.

"That's Kate's department. Ask her."

"Flat shapes with markings that could be from a clay tablet, curved shapes that might be pottery, stones with symbols carved on their surface, anything that looks handmade or out of the ordinary. And look for caves. Look for openings behind dense brush; and check between the boulders. Many relics have been found wedged into crevices. I'm going over the hill to the coast, to the place where Jake's pendulum said I should begin."

Without waiting for agreement, I walked up the slope, carefully finding my way through the boulders and smaller rocks. Jake headed northwest up over a hill, Tina went due west along the coast, and Theo stayed along the southern shore, which would be extremely difficult. Considering the rocky terrain, it would involve some climbing which was no problem since Tina said Theo was part mountain goat.

We all walked with heads down, eyes on the ground.

Like me, Jake wanted to explore the northern part of the island, so he walked at an angle up the rolling hills and headed toward the coast.

I saw nothing of any interest, and when I reached the cliffs, I stood at the edge looking down at the incoming waves crashing against the base. Looking north, I searched the horizon for Santorini, Crete's sister island.

By the time Jake circled around and reached the place where I was along the cliffs, I had moved even closer to the edge, leaning out to better see the rocks and surf down below.

"Kathryn," he yelled. "Back away from the edge!" Jake's voice was sharp with concern, and he was rubbing and shaking his arm as if it had gone to sleep.

Surprised that he had followed me, I turned, saw the concern on his face, and took his advice. I moved away from the edge and sat down on a small boulder in the middle of a patch of grass.

Heat from the sun-baked stone quickly penetrated my shorts and made sitting very uncomfortable, but not uncomfortable enough to make me move. I unscrewed the top of my water bottle, but before I drank I felt the urge to perform an old ritual honoring Mother Earth. I spilled a little of the precious liquid on the parched ground and that small gesture of respect gave me a feeling of kinship with the island. I placed my palm against the dirt and gave the warm, gritty soil an affectionate pat.

Jake poked here and there with the toe of his boot, walking a hundred yards in either direction along the rim, while I watched seagulls swoop down from their roosting places on the cliffs and skim the surface of the water in search of fish. Their raucous calls cut through the busy sound of bees working over a patch of weedy flowers. The whole island smelled of hot rocks and wild herbs.

"We'd better head back," Jake said. "I want to come here again, tomorrow. I think this place is ripe. It feels hot. Very hot."

"Like *hot* in the game we played as kids?"

"Yeah. Something like that." But there was no hint of playfulness in Jake's eyes. He was serious. This was business.

"You know, I've been sitting here puzzling over those rust stains coming from beneath that stack of flat rocks over there near the edge. Don't you think that's an odd place for rust?"

The two of us walked onto the sloping table rock to take a closer look at the rusty wash spilling out from under an untidy pile of stones.

"Let's see what's underneath," Jake said. Working together, we quickly moved the stones away.

"Bolts. Threaded bolts set in a metal plate. I've used smaller stuff like that in the concrete walls in my laundry room back home."

"It's the remains of a base support for a lifting device."

"You don't know that. You can't know that just by looking."

Jake wasn't listening. He wanted to see the face of the cliff. He dropped to one knee and was about to lie down on his belly to look over the edge when I stopped him.

"Wait a minute. It would make more sense if we traded places, just in case the edge is undercut. Less weight out on the edge would be safer. You hold my ankles and I'll do the looking."

I crawled far enough out to scan the face of the cliff. "I don't think there's any danger of collapse at this point. You could put weight, heavy weight, right out onto the rim. There's a ledge about a third of the way down from here, but it's very narrow. One misstep and it will be good-bye explorer."

"A ledge? That's where I want to look. Let me see." Jake crawled out beside me. "It's pretty steep. We'll need some climbing gear."

I scrambled to my feet, brushing hard at the gravel and

weed stems clinging to my clothes. I was thoroughly disgusted. I was angry and disappointed.

"What's wrong with you?"

"Ancient Minoans didn't have bolts or metal base plates. I came here to find clay tablets or potsherds—some kind of relic. I didn't come all this way for iron bolts and base plates."

"How do you know what you came here to find? Only time will reveal why you were drawn to this island. I think we're close. I feel there's something on the face of the cliff. We just need to find a way to get down there and take a look."

We returned to the dinghy, and the four of us motored back to the *Crystina* where we shared the news of our discovery. The decision was quickly made to return immediately to Heraklion and find proper climbing gear to inspect the face of the cliff.

As we motor-sailed away from the shallows, a white yacht came speeding straight toward us. It looked as if the boat could have been standing off, waiting for us to leave the anchorage. In an aggressive move, they cut across our bow and forced us to tack although we had starboard right-of-way.

"That looks like the *Sheitan*," Jake said. "That's the boat we chartered yesterday in Venetian Harbor. We had a slight altercation with one of their crewmen this morning. He and his friend were drunk then; by now he must be four sheets to the wind."

As the *Sheitan* passed us to port, one of the crewmen gave us a one-armed salute holding the black shape of an automatic weapon in his hand.

"I don't believe this," Theo said. "Tina, hand me the glasses."

Focusing on the speeding yacht he shouted, "Those

bastards are flying a Corsican Rebel flag. And that idiot is waving an Uzi. They must be revolutionaries. Damnit! The only weapon I have on board is an old thirty-ought-six and half a dozen cartridges."

Theo lowered the glasses and glared at Jake.

"Surely you know that *Sheitan* means Devil in English. Look at them! That bastard is still waving that God-damned firehouse at us."

"Please, don't blame Jake. It's not his fault," I said. "I'm the one who found them. Jake didn't want to talk to them, but when we first saw them they were flying an American flag, and the boat looked so clean compared to the rest. I'm truly sorry."

"Don't be so ready to take all the blame," Jake interrupted. "I went along with the deal. Besides, it looks like they're turning away. They only wanted to force us to change course."

The stern of the big cruiser dug into the water as their helmsman pushed the powerful engines full forward. Wings of white water flew in the air on either side of the boat as they sped away. Although the *Sheitan* was leaving, Jake's brow was creased with worry. Once again he was rubbing his arm and flexing his fingers as if they were in a cramp. "When we return tomorrow, I think it would be wise to come armed. We'd better be prepared to do a little hunting."

"Hunting could pose a problem on Dhia. There is always a matter of permits and licenses, limits and fines, but luckily I brought some business friends here to hunt wild goats a few weeks ago. I know someone who can renew the documents. I foresee no problem. It's been some time since we last did a little hunting. Kate, do you know how to shoot?"

"My dad taught me to hit tin cans with a .22 rifle, if you call that shooting."

"That will do. I have a pretty little Finnish Sako that you should find comfortable. It's a fortunate coincidence that we have a small stash of weapons back at the Villa. As for you, Jake, I have a Ruger you should find very sweet. I have used it to hunt ibex in the mountains in Italy. It's scoped, but you can use the iron sights if you prefer."

"That fine for me. Sounds like a good plan. But, I think the women should stay behind."

Jake continued to flex his left hand, shaking it as if to stop it from tingling. "I'm feeling that we're in for a bad time. Lots of negative energy. Not just from the *Sheitan*. Something more."

"I'm not staying behind," Tina stated emphatically.

"Neither am I," I said firmly. "And before we go any further, I need to make something clear. Without your help, and the use of the *Crystina* I would never have been able to explore the island, at least not at this time. I have no idea what we may find tomorrow, but if we do find something important, I think that we should share the fame of discovery equally. I also want an agreement that we will keep everything legal. No ignoring the Greek antiquities laws. Penalties for even minor infractions can be as bad as they are in the States for selling drugs."

"No problem," Theo said, and I was relieved when Tina and Jake both nodded their heads in agreement.

"One more thing. As for leaving Tina and me behind, unless Theo wants to include a deckhand in your exploration, you need me. I've done a lot of heavy weather sailing. One last thing. In case Jake hasn't already told you…this is *my* expedition."

I stood with my feet planted and my fists clenched. I was staking my claim and it was not for the right to hunt *kri kri* goats. No one was going to do me out of my right to search for my destiny, not the *Sheitan*, and most certainly not Jake and his quaint need-to-protect-the-little-women attitude. He was worse than Dan and Letty Marie put together.

"Agreed," Jake said almost too easily and immediately turned to Theo and asked, "What about climbing gear?"

Jake had barely acknowledged my little speech. He resumed his conversation with Theo as if nothing out of the ordinary had been said. I wasn't sure I had made myself clear, but as long as they included me in their plans, I would wait before restating my claim.

"We have plenty of line on board, and safety harnesses, but no carabineers or jumars, not even one piton, which is to say that I have nothing to do any real climbing. Although I've talked about it for years, I've never climbed in Crete."

"Excuse me. Sorry to interrupt," I said, "but I know where we may be able to get the climbing equipment you need. I met a woman whose brother is a climber. She said he had been in a climbing accident with the man who worked in her shop. In fact, he was the one who directed me to Venetian Harbor to hire a boat."

Jake glared at me vehemently. "You are something else!"

"What did I do now?" I was baffled by Jake's reaction. Lately, he seemed to be in a perpetual snit over everything I did.

"Tell me something," he snarled. "Why did you come to me saying that you needed my help with your exploration? You continually have information before we need it. You go to the exact spot where I'm led on the island; in fact you're there before me. Are you some kind of ringer? Why did you bring me into this, if you can do so well on your own?"

I'm sure I visibly shrank in size, curling inside myself, unable to disguise any longer the painful insecurity I tried to hide. Honesty was my only defense.

"I don't have any special abilities. Without your help, I might never have come back to Crete. I would probably never have found a way to sail to Dhia on my own. Without a safe way to reach the island, I would be on my way back home, dreaming dreams of doing. I'm only trying to help with the search. If you give me a list of the gear, I'll go back to the antique shop and see if I can beg or borrow the stuff you need. At least, I can try to find a place that sells climbing supplies."

"I'll go with you," Jake snapped. His response was a little too sharp and a little over-tough. He sounded as if he might be trying to cover up feelings that might have been stirred by my confession.

The sail back to Venetian Harbor was without further incident, however Theo was more than a little concerned by the confrontation with the *Sheitan*. There had been an attempted hijacking a few months earlier off the western end of Crete that had ended with a fatality. Determined to be prepared for any eventuality, he and Tina drove back to the villa to assemble guns, ammunition, permits, and provisions.

Jake and I walked up the sloping hill into the city. The busy shopping pace had slowed and many of the stores had already closed for the evening. When we approached the antique shop, the lights in the window sparkled and winked behind the wavy panes of glass, adding a touch of magic to the narrow alleyway. The tinkling doorbell and the ever-present aroma of coffee were a friendly welcome. This time Elana was sitting at a small desk writing in a journal. She immediately recognized me, extended her hand, and kissed me on both cheeks with the warmth you might offer an old friend.

Jake once again posed as an amateur botanist who wanted to turn his trip to Crete into a working holiday.

"I am certain my brother has climbing equipment you could borrow, or he will know where it can be purchased. He lives in a small village just east of the city. I was about to close the shop and go there to a family celebration. He will be sure to attend the feast since he was *Koumbaros*, what you call the best man, at the wedding of the cousin whose child is being honored. Why don't you come with me?"

Jake winked at me and said, "Well, why not? It's been a pretty boring day."

CHAPTER SIXTEEN

PARTY TIME

Since Elana would be staying the night with her family, we followed her in Jake's car. She led us to a place in the nearby hills. Our destination was a beautiful home, the largest in the village, with a cobblestoned courtyard dressed for a party that had already begun.

The side patio was strung with colored lanterns glowing like giant fireflies caught in the boughs of the trees. The night air was warm and carried the fragrance of roast lamb and the happy sounds of laughter.

Most of the guests were already seated at three long tables covered with white tablecloths dotted with flickering candles inside luminous globes of red glass. The tables were set with plates, and wineglasses, and a multitude of bowls, platters, and trays piled high with food.

"My brother is not yet here, but he will come. In the meantime, please, you must join us and eat."

We were presented to the ranking elder, a tall, dignified man with an iron grip and dark magnetic eyes. He insisted that we sit with Elana at the head table. We were each handed a knife and a fork, and with unrestrained *panache* everyone began serving themselves from the dozens of communal bowls spread all along the table.

"Think of it as a duel with forks," Elana said with a broad smile.

An enthusiastic white-haired grandfather lunged forward, having speared a tasty piece of lamb, offering it to me to eat straight off his fork, which I did, since everyone else was doing the same. The delicious morsel was followed with a toast and a chaser of wine.

"*Panta yia!* May you always be happy!" the grandfather said with a sly wink and a seductive smile.

Elana returned the toast for me saying, "*Epissis!* Same to you."

Since we were honored guests, we found we were receiving more than our share of attention and a generous amount of food and drink. After several rounds of toasts, we began to imitate our hosts, using our forks aggressively, offering bites to our laughing companions.

Most of the celebrants spoke a little English and they all welcomed us to their feast, urging us to eat the dolmathes and little phyllo pastries filled with spinach and cheese, tiny meatballs, marinated squid, cucumbers in garlic yogurt. There was flat bread, summer salad, olives, tender chunks of roast lamb, and wine drunk from glasses that were never less than half full.

While the guests talked and ate and laughed, a bandy-legged fiddler moved from table to table singing impromptu couplets, *Mantinadhes,* which Elana interpreted.

He sang a poem to a young girl praising her pretty eyes, and another teased a shy, lovesick young man about his faintly beating heart, and yet another slightly bawdy verse extolled the virility of the new father and praised the health of his firstborn son, the infant they had come together to fete.

This was a celebration of family, and true to the spirit of Crete, strangers like us were honorary kin.

More than an hour passed. We watched the entrance to the courtyard, anxiously awaiting a man who looked like he could be related to Elana. The relatives kept assuring us that the brother would soon arrive, "No problem."

"I think we're wasting our time," Jake said. "We'll have to make do with the safety gear we have. I think we'd better go."

Just as we started to leave, a drummer and a flamboyant *bouzouki* player joined the wandering fiddler and the dancing began. The persistent beat of the drums was irresistible to me.

"Let's wait just a little longer," I said when Elana asked me to join the circle dance.

"You shall dance the *Pendozalis* like a true Cretan," Elana said as she took my hand and pulled me toward the open space set aside for the dancing. "We will dance together. Only the women. Come!"

When the male dancers left the floor, Elana and her friends led me through the *Syrtos*, a traditional Cretan dance. Head erect, back straight, the women danced the patterns with grace and dignity. When the *bouzouki* trilled the exuberant finale, the party-makers cheered, and clapped, and threw flowers at our feet.

Radiant and out of breath, I fell into the chair, fanning myself with my hand. I was telling Jake how much fun he was missing, when he stiffened and his face turned dark and somber. Alarmed by his expression, ready at a word to leap from my chair, Jake pointed his finger at something behind me. Turning, I expected to see Elana's brother; instead I saw Demetri once again standing at my back.

Dressed in tight black pants, black boots, and a black shirt unbuttoned to the waist, all he needed to complete the pirate look was a curved Cretan blade stuck through a loop in his wide leather belt.

Although his manly dress was striking, it was the ornate gold replica of a labrys, the Minoan double ax, hanging from a heavy gold chain around his neck that caught my attention.

A smaller version of the gold double ax was also worn by the two men, also dressed in black, who stood at his side like subalterns. I recognized the man on Demetri's left as the drinking companion of the loud-mouthed crewman we had encountered that morning at the boat harbor.

While I assessed the three men in black, Demetri glared at my chest. The once hidden blue lapis beads, thanks to the lively Greek dancing, were displayed for everyone to see.

Demetri pointed an accusing finger at me and shouted, "*You* are the one who stole my beads."

I could not let such an accusation go unchallenged. I was instantly on my feet, standing nose to chin with my accuser. I was fully prepared to defend my honor, but before either one of us could move or speak, Elana stepped between us.

"Demetri! Have you no shame? Kate has come to this village as my guest."

"She has no right to my beads," Demetri shouted. He tried to push Elana aside. Although she was barely tall enough to reach his shoulder, she was firmly rooted and did not budge. "They are my property!" he yelled at me over Elana's head.

Trying to step around Elana he shook his finger at the stars and declared solemnly, "They are stolen property!"

"I stole nothing from anyone," I said. "I bought these beads. I paid Elana's grandfather a fair price for these blue stones."

"Then I will buy them back from you. What did you pay that old thief?" He dug in his pocket, struggling to remove his money from his tight-fitting pants.

Jake moved up to stand at my side and placed a supportive hand under my elbow. In a strong, clear voice he said, "The lady's beads are not for sale."

His voice was calm, but his eyes were veiled and his mouth looked dangerously controlled. He whispered to me, "It's time for us to go."

"I'm not leaving!" I lifted my arm, trying to remove it from Jake's hand while throwing a defiant look of warning toward Demetri.

"He owes me an apology."

"Forget it," Jake muttered and in a loud stage voice he said, "Thanks for inviting us to a great party. Sorry, everybody, for all the commotion. We'll meet your brother another time, Elana. We have to go."

Jake ushered me through the courtyard while I jerked and pulled, but he held my arm in such a tight grip I could do little more than bluster and fume.

"Why are you always manhandling me? Let go!"

Demetri would have followed us, but he and his companions were being detained by a short, stout man whose features marked him a close relation. Elana, once again, shook her finger under Demetri's nose. We could hear the elders protesting his bad manners, denouncing his wild accusations against a man long dead. Speaking in English for our benefit, they declared that Elana's grandfather was a true and honorable Cretan of fine reputation.

Jake opened the car door and pushed me inside. "Stay put."

"I will not! You can't tell me what to do! No one gets away with accusing me of thievery. Why do we have to make such a speedy retreat?"

"Demetri is the one who ransacked your room last night. Those thugs from the *Sheitan* distracted me. I should have known it before now."

"You don't know that. How do you know that?"

"What kind of lock is on the sliding door to the balcony in your hotel room?"

"I don't know. I never lock it. No one could come in through the balcony. I'm on the ocean side of the hotel. It's at least a hundred-foot drop onto the rocks below."

"It would be no trick at all for an experienced climber to rappel down from the roof, search the room, and leave through the door after he had what he came for, which would have been your lapis beads."

"Demetri has a game leg."

"A stiff leg would be a nuisance, but not a real problem for an experienced climber. You must come back to the villa with me tonight."

"Tina may not have an empty bedroom."

"That's a technicality. You can't stay in your room to-night. We'll stop at the hotel and collect what you need. In the long run, it will save time. We can go directly to the boat from the villa in the morning."

"But my husband may call tonight."

"You could leave Theo's phone number with the hotel, but I don't advise it. Desk clerks are honest to a point, but most people can be bought or threatened into divulging in-formation. I think it would be best if there are no clues to tell Demetri where he can find you."

"What will Tina think when she wakes up and finds me on her couch?"

Jake threw back his head and laughed with genuine amusement. "She will be shocked. She would be less surprised if she found you in bed with me." Jake momentarily took his eyes off the road. "After seeing you dance tonight, I think that could be a very pleasurable experience indeed. Your husband is a very lucky man."

Thinking about Dan's anger when we parted, I responded with a grunt. From the understanding look on Jake's face, I felt I didn't have to explain. This unspoken understanding between us was beginning to really frighten me. I felt confused and apprehensive, afraid that it could become addictive.

We stopped at the hotel to collect my things, and just as we walked through the door to my room, the telephone rang. I took a deep breath, picked up the receiver, listened a moment to the silence before saying a faint, "Hello?"

Sighing with relief I cried, "Letty! Oh, it's so good to hear your voice," and I meant every word. I sat down on the edge of the bed, preparing to have a much needed chat with my dearest friend.

Jake stepped out on the balcony into the starlit night, and watched the breakers throw a spray of silver moonshine onto the rocks below. The telephone conversation with Letty was abnormally brief. Way too soon, I joined Jake at the rail of the balcony, where I, too, looked out at the moonlit sea.

"Bad news?" he asked.

"I'm not sure. Letty says that my husband had tried to reach me all day; she said she's been trying for hours. She called to tell me that Dan is arriving at the Heraklion Airport early tomorrow afternoon."

"Your husband is coming to Crete to help you with your search?"

"No. He's coming to collect me. It seems that since I insist on taking a vacation, he's booked us on a tour of Egypt. We leave for Cairo day after tomorrow. We're supposed to join a travel group from the Cincinnati Art Museum."

"Surely, you're joking."

"Not hardly. You'd better go. Letty said that Dan may call me from the plane, and I need to be here so I can tell him my plans. I'll be fine. I'll keep the balcony door closed and locked. It'll be hot, but I'll be fine."

"Do you want to go to Egypt?"

"No. This isn't about going to Egypt. It's about Dan making all the decisions in my life. Don't get the wrong impression. I've brought it on myself. I've always relied on him to make the major decisions in our family, and I usually agree with his choices. By coming to Crete to get me, he probably thinks he's offering a compromise. He still doesn't understand how important it is for me to find out what happened to Ariadne."

"So you're going to drop everything and go to Egypt? What about your book? Are you going to quit when you're about to reach a goal you've pursued for years?"

"You'd better get going. It's a long drive and it's late. Call me in the morning when you leave the villa, and I'll be waiting for you in the lobby. I'll go with you tomorrow, but later…I don't know. I have some serious thinking to do."

I spent the night locked inside a stuffy room waiting for a call that never came.

HAVE YOU SEEN MY WIFE

The following afternoon at exactly ten minutes to two, a sandy-haired man, an American, dressed in rumpled pants and shirt, stood before the mahogany reception desk at the Minoa Palace Hotel.

"I believe you have a Mrs. Daniel Marshall registered here."

The clerk glanced at the book, and then at the rack of keys behind the desk.

"Yes, sir. Ms. Kathryn Marshall is our guest."

"Is she in her room?"

"No, sir. Ms. Marshall is not in her room."

"Then give me the room key, please. I'll be joining her. I'm her husband."

Tired and with his patience stretched thin, Dan slapped his passport on the counter, followed by a business card that announced that he was the senior partner in the firm of Marshall, Parks, Kramer and Reynolds, Attorneys at Law, Cincinnati, Ohio, United States of America.

"Ahhh yes, Mr. Marshall. To give you the key might not be wise: not since the upset of the intrusion into your wife's room the other evening. We would not wish to surprise her, of course. A pity she did not alert us to your arrival. However, under the circumstances, perhaps we could offer you a courtesy room until she returns. I'm sure you understand our concern, dear sir."

"What intrusion? Why isn't my wife waiting here to meet me?"

Dan's questions were spiked with anger. He had expected to find Kate waiting to greet him at the airport, and when she wasn't there, he assumed she would be waiting for him at the hotel. Now, she wasn't even in the hotel. This was not like Kate. Something must definitely be wrong.

"Perhaps there is a message for you in her box," the clerk suggested. He returned with an effusive smile of success and presented Dan with a sealed envelope addressed to him in Kate's handwriting.

Sorry I can't be there to greet you. I'm still searching. See you this evening when I return. Love, Kate.

Dan crumpled the note. Then he smoothed it out and read it again.

"Is that all there is? Nothing to tell me where she is?"

"I'm sorry, sir. The only other thing in her box is a calling card from a Ms. Elana Demopolis."

"Let me see it."

There was no telephone number on the card, only the name and address of an antique shop in downtown Heraklion. Since there were no other clues to act on, Dan left his luggage with the clerk and took a cab into town.

"Can't you go any faster?" he complained to the driver.

Traffic was heavy and the taxi crept along. The streets were clogged with discourteous drivers, every light red, a donkey could have made the trip with more speed. Dan told the taxi driver exactly what he thought of Crete, and how backward Heraklion was compared to the rest of the world.

Following the taxi driver's surly directions, Dan easily found the address on the card.

The shop was at the end of a narrow alley lined with

old buildings whose stucco walls were cracked and badly in need of repair. To him, the antique shop was even shabbier than the others. The bare bulb lighting magnified the distortions and imperfections in the cheap window glass. He thought the whole town could use a fresh coat of paint.

He pushed open the door and heard a bell jangle somewhere in the rear of the shop. The place was dingy and dark and stuffed to the rafters with moldering junk that smelled of dust, dry rot, and boiled coffee. He sneezed as he walked between two rows of display cases filled with fake Minoan artifacts. Looking for someone to talk to, he wondered how Kate had gotten herself involved with anyone associated with such a tawdry place.

Finally, a dark-haired woman dressed in black, wearing far too much jewelry for Dan's taste, pushed through a curtain of clattering wooden beads and asked if she could help him.

"Thank God, you speak English. My name is Daniel Marshall, and I'm looking for my wife. Evidently, someone from this shop visited her at the Minoa Palace Hotel this morning. I need to speak to a Ms. Elana Demopolis. I need to ask her some questions."

"You are Kate's husband?"

Dan saw a flash of apprehension in the woman's eyes, but with a blink the look changed to one of concern. Elana introduced herself as the owner of the shop and told Dan that she had gone to the hotel that morning around nine o'clock.

"I went there to invite your wife to join me for afternoon *mezes*, uh, a bite to eat. It may seem odd to you, Mr. Marshall, but your wife has become to me in a very short time like an old, old friend. Please, let me make coffee for you and I will tell you what little I know of her visit to Crete."

Elana insisted that Dan follow her into a garden at the rear of the shop.

Christ, the last thing I want is a cup of thick, Greek coffee, but Dan grudgingly followed Elana through the beaded curtain. Although he complained to himself, he knew that he might get more information if he accepted the woman's hospitality.

Three-quarters of an hour passed.

"You say she was at a party with you and some of your women friends last night?"

"Yes."

Elana lowered her eyes, hoping that Dan would not guess that she was not telling him all she knew. She felt that she was caught in the middle of a very delicate situation.

Since there was no reason to think that Kate was in any immediate danger, Elana felt it was her duty to protect her new friend from what seemed to be an inquisitive husband who had come looking for his errant wife. Elana did not fully understand what Kate's relationship was with Mr. Deupree, but she felt that no husband, Greek or American, would want to hear that his wife had attended a party with another man.

"Mr. Marshall, I assure you that if I hear from Kate I will tell her you have arrived. Your wife seems a very capable person to me. I feel certain that she is off doing the things that tourists always do when they visit Crete. For now, I suggest that you return to your hotel to rest and recover from your flight."

"I don't think I have any other choice. But if she's not back by nightfall…" Dan left the threat unfinished because he wasn't sure what his next move should be. As he was leaving the shop, he remembered his manners and said, "Thanks for the coffee."

CHAPTER EIGHTEEN

OMG, WE FOUND A CAVE

It would have been interesting to see Dan's reaction if he had known that at the very moment he was climbing into a taxi for the return trip to the hotel, his adventurous wife was getting ready to rappel down a rock-faced cliff on the northern coast of Dhia Island.

Jake was already standing on the ledge below, waiting to enter a cave that was concealed behind a thick screen of dry brush.

Always the attentive husband, Theo had carried a light-weight folding chair with an umbrella attachment so that Tina could wait in comfort. She refused to have anything to do with rappeling or spelunking.

"Theo," Jake yelled up. "You won't have any problem with the descent at this point, but I'm not so sure about Kate. Hold on a minute."

"What do you see?" Theo called to Jake. "I'll be down as soon as I pull up the rope."

"The cave entrance is directly below where you're standing, but if Kate wants to come down, you should move the drop point about thirty feet to your right. The ledge fans out considerably and the slope is very gentle: much less intimidating for a first-time climber."

Theo was impatient to join Jake on the ledge. The cliff was no challenge at all for a real climber like himself, but he didn't want to risk any mishap with someone who had never rappelled before. He was doing a jigging two-step like a toddler about to wet his pants, waiting impatiently for the rope to change hands.

"Don't hurry," Jake yelled up. "I need to clear away some of the brush from the entrance. I won't go in without you."

"Tina, my heart," Theo said with carefully controlled excitement. "Are you absolutely positive you don't want to go below? It's perfectly safe. The slope is gentle, and the lines and harnesses are in good condition. I can be the one to stay here on top."

"Not on your life. I've never liked climbing, no matter how easy. I know this is only mildly dangerous, but my *Curiosity Cat* was put to rest many years ago. I'm quite content to stay up here and admire your brave efforts. Just don't take any unnecessary chances."

Theo helped me into a harness and attached the belaying lines. Easing myself over the rim of the cliff was terrifying; there was nothing but crashing surf and boulders below if I went into freefall. When I finally stood beside Jake on the ledge, I was weak-kneed but ecstatic.

"I did it," I said with a self-satisfied giggle. "Going down was not any more challenging than being suspended from one of those manmade climbing walls in the amusement parks. Climbing back up will be a different matter. It may take all hands to get me back on top. Thanks to Theo's good instructions, I actually rappelled down a cliff. My kids aren't going to believe it."

While he was waiting for us, Jake had hacked at the brush with his hunting knife, stomped on some of the bigger stems, opening up the entrance to the cave. I cautiously shook the bushes and moved a few stones with the toe of my hiking boot.

"I remember reading that there are no poisonous snakes anywhere on Crete. I hope they didn't ship them over here to Dhia."

As soon as Theo joined us, cautious, all senses alert, the three of us entered the cave. We slowly crept into the chamber, remembering every fabled tale of treasure caves we had ever heard or read.

"Just like Indiana Jones in *Raiders of the Lost Ark*," I whispered.

"Stop that!" one of the men commanded.

I wasn't sure if it was Jake or Theo—whichever one—my guess was they didn't want to think about cobwebs and trapdoors and skeletons impaled on slime-covered walls.

The cave was shallow and curved inward toward the center of the island. It smelled musty and at first appeared to be empty. We examined the floor, ceiling, and walls, and the narrow beams of our flashlights crossed like searchlights in a nighttime sky.

"Look! Over there!"

Jake pointed the beam of his light at a mound of dirt on the floor that rose partway up the back wall. It looked manmade.

"I bet my Aunt Fanny's farm there's something buried under that pile of dirt." Jake clawed at the earth with his hands and came up with a piece of rotted canvas. "There's something hard under here. Feels like wood. Have Tina send down the tools."

"Maybe we shouldn't do any digging," I said. "Maybe we should contact the Greek authorities before we disturb anything. It could be a really important *Tell*."

"Nonsense. This is no *Tell*. As you so rightly said before, ancient Minoans didn't have threaded bolts and metal base plates; and they most certainly didn't use government issue green canvas."

All three of us scraped away the dirt using a screwdriver, a hammer, and a small entrenching tool. Ripping away the rotten canvas cover, we exposed the top of a moldy wooden crate and several heavy, metal boxes.

With three of us working, we soon freed the first crate from the mound, and as we moved the box and dirt away, we could see that there were more crates buried beneath the first—how many more was impossible to see.

Setting aside my initial reservations, I felt giddy with anticipation. I tried to read the lettering stamped on the side of the box, but it was masked by a layer of moldy dirt.

"The suspense is awful," I said. "I wonder what's inside." I brushed at the printing but the lettering was still obscured. Spitting on my finger, I rubbed the wood until the faded symbol was fully revealed.

The terrible meaning slammed me in the stomach like a fist, and I recoiled in horror from the emblem. I fell backward as if someone had given me a shove. Stumbling to my feet, I must have looked as if I had been attacked by a swarm of giant spiders.

"What's wrong?" Both Jake and Theo jumped to their feet, ready to defend and protect.

"*Swastikas!*" It's marked with *swastikas.*"

I backed away as far as I could from the jack-legged cross and wiped my hand as if I had touched filth, frantically scrubbing my palm against my shorts.

"Nooo," I moaned. "That's not what brought me to Dhia. That's not what I came all this way to find."

I bolted from the cave, out into the bright sunlight, and sat down hard in the dirt. Wounded in spirit, my soul was cut to the quick. I pulled my legs up against my chest, wrapped my arms around them, and pressed my head against my knees.

Jake and Theo viewed the *swastika* with an equal amount of disgust but, unlike me, they had not come to Dhia to search for truth. They hesitated for only a moment and then pried the lid off the crate, anxious to know what was inside.

"Rifles. Damn it to Hell."

"That's just the first box. There are more to be opened."

After a while, I set my feelings of repugnance aside and walked back to where the two men were unearthing still more wooden boxes. So far, they had uncovered a dozen steel canisters filled with ammunition and half a dozen crates containing German Mausers in perfect condition, still wearing a greasy coat of Cosmoline.

Jake wasn't impressed but Theo was more optimistic. "If we don't find anything else, the guns will be worth thousands of dollars to private collectors."

Jake rapped his shovel on a box that was buried at the very bottom of the cache. "This one looks different. It's completely wrapped in some kind of waterproof covering."

Theo jumped down into the hole and cut away the wrapping.

"It looks like an iron-bound chest with an enormous internal lock. It's bigger than the rest and it's buried almost to the lid. I can't budge it. We'll have to do a lot more digging. Whoever did this, it was a major project. Cutting this hole in the stone was no easy job—you can see the chisel marks. The dirt must have been hauled down from the top to cover it all. This was a difficult operation. Took a lot of manpower. It's amazing that it's still intact."

After more intense labor the iron-bound chest was finally free, but before we pulled it from its resting place, Jake closed his eyes and just as he had done with my chart, he used his hands as sensors, passing them over the lid; first the top and then the sides. When his eyes returned to normal, he looked very serious. He wore a poker face—he had switched to business mode but he couldn't completely conceal his excitement.

"I can't tell what's inside. Lots of energy. Could be more guns, but I don't think so. Grenades. Maybe some kind of explosive. Something dense. There's only one way to know for certain. Open it! But with that internal lock, a good whack with a shovel won't make a dent. This is heavy-duty hardware, my friends."

"Nonsense," Theo said. "We just have to give it some thought. It may be iron bound, but it's still made of wood. We could burn a hole in it, or cut into it with the screwdriver and a hammer. It'll take some time but with a little ingenuity, we can do it."

"Since we don't know what's inside, burning would be too risky. Maybe we could cut through the wood. We can at least give it a try."

After a lot more digging, it took all three of us, using ropes and straining muscles, to slide the box up the sloping ramp the constructors had built to push the box into the hole. We pulled and pried and once the box was all the way out of the hole, we shoved it to the mouth of the cave. It was only then that we realized how much time had passed.

Theo's eyes were on the setting sun. Knowing the capricious nature of the Greek wind, aware of its penchant for playing devilish tricks on the most diligent sailor, he was worried about the *Crystina* riding at anchor with no hands on board.

"The three of you go back to the boat," Jake said. "Cutting through this thing is a one-man job, but I will need a fire to see what I'm doing. The lids from the gun crates should burn without making a lot of smoke. Does anyone have a lighter?"

"Oh, Lord," Theo said and hung his head in despair. "Tina and I just gave up smoking."

"How about a match?" I asked, and pulled a small waterproof tube from one of my vest pockets.

Jake looked at me with admiration. "Girl Scouts?" he asked.

"No. Den Mother. Look, you guys. I made it down the cliff once without mishap, but I don't want to push my luck. I'm the logical person to stay behind and chip the wood. I hate the fact that this is a German cache, but the war was over a long time ago. There is still a chance, a slim chance, that what I'm looking for is inside the chest."

Jake was the one who made the decision.

"We can't risk losing our transportation. I think the most sensible plan would be for Theo and Tina to take care of the boat, and you and I, partner, will stay behind and try to open this Chinese puzzle box."

The light was going fast and Theo was much too concerned about the *Crystina* to waste time discussing the pros and cons of Jake's proposal.

"I'll send down the picnic basket. There are a couple of bottles of water, and some cheese and bread and even a bottle of wine. I brought it in case we had something to celebrate. We'll return at dawn with more supplies."

Theo climbed the cliff in a half-scramble, barely needing Tina to belay him.

"Theo," I called. "Please, use your radio to get a message to my husband at the hotel. Tell him…" I hesitated.

What should I tell Dan? I knew he would be angry and concerned. Then I thought of the hundreds of messages I had received from him over the years telling me he had to work late, or go out of town; that I should go to the play without him, that he couldn't make Suzie's recital, or help me take Steve to the hospital when he broke his leg. I even drove myself to the hospital to have one of the babies, but I understood. He was taking care of our family; he took his job seriously. Perhaps it was time for a little role reversal.

"Tell my husband I'm sorry. I've been delayed. Tell him I'm working on a very important project. Tell him I'll return sometime tomorrow afternoon."

CHAPTER NINETEEN
STARLIGHT STAR BRIGHT

The plan was to cut through the largest rectangle of exposed wood on the back of the chest, and it really was a one-man job.

When Jake refused to relinquish the hammer, I took my flashlight and went back inside the cave. I looked carefully behind and between every boulder and stone, and when I returned, I was carrying a small treasure in my hands.

"I found this old stone lamp wedged into a crevice between two of the boulders. Someone must have put it there long before the guns were buried."

I rubbed the pitted stone sides just as Aladdin must have rubbed his magic lamp, but my genie did not appear.

Turning it over and over, I inspected it carefully.

"It doesn't look like it's ever been used. The oil well is packed with mud. I can't tell if it's new or old, but it looks old. Do you think maybe this is what I came to Dhia to find?"

"Not much of a find, if you ask me. I relinquish any claim to that bit of everyday house ware, madam. The find is all yours."

Jake continued to chip away at the wood.

"I think I'll take it to the museum. I'll say I found it somewhere else so they won't know about the cave."

"We would appreciate it if you would wait until after we're finished here before you start making any donations to the Greek Department of Antiquities. We don't need any complications."

"I know. I know. I was just thinking ahead."

I tucked my precious relic into the picnic basket, unpacked the food, and laid it out on a green cloth.

"We have cheese and black olives, flat bread and wine. What more could anyone ask."

The last rays of the sun brushed a wide band of gold across the horizon. The heavens were dotted with more and more brilliant points of light as darkness flowed in from the east, washing away the heavenly blue, taking all the color away and turning everything into shades of gray, becoming more and more dense, until the final curtain of indigo gradually locked the rest of the world away.

We were alone.

Except for the face of the cliff, the chest, and the fire, the rest of Dhia Island was hidden from sight. It took only a few heartbeats for my euphoria to fade.

The excitement of the moment had masked all the whistles and bells that should have sounded an alarm. Curiosity and naiveté had prompted me to stay. My judgment was understandably dulled, since this was certainly not an everyday kind of thing. However, now, I found myself alone with a man whose strength was far greater than mine, confined in a place from which I could not escape, and to make the situation even more precarious, I was alone with a man I was beginning to find extremely interesting.

"Would you like to eat?" I asked, trying to sound normal, struggling to keep my overactive imagination in check, praying that Jake could not hear my pounding heart.

"Let me get this chunk out first and then I'll see just how well you can cook."

His cheery words did nothing to quell the turmoil

churning inside me.

I walked as far away as I could to put some distance between us. When I came to the end of the ledge, a small stone
bounced down the side of the cliff and landed at my feet. It
was quickly followed by a shower of pebbles and shale.

Dodging to one side to avoid being hit, I came nose to
nose with a bewhiskered young goat whose inquiring nature
had caused the small avalanche.

I jumped aside, startled as a rabbit flushed from its hiding
place, and the kid bleated a screech that sent both of us into
wild gyrations of panic. The little goat scrambled frantically,
trying to escape the peculiarly formed creature making loud
noises in its face, but its small hooves kept sliding on the
loose rock.

The instant I yelled, Jake began to move, advancing,
hammer at the ready, prepared to protect us from a demon
that had slithered in out of the darkness.

When he saw the poor little goat in action, he roared
with laughter, which of course only terrified the poor animal
even more. Its spindly young legs were a furry blur, working
hard and fast, trying to gain a purchase on the slippery shale.
Finally reaching a bit of solid stone, he scampered away.

With laughter and shared relief in our hearts, Jake's
eyes glistened in the light from the fire, and for a moment
I thought he was going to open his arms and invite me inside, but before that could happen I turned away. I could feel
the warmth of him, although he never made a move in my
direction.

"In the movies, this is where the love scene begins," he
said. I knew his eyes were full of need but I wouldn't look at
him. I could not, would not, respond in any way.

"Then again," he said, keeping his voice light and soft, "everyone knows that a love affair can ruin a good partnership. And good partners are not that easy to find."

I was afraid to speak. I was selectively deaf, dumb, and blind. With a sweep of my hand I silently invited Jake to our simple feast.

After we ate, we sat for a while, listening to the combers roll in from the north. They made a sound like a giant rushing wind. And we talked. We told stories triggered by the smell of the wood smoke: about campfires and roasted marshmallows, about autumn hay rides and laughter with old friends. And I told him about my grandmother, who made a chocolate pie for my grandfather every day for over sixty years. I talked about Dan and Suzie and Steve, about Letty Marie, and my mom. Without any real emotion, he mentioned a failed marriage that ended without children.

"Do you have any idea what might be inside the chest?" I asked, and the question returned us to the present.

"Gold, of course, and pearls beyond measure," he said with a dry laugh. "I don't know. I just hope it's something extremely valuable."

"What will you do if it is full of treasure? What would you do if you became incredibly wealthy?"

"I think I might buy a farm. I've always had an affinity for the land. I would like to grow animals and wheat and corn. I guess I would like to be the lord of a manor. How about you?"

"I'm satisfied with my life as it is. I'm still hoping to find some kind of Greek relic that will help me finish my book. Possessions don't mean that much to me. That's not totally true. Deep down, I feel I do want something more—it's just that I can't quite put a name to it."

"Look at those stars. Hey, a shooting star. When I was a kid I used to keep count of how many I saw, but after a while you grow up and you forget to look up at the sky. Your priorities change. Moon's up. Wow. The peace and beauty of this place certainly give words like vast and grand a whole new meaning. THIS," and Jake raised his arms to the sky, "is surely what God is all about."

I rubbed my eyes, stifled a yawn. "Let me take a turn with the hammer."

"Not necessary."

Jake stood up, stretched, and walked to the side of the ledge where he gathered an armful of sweet-swelling grass. He stuffed it into his discarded sun-shirt, and created a pillow of sorts.

With a sweeping bow he said, "Your couch awaits, my princess."

"Ha! I'm about the farthest thing from a princess you're ever going to find."

"Maybe yes. Maybe no. Your past, as well as your future, have yet to unfold."

Once again, I fingered my strand of blue beads. I was feeling more at ease with Jake, less self-conscious, more in control.

"If you won't let me help cut through the wood, maybe I could try another regression. I would like to find out more about that fierce-looking helmsman. I wish I could learn why I saw him with a small strand of blue beads just like mine tied to his wrist."

"If you listen to the tap of the hammer, it will lead you into a trance. I'll be your drummer. Remember, the more you trust yourself, the longer you will stay with the images, and the more you might learn. You can have the whole night to dream. I promise no harm will come to you."

I trusted Jake to be a man of honor. I took my homemade pillow stuffed with fragrant grass and curled up just inside the entrance to the cave. I listened to his soothing voice accented by the tap of his hammer and held my blue beads in my hands. I set time aside and allowed the present, with its disturbing thoughts of family and treasure, needs and desires, to drift along without me. I allowed my spirit to listen for the messages held within the beads of lapis lazuli.

This time, instead of taking me to a warm, sunny beach, Jake led me to a stairway where I descended, down and down, into a tunnel that glowed with an iridescent light. I was in a place where shadows took on human form.

This time the image of the bearded helmsman did not come to me. Instead, I saw a strand of blue lapis beads around the neck of a fair-haired young woman standing in the middle of an arena. The strong, bare-breasted woman was dressed like a bull dancer in loincloth and boots, and she was standing directly in the path of a charging, ginger-colored bull.

ψ

"Kate."

It was sunrise. Jake was sitting beside the dying fire, poking and prodding it back to life. The fingers on his left hand were black with soot.

"Why didn't you wake me? Did you open the chest?"

"No. Like you, I slept most of the night. I was able to remove a section big enough to see that the chest has a black metal liner. You can look for yourself. I'm not sure what to do next. It'll take a block and tackle to lift it out of here. And even if we managed to get it up on top, I'm not sure how we'd get it back to the boat. The better plan might be to bring in some tools and a small gasoline generator and open it here on the ledge. Theo is very resourceful."

We finished the few bites of food left in the basket, and while we sat waiting for Theo and Tina to arrive I told Jake about my regression.

"This time it was Ariadne who wore my blue beads. I thought I knew what she suffered, seeing her peaceful way of life destroyed, living with a lecherous mother who didn't love her. I knew she lost her battle against a world overrun by religious fanatics, but I never really felt her hopelessness, her anger, her desperation—not until now. Now, I think I understand."

My heart and mind were still caught up in the past. "I can't shake the feeling that I must find the bearded helmsman. I wonder if I could go back again."

"Suit yourself."

With a distinct lack of enthusiasm, Jake tried to lead me again, but it was wasted effort. The doors to the past were closed and locked against anymore intrusions.

"Stop worrying it," he said wearily. "What's past is past. The only reality you can count on is the one you can touch, so enjoy it the best way you can. I'm going to try and get some shut-eye. Theo and Tina should be here within the hour."

CHAPTER TWENTY

HELLO, MY SWEET

Theo was disappointed that Jake had not succeeded in breaking into the chest, but he had urgent news that presented a more serious problem.

"There are many ways we can open the chest, but we need to leave and return later with the proper tools. There is a complication. Just after we left the beach to come back here to you, our friendly fanatics in the white yacht motored into the harbor. We watched them for a while from top of the hill, at a place where they couldn't see us."

Jake was rubbing his arm again, and there was a worried look on his face.

"I had hoped to carry out some of the Mausers," Theo said, "but with those bastards watching, we can't do anything suspicious. I think it would be wise to leave the few tools we brought inside the cave. We don't want to give them any reason to think we've been looking for anything more than plants and goats."

We dragged the chest and Tina's chair and umbrella back inside the cave, and erased all evidence of our presence from the site. We created a false campsite about half a mile from the cave, a photogenic spot, where we left cups and plastic bags. I felt bad trashing the island, but considering the gravity of the situation I would have to sooth my guilt with an apology to Mother Nature.

Jake took pictures of every kind of weed he could find to support his interest in botany. We deliberately flattened the brush, leaving a trail back to the *Crystina* that was so obvious a child could follow.

It was not an easy trek. Each of us had a rifle and ammunition. Jake carried a knapsack of water bottles. Tina carried the camera and tripod, Theo lugged the extra food, and I carried the picnic basket. However, the most difficult burden each of us carried was our fear of confrontation.

We expected at any moment to be ambushed by the crew from the *Sheitan*, but there were no signs of our visitors until we topped the crest of the last rolling hill. From our vantage point we could see the *Crystina* floating peacefully in the clear blue water, and the *Sheitan* was anchored well off on her starboard side. A rubber Zodiac was pulled up on the beach next to the *Crystina's* dinghy.

We counted four men spread out along the beach: two standing, one hunkered down taking a smoke, another sitting on the topside of the Zodiac. All four appeared to be waiting for us to return.

"What do we do now? Do they have any weapons?" Tina asked.

"I wish I had the binoculars," Theo said. "I could use the scope on the Ruger, but the last time I tried to take it off, the screw was frozen, and if they spot us pointing a rifle at them it could be provocative. At least they aren't showing anything like that Uzi they waved at us yesterday. No way to know what they may have stowed inside that Zodiac."

Jake seemed unusually calm. "We have to pass them to reach our dinghy. I guess we may as well get to it."

I was frightened. This certainly wasn't what I had envisioned back in Cincinnati. All I wanted was to take a look at the island. Was that such an outlandish need? This was supposed to be a simple exploration trip, a little reconnoitering, just a walk across a dried-up piece of dirt and rock. It was never supposed to be dangerous.

When the crewmen waiting on the beach saw us come over the crest of the last hill, they moved apart, opening a path, inviting us to come down to the sea. The man who had been sitting on the Zodiac moved over to join the others, and when he walked, he dragged one stiff leg.

"It's Demetri," I said. "I should have known. Hindsight says I should have given him my beads. I can't believe he followed me here."

"I don't like it, Theo," Jake said.

"I still don't see any weapons."

Jake rested the barrel of his gun on his shoulder. "I think you should take the women to the *Crystina*, while I stay here on the high ground. I'll cover you with the Ruger. Once you reach the boat, you and Tina can keep your weapons on them while Kate returns for me in the dinghy."

None of us liked leaving Jake behind, but it was a sound plan. The three of us walked down to the beach and began stowing our gear in the dinghy, acting as if Demetri and his companions did not exist.

However, Demetri was not about to be ignored. He moved up to stand by the Zodiac, using its inflated body for protection which was a ludicrous: he was hiding behind an oversized balloon.

"How was the hunting?" he asked.

"Great," Theo said with a slight smile. "We shot lots of goats, but then I dropped the camera so we're not sure what we got. Because of my clumsiness, we may have little to show for our efforts."

I thought Theo sounded convincing.

"And the climbing?"

"We did some. But without any real equipment, it was no challenge. Not like the Alps."

Tina sat in the middle of the dinghy, Theo moved to the rear ready to start the motor.

I picked up the picnic basket and was about to hand it to Tina when Demetri asked, "Why is your friend sitting up on the hill with a weapon across his knees?"

The tone of his voice, or his stance, or the pressure of the deceit triggered my temper.

"Because we don't trust you. Because you act like a bully. Because you are here to steal my beads."

"I am not the one who is the thief," Demetri shouted. "I think I shall tell my friends in the Department of Antiquities to come and see what else you steal that belongs to Greece."

"What belongs to Greece is not what bothers you. It's what belongs to me that's eating at you. The blue beads are mine. I have a bill of sale."

"What else did you find on Dhia to steal? What do you conceal in that basket?"

A clutch of fear squeezed the pit of my stomach when I remembered that the lamp I found inside the cave was in the picnic basket.

Recovering quickly I answered boldly, "We have many treasures in the basket, but surely you want to check my pockets first."

I dropped the basket on the ground, pulled my pockets wrong side out, and left them dangling in the wind.

"You see? Nothing. But we do have a great treasure in the basket. Behold! A stone lamp I bought yesterday from a street vendor. Here! Take it! It's yours."

Momentarily flustered, Demetri automatically accepted the lamp, looked at it with suspicion, and then pushed it back at me.

"No," I shouted. "Take it. Take the food. Take the basket."

"I don't want your stupid lamp," Demetri shouted derisively.

"Then give it to Elana. She deserves something for the way you treat her. She warned you to stop behaving so foolishly. Now, I'm warning you. If you don't leave me alone, *you* are the one who will answer to the Greek authorities. Maybe I will contact the American Consul and let you explain your actions to them."

Leaving the basket on the beach, I shoved the boat into the water and climbed in over the bow. Demetri kicked the basket, spilling the picnic remains onto the gravelly beach. Seeing nothing of importance, he turned and stared up at Jake, who was still sitting on a rock with the rifle balanced across his knees.

Muttering obscenities, Demetri motioned for the men to leave.

Just as we planned, I returned in the dinghy for Jake while Theo and Tina stood on the bow of the *Crystina*, rifles at the ready. Even before we raised the *Crystina's* anchor, the *Sheitan* roared noisily out into open water where it waited, menacing, in the distance like a patrol boat guarding access to the bay. As soon as we entered open water and raised the sail, they sped off with a roaring display of horsepower.

"That's a relief. We would probably have left soon anyway, but I don't like being threatened." Theo's face looked grim as we motored away from the anchorage.

Once we shut down the engine and had the sails trimmed, Theo engaged the self-steering mechanism and we all went below to talk about the German Mausers and the unopened chest.

"I don't like any of this," I said. "I thought we were in for real trouble when I remembered that I put the lamp in the picnic basket. It's a good thing Demetri didn't bring the Greek authorities; I don't think they would have been convinced that the lamp was a souvenir."

"It wasn't a souvenir?" Theo looked surprised.

I told them about my discovery of the lamp in the cave, and I couldn't conceal my disappointment over its loss.

"It's the only part of this whole experience that seems real to me. It has to be what drew me to the island—it must be."

"We'll get your lamp back," Jake said. "Demetri is all talk. Right now, we need to decide what to do about the guns and the chest."

"I have several clients who are avid gun collectors," Theo said. "I estimate that the cache is probably worth a quarter of a million dollars to collectors of World War II relics."

"Wait!" I spread my hands and physically released my share of the booty. "Before you talk about disposing of anything, I have something to say. When I left home, I had no idea we'd find anything like this on the island. I have never thought of myself as a coward, but I won't risk getting caught smuggling that stuff out of Greece. Nothing is worth spending even one day locked up in a Greek prison."

The trio looked at me with solemn faces.

"The three of you can do whatever you want, but from this point on count me out of your plans. As far as I'm concerned, those guns can stay in that cave until they turn to dust. If you decide to smuggle them through Greek customs, it's your affair. I want nothing to do with it."

When the three treasure hunters did not respond, I felt like an alien, an intruder. To leave no doubt I added, "I've never been a risk-taker, and it's too late for me to start now. Whatever you decide to do, it will be better if I don't know anything about your plans."

I backed away from them, climbed the stairs up to the cockpit, disengaged the auto-pilot, and took the wheel.

I really am a coward, I thought. Tears filled my eyes. *The Goddess of Good Fortune has presented me with a gift, and I don't have the courage to reach out and take it.*

The wind whistled across my ears but I didn't hear it; spray soaked my clothes but I didn't feel it.

If I get caught smuggling, I might never see my family again. Never see my children, or hold my grandchildren, never feel Dan's arms around me. How could I grow old without him beside me?

These were the real treasures in my life and they were more precious than all the riches the world could offer. This was my truth, yet the thought of turning my back on the possibility of coming home with found money felt like self-betrayal. With the money the guns would bring, I could be like Dan: I could have an office and write full time. I could pay someone else to be wife of the house.

"Why?" I moaned and looked skyward. "Why couldn't we have found broken clay tablets, or potshards, or beer cans? Why did you have to make it so complicated?"

As I struggled with my fears, common sense kicked in and managed to insert a touch of reality into the mix. *Would Dan turn his back on an opportunity to salvage a cache of valuable weapons? Would he be bold enough to take a chance he wouldn't be caught?*

"Hey, mate! You're sailing her a bit hard, aren't you?"

Coming up from the salon, Theo had to hang onto the handrails and walk on the sidewalls of the companionway just to keep his feet under him.

"I'm sorry. I'm upset. The wind picked up. I guess I should ease the sail. Better still, *you* take the helm."

I dropped my hands from the big wheel, and the ship quickly righted herself and came head to wind. Without asking Theo's permission, I went forward, picking my way cautiously along the deck to claim my precarious seat before the mast. Catching a line in the crook of my arm, I cradled my head on my knees. All sound was swept away by the rising wind, and I wasn't aware that Jake had followed me until he eased himself down against the other side of the mast.

"You know, partner, you're not the only one who's afraid of getting involved with the Greek authorities. No one wants to run the risk of getting caught smuggling this stuff through customs, so we won't do it that way."

"What do you mean?"

"We'll hide the guns in the secret compartments Theo had built into the *Crystina* when he commissioned her. Once the guns are safely stowed, a professional crew will sail the boat directly to Italy where Theo's people will dispose of the weapons with no risk of discovery. All we have to do is carry the stuff out of the cave and onto the boat. Then we sail to a place where the crew can take over. We could probably do this without you, but Theo thinks it would be best to have someone else on board who knows how to sail, just in case we have an emergency."

My spirits brightened somewhat. It sounded like the chance of getting caught would be minimal, although nothing could ever be foolproof.

"I think I need to move back to the cabin," Jake said. He was turning a bilious shade of pale. "I don't like this slanty deck."

In only a matter of minutes, the unpredictable Cretan wind had increased another five knots. Carefully, we made our way back to the safety of the cockpit. Theo wore his captain's face, and his eyes were pinched with concern. "I don't want anyone on deck in this wind without a safety harness."

Jake and Tina went below, where they each heaved into their own personal bucket. Theo and I put on storm gear and safety harnesses.

A saltwater crust quickly gathered in my eyebrows and eyelashes, and the persistent flow of seawater streaming down my face and chin sent a wave of chilly shivers across my skin. The salty spray ran all the way down my neck, flowing into the channel between my breasts, and catching in a puddle at the waistband of my shorts.

With an occasional slam and wiggle, the *Crystina* sliced through the waves, but as sleek as she was she struggled to make headway in the building sea.

"I don't like it. Has the makings of a full-blown Meltemi. It's early in the year, but the Cretan wind is all female and abides by no man's calendar."

It was difficult to see through the spray, but ahead and off to port, I thought I saw a boat wallowing in a trough between the waves. When we topped the next wave, I could see that it was the *Sheitan*. She looked to be dead in the water.

"What are they up to now? We should ignore them and

sail on past, but no real seaman fails to lend assistance to a vessel in distress; no matter who they are or how foul their behavior. Ask Tina if she can pull her head out of the bucket long enough to raise them on the radio."

I stuck my head down the companionway and relayed the message.

The *Sheitan* replied instantly.

"They say that one of their crewmen fell overboard... probably the drunk. They're trying to rescue him and warned us to stay clear."

"I can't in good conscience sail off and leave them. We'll circle. Ready, Kate? Hard alee!"

It took about twenty minutes to close the circle and by then the crewmen on the *Sheitan* had hauled their man back on board. Still standing off, we watched as their helmsman once again rammed his throttle full forward, digging the boat's stern into the sea. First, we saw a puff of smoke; then we heard a loud pop. The boat settled into the trough between the white-capped waves like a wounded albatross.

"Damn fool. I bet he's blown his engine. Hail them again, Tina. See if they want help. I wouldn't desert my worst enemy in a blow like this. You can bet all of them are seasick. We may not be able to drag them all the way back to the harbor, but we can at least tow them closer to port."

It took three tries before a line could be secured between the two vessels.

"Tell those idiots to get off the deck and stay clear of the towline. If it breaks, someone could lose an eye. The same goes for you, Kate. I want you down below."

Theo used both engine and sail to pull the crippled white boat back to Venetian Harbor. The port police must have been monitoring our transmissions, for when we approached the entrance, two fishing boats came out to meet us. Once they took the *Sheitan's* tow, the *Crystina* could safely motor into the calm water behind the breakwater that protected the harbor. As the line was passed over to a fishing *cacique*, Demetri came out on deck and gave us a halfhearted wave of thanks.

"I hate heavy-weather sailing," I confessed to Theo, "but I'm always so thankful for safe harbor after I've survived a blow. Do you want help clearing the decks and stowing the gear?"

"No. The dock crew will come on board and tidy up."

"Then, I'll take a taxi back to the hotel. My husband must be wondering what's happened to me. Be assured, I don't intend to say anything to him about the guns, or the chest, or the cave. He's a lawyer and understands confidentiality. I'll tell him we explored the island. I'll tell him I found the lamp and that I lost it to Demetri."

"We'll call you when we get back to the villa, after we've sorted out the best way to proceed. You're good crew, Kathryn Marshall. You will always be welcome on board the *Crystina*."

Theo gave me a fierce hug around my shoulders, and an encouraging pat on the back. Tina moved up to stand by Theo. She was still pale, but the nausea had diminished as soon as we entered calm water.

"I guess you know by now, I'm not much of a talker," Tina said, "but I enjoy your company. The guys don't want to pressure you into helping us move the guns, but I sure hope you stay with us. You deserve a share of the treasure. After all, it was your hunch that led us there in the first place. But whatever you decide to do, we still need you as a friend," and she gave me a big, warm, mama-bear hug.

When I stepped off the boarding plank, Jake was sitting with his legs dangling over the edge of the concrete mole. He still looked a little gray around his mouth.

"I'll be keeping my eye on you, partner. Call me if you need help. You take good care of yourself," he called as I walked away. Maybe I was just being super sensitive, but Jake's words gave me an uneasy feeling of foreboding.

CHAPTER TWENTY-ONE

HONEY, I'M HOME

The taxi arrived at the hotel much too fast. I could have used about a week to prepare for my meeting with Dan. I wondered why it was that happy things seem to arrive at such a pitiful slow pace, and dreaded things always approach with such incredible speed.

Resisting the urge to drag my sea bag instead of carrying it, I gathered my spray-soaked gear and entered the lobby, stopping at the desk for my room key.

"Madam. A gentleman, your husband I believe, awaits you in the seaside lounge."

Dan was sitting in the same chair Jake had occupied only five days earlier. Could it be only five days? From the down-turned corners of his mouth, I knew he was angry.

"Where have you been?" he asked accusingly.

"I was on my way upstairs. I'm soaked through. I need to change my clothes."

"I've been waiting for you for two days."

It took all the strength I could muster to keep from saying, *poor baby*. Instead I answered carefully. "I didn't expect you. When I got the message that you were coming, I had already made plans to sail to Dhia."

My response was concise and so out of character, Dan's eyes widened with surprise.

"They wouldn't give me your key. They put me in a room at the end of the hall."

He was looking at me in a peculiar way, assessing me, as

if he might be searching for just the right words to say, which was weirdly out of character. There was never a time when Lawyer Dan Marshall was at a loss for words—maybe with someone else, but never with me.

"I have to change," I said wearily. "I need to wash the salt out of my eyes. You can wait for me here, if you like." Deciding to temper my tone I added, "I could use a hot cup of coffee. I feel chilled. It'll take me only a few minutes to shower and change. Would you order me a Nescafe?"

"Not hardly," he said irritably.

He wasn't about to spend another minute waiting. As he followed me up the stairs, he found his voice and began bombarding me with questions, never offering to help carry my things, not bothering to open the door, never giving me a hug, never asking, "Are you okay?"

He spoke only in sentences beginning with I and My, and I wondered if I could be having a delayed attack of seasickness because I was feeling slightly nauseous.

"How was your trip to Atlanta?"

"I didn't go. Someone had to stay home and look after the family."

Dan went on and on with his diatribe about his interrupted work schedule and I couldn't believe how much had happened in the six days I had been away from home. The more Dan railed, the redder his face became. He could see that he was failing to impress me with how much he had suffered. He knew he was not even close to winning his case.

"Well, I didn't want to tell you this way, but there's a problem with your mother."

"What's wrong with Mama?" I was instantly on guard.

"It's her house. We had a bad storm the night you left:

lots of damage to the big trees in her front yard. The power was out for two days. I had to get an electrician and tree trimmers. I made dozens of calls. Joyce had to reschedule all my appointments, and your mother was really upset that you weren't there to take care of things. Someone had to give her a hand, so we talked it over and decided that the time had come for her to move to that new condo she's been looking at in Green Meadows. She's putting her house on the market as we speak."

"The two of you decided something, together?" I was stunned. In the past, whenever I asked the two of them to talk directly, they refused. "I have tried to get Mom to move to a retirement center for at least three years, and she has always insisted that she couldn't stand to part with the house. And you, *you* kept insisting that she should stay where she was as long as possible to keep from draining her finances."

"Well, when I drove her over to the new complex, I could see that it's very nice. And the price is reasonable. Your mother shouldn't have the strain of keeping up that big old house anymore. The movers are coming the second Tuesday after we get back from Egypt."

I was speechless. The pressure of keeping two households had been on my shoulders for years. Everyone automatically looked to me to solve all of the family problems. I was chief in charge of fixing potholes and installing guardrails on the family's road of life. I was the one who helped Dan's mother before she moved to Florida after his dad passed away. Familial duty was my job. Dan was always too busy to participate.

"There was an opening," he said matter-of-factly. "It's too damn much work keeping up two places."

"Oh, really?"

"But that's not the worst news. There's more!"

I held my breath, expecting to hear a black-bordered announcement.

"Susan is pregnant and they've called off the big wedding."

"Suzie is pregnant? She and Jim split up?"

"Not exactly. Three weeks ago, they were married by a justice of the peace. They said they didn't want to wait and blow a pot of money on a big ceremony, with the baby and all. Instead, they used their wedding money as a down payment on a house they found near the hospital. They dragged me over to see it. It's an absolute mess. Damn fools. I don't know why they couldn't wait to get pregnant. Didn't you teach her anything about birth control? Loading themselves up with responsibilities—just like we did—while they're still just kids. Now they're stuck. No way out."

"They're buying a house? You've seen it?"

"Yes. And she has morning sickness, just like you. I told her to eat crackers and watch her fluids. You should be there with her. Susan needs you. The house is hopeless. She's trying to paint and wallpaper, and she's determined to keep working, and she intends to go back to school. She won't listen to me. And where is her mother? She's off chasing moonbeams when her daughter needs her most."

"Sounds to me like she needs a house painter and a carpenter more than she needs her mother. Our little Susan... married. Ohhh, she always wanted to wear a white wedding dress. When she was little, we had to stop and admire all the bride dresses in the shop windows. And you told her to eat crackers? I remember how you used to complain about the crumbs in the bed. Why didn't she tell me she was pregnant?"

As soon as I asked the question, I knew the answer. If she had told me, I would have canceled my trip and she knew how important it was to me. If it were Dan going off somewhere, he would continue with business as usual, but I would probably have chucked the whole adventure just on the chance that she might need me.

"A baby. Our little Suzie—a mother." My chin trembled. I was close to tears.

"You'd better hurry up and change. The plane leaves for Cairo at four. That doesn't leave much time for you to get your stuff together. If you'd been much later, we would never have made the flight."

"At least Steve and Letty seem to have survived without me."

"Well, since you brought it up."

"Don't tell me. Steve wrecked my car. I knew I should never have loaned it to him. Is he hurt?"

"No! Steve didn't wreck your car. The guys who stole your car are the ones who wrecked it. They took it from in front of his apartment. He wanted to borrow my car while I'm away, but Pete's still using it."

"Why is Pete using your Jag?"

"His car crapped out. He came home to borrow Letty's and caught her shrink-wrapped to some muscle builder in bib overalls. He walked out on her and is bunking in our guestroom."

"Oh, my God. The WanderWeed man." I had to sit down on the edge of the bed.

"You knew about it, and you didn't say anything?"

"No. I didn't know. But I should have guessed. My God, the WanderWeed man."

"Get packed. We need to get to the airport, now."

"Wait. Hold on a minute." I stood up. "I'm not ready to leave here yet. I'm just now beginning to sort through some things. Last week, you couldn't drop what you were doing and come with me to Crete and I understood. You had commitments. Now, the same thing is true for me. You should have asked if I could go with you to Egypt instead of assuming you could just show up and take charge. I've made plans that include other people."

"You've gotten yourself involved in some shady scheme involving that faker, Deupree."

"That's not true. How can you say such a thing? I haven't finished what brought me back to Crete. I need a few more days."

My stubborn resistance was more than Dan could handle. "You're my wife and you're coming with me."

He grabbed me by the shoulders and shoved me against the wall.

"Let go!" I cried, pushing at him, throwing my knee at his crotch, forcing him to back away to keep it from connecting.

Breathing hard, we eyed each other warily. I was the first to regain a modicum of control. Never before had either of us gone so far over the edge of reason, and when I relaxed my aggressive stance, he backed away.

Dan's anger was spent. He fell into a chair, leaned forward, holding his head in his hands. I couldn't tell if he was feeling despair or shame. At that moment, I really didn't care.

Walking to the window, I jerked the drapery cord and flooded the room with light. Still struggling to harness my raging temper, I shoved the sliding door open and stepped out onto the balcony. The sea air helped clear my mind and rein in my runaway emotions.

After a time, I came back inside the room and in an effort to be conciliatory I said, "I'm ashamed. What I did was unforgivable."

"I feel the same. But you pushed me too far."

"I pushed *you?*"

"It's that Deupree. You've never acted like this before. He's changed you. It's either him or me. You're going to have to choose between us."

I laughed without humor at the absurdity of such a suggestion.

"How can you say such a thing? Jake is a business partner. He's been helpful to me and I think he's becoming a friend. He's nothing more to me than a business associate."

"Choose!"

Dan's lack of trust wounded me deeply. I felt as if a barbed stone had been thrust into my chest.

"How can you compare our marriage to a business partnership? I thought we at least had faith in each other. How many close working arrangements have you had with women over the years? Dozens! In fact, you've spent more time with your secretaries, your administrative assistants, than you have ever spent with me. But then of course *you* can be trusted and I, obviously, cannot. Letty is right. I'm unrealistic. I'm nothing but an idealistic fool."

Dan couldn't hear a word I was saying.

"CHOOSE! Deupree or me."

"All right. I will choose. But I will not choose from the choices you give me." I raised my chin and said, "I choose *me*. And the stupid part of this whole thing is that I don't even know who *me* is. All I know is that at this point in my life I need to finish my book, and that's what I intend to do. I'm not my mother's keeper, I'm not Susan's house painter, and I don't get one penny's worth of satisfaction being your audience, waiting offstage in the wings while you play your big scenes."

Dan looked at me with mean eyes and said, "My mother did it; your mother did it; why can't you?"

"Because I'm not your mother, and I'm certainly not *my* mother. I want something more than scrubbing toilets, and killing dandelions, and waiting while you do as you damn well please."

Dan looked like he couldn't believe what he was hearing…and I didn't care. My words were painfully pulled from a growing ego that was just setting its buds.

"I had hoped you might be coming here to Crete to help me, to encourage me, but I was foolish to think such a thing."

I looked at my watch: the old puppet-master was alive and ticking. "It's getting late. You'd better go. You're going to miss your plane."

I opened the hall door wide.

"Have a nice time in Egypt," I said with a forced smile. "I'll be home when my business here is finished."

Dan stood with his shoulders hunched. "I don't want you to get hurt. Deupree is a liar and a charlatan. He's using you to get what he wants."

"I don't know what you think he wants from me, but I didn't come to Crete because of Jake Deupree. I came to Crete because of me."

After I closed the door, I peeled off my wet clothes, took a quick shower, wrapped up in a blanket, and lay down across the bed. I was completely exhausted.

When the tears finally stopped, I was drained. I was appalled at the pain Dan and I had inflicted upon each other—all because I wanted to explore, to stretch, to look on the other side of the mountain. Why couldn't he understand? He had been my love for so many years; I couldn't imagine how he could believe that I would turn to a stranger.

I should give up and go home...stop tormenting everybody. I don't even have the courage to claim my share of a prize some people would die for. And there's probably no great truth waiting to be found on Dhia Island. Who am I fooling? Not Dan, certainly. I'm only fooling myself.

Doubt swelled and grew, widening the cracks in my fragile self-esteem.

The sun shining through the sliding door was low on the horizon and it illuminated the top of the nightstand, spotlighting the little Goddess of Snakes and my strand of lapis lazuli beads. The tiny woman looked so brave standing there holding a snake in each of her hands.

I reached over and picked her up and looked into her eyes.

That's just how I feel, I thought. *I've grabbed hold of something dangerous, and even if I let it go, it may turn around and bite me.*

Thoughts of quitting my search when I could be so close to solving the mystery of Ariadne and Theseus caused anger to rise like bile in my throat. Dan had no right to treat me like he was my lord and master—that was archaic.

One thing was clear. If I wanted to be treated with respect, I would have to demand it. And I had to see this thing through to some kind of conclusion.

The phone rang and I covered my head with the pillow to shut out the sound. I didn't want to talk to anyone, but the ringing persisted so long I finally picked up and listened, afraid to answer.

"Kate?" a female voice asked. "Are you there? This is Elana Demopolis. I have your little stone lamp. I called to ask how I can return it to you."

CHAPTER TWENTY-TWO

LOST AND FOUND

The lane to the antique shop was becoming comfortably familiar. The black-and-white house cat that lived in the corner courtyard meowed as I approached. Tired as I was, I stopped to let the warm body purr and wind its slick fur around my bare legs. The old woman dressed in black stopped watering her geraniums, beamed a motherly smile, and bobbed her head in greeting.

The shop was dark and the tinkling bell summoned Elana from the workroom. With a great deal of bustle and flurry, she gave me a welcoming kiss on each cheek.

"I am so happy that you are all right. First your distraught husband comes looking for you. Then Demetri tells me how you and your friends rescued him from that howling wind storm this afternoon."

"It was nothing. Any sailor would have done the same."

"I think not. If your places had been reversed, I think the men you saved would not have helped you. The owner of that boat is an in-law of Demetri's; a man with a clouded reputation. He is a poor choice of companions; a regrettable involvement."

Elana was vigorously shaking her finger as she spoke, just as if Demetri stood before her to take his scolding. I heard the beaded curtain part again and a husky Greek voice said, "I would like to offer my sincerest thanks in person, if you will allow it, my lady."

Demetri and his flowery greeting surprised me, especially

since every other time we had met, he was rudely belligerent. For the moment, his intense black eyes were so filled with gratitude I thought that he might drop to one knee and kiss my hand.

"Your gallant rescue meant more to me than you know," he explained. "I have tamed many wild mountains, but I have never conquered the sea. I never learned to swim. You and your friends showed great courage when you helped rescue us from the waves and the wind. You put your own vessel at risk. Your actions made me regret that unfortunate incident on Dhia. I asked Elana to call you so that I could return your small lamp, your small souvenir lamp, filled with mud. We set it in a pail of water to soak so that we can clean it for you."

Elana led the way back through the beaded curtain to the worktable where the restorations were made. She put on an apron to cover her dress; she never wore anything but black. She removed her seal ring and was about to dip her carefully manicured hands into the bucket of muddy water, but before she could act, I stopped her.

"Please. Your beautiful lacquered nails; you must let me."

Elana reluctantly gave way and allowed me to put my sturdy hands into the mucky water. I dug my finger into the belly of the well where the clay was most resistant.

"Demetri, I apologize for telling you this was a souvenir lamp. I must confess that I found it on Dhia when we were exploring the island a few days ago. It was wedged between two large boulders not too far from St. George's Bay."

The admission was a gray truth, but I felt it was the only safe path I could travel to keep my promise of secrecy. St. George was a popular place for day sailors.

"Do you think it's old? I can't tell the difference between

this one and the reproductions out there in the shop. This mud is really hard. I think I'll need something sharp to work it loose."

Demetri handed me a stiff palette knife.

"Be careful. Do not scar the sides with the blade. Such lamps are usually cut from very soft stone. As to the age, it would have to be tested. But even if it is very old, it would have little value since they are so common."

Working with care, I kept my hands just beneath the surface of the murky water, making small swishing motions to help wash away the sandy mud.

"The lump is out of the well. It's really hard, almost like a rock."

When I tried to crush it, I caught the glint of yellow metal through the dirty water. I rubbed harder and faster, and after some effort I exposed a large gold ring similar to the one Elana wore on her right forefinger.

With the appearance of the ring, all traces of gratitude were washed from Demetri's face, Once more his dark eyes burned with rage, and an aura of hate surrounded him.

"First, you take my beads, and now *this*."

The momentary flush of pleasure I felt when I found the ring instantly changed to resentment. My feelings were still raw from the quarrel with my husband, and I was not about to take any more abuse from anyone.

"Demetri, you continue to accuse me of things I have never done. I came to Crete to search for answers to an old story. I came here to find something that would help me solve the mystery that shrouds Princess Ariadne's death. I believe an injustice was done and for reasons I can't explain, I feel compelled to do all I can to expose the truth. I didn't come here to steal anything. *All* that has happened to me has been beyond my control. Fate led me here, and Fate put this ring into my hands instead of yours. I need your help, not your baseless accusations. What I need most are answers."

Demetri responded with a sinister look. I moved toward him and, just as I had done with Dan, I looked him straight in the eye.

"Tell me why Elana's grandfather sold me the beads. Tell me why he insisted that he knew me. Tell me why you are so determined to reclaim a strand of beads that legally belong to me."

The rapid-fire questions caused Demetri's eyes to waver, but the interrogation prompted Elana to respond.

"I will tell you what I know. My grandfather was the leader of a secret society called the Brotherhood of the Double Ax. Eh, Demetri, do not give me one of your black looks. None of their members may reveal what they do, but it is common knowledge that they use ancient relics in their rituals. The beads of lapis lazuli are thought to be a very powerful talisman."

Demetri glared at both of us with arrogant eyes and spoke with great pride.

"I am the new leader of the Brotherhood, and it is my duty to reclaim what was lost. Since you, cousin, choose to reveal my secret fraternity, perhaps you would like to disclose to us the mysteries you celebrate in your women's society. Tell us what relics the Daughters of the Veil hold sacred in your rituals?"

"Stop it! Both of you," I ordered impatiently. "I did not come here to pry into your secret societies. I came to Crete for answers to an old mystery. Demetri, if you want the beads returned to you, then you must agree to do something for me."

With a flash of insight, I made a decision.

I put the gold ring on my forefinger, untied the blue beads from around my neck and placed them over the stone lamp. I threw down a gauntlet with my husband, and now I was going to issue a challenge to Demetri. When I raised my eyes, they were so fierce it caused him to blink.

With great solemnity, I covered the beads and the lamp with my ringed hand and placed my other hand on my heart. I spoke in a full, clear voice.

"I swear, by everything I hold dear, unless you help me find the answer to one important question, I will do everything in my power to prevent you from taking these beads from me."

My eyes were cold, and the muscles in my jaw were hard as the stone lamp beneath my hand. No one observing my actions could have any doubt that my oath was sincere.

Excited by my own audacity, I felt a great upsurge of courage and pride because I knew that my words were not an idle threat. This was a cause worth fighting for and it was nobler than a battle over guns or treasure. This was a matter of honor, and it felt right and good. There could be no compromise when it came to my integrity.

"And…I swear that I will return the beads to their rightful owner, if you will help me learn why Elana's grandfather sold them to me."

After a moment of tense consideration, Demetri eased his stance and lowered his eyes. He pulled at his mustache for a moment and then grudgingly dragged a chair up to the work table and slowly sat down. He was ready to bargain.

"I will make coffee," Elana said and hurried from the room.

It took the better part of an hour for me to reveal the many events that had led me to return to Crete. I told them about the years I had spent researching and writing my book, about my efforts to recreate the old Minoan culture, about my search to find the truth surrounding Theseus' abandonment of Ariadne. I even told them how I had been struggling helplessly for months, trying to write an ending to my novel.

"But why?" Elana asked softly. "Why are you so concerned about the fate of Princess Ariadne?"

"All I know is that the more I search for answers, the more determined I am to succeed. The myth deals with archetypes that represent basic human motivations. Psychologists like Carl Jung have written extensively about the subject. When Ariadne gave up everything she held dear to save a handful of Athenian children, and the man she loved, she represented the best in every woman. Theseus accepted her sacrifice, she gave him the gift of life, yet he broke his vow and betrayed her. If that is the truth, then why does the world still honor him as a hero?"

All the feelings of injustice that had been stirred ever since I first read the mythical story about Ariadne and Theseus burned inside me like a raging fire. My hand curled into a fist and I slammed it down on the table, rattling the coffee cups in their saucers. "It wasn't fair," I shouted. "Theseus should have been the one to die on Dia, not Ariadne."

Demetri couldn't conceal his surprise. He never expected to see a woman display such strong feelings about a matter of honor, especially an American woman.

Elana smiled and said, "You have a passionate soul. You

must surely have Greek blood in your veins. But I am puzzled. Why do you go to Dhia Island to search for Ariadne when she died on Naxos?"

"That is the confusing part. Dia is the name given to two different Greek islands. In the past, Naxos was called Dia, and today, Dhia is also called Dia. Storytellers say Naxos is the place where Ariadne died, but I can't help feeling that Dhia also has some connection to Ariadne. I have this persistent feeling that something is there that will reveal the truth about why she was abandoned by Theseus. All I have found is this lamp and ring and I don't know the significance of either one. The ring doesn't look like any Minoan seal ring I've ever seen in any of the collections. It will take some work to learn if it has any connection to Ariadne."

"Perhaps you should not be so quick to call Dhia the wrong island," Elana said. "Dhia may be the wrong island for Ariadne, but it could be the right island for you."

"If only I could rid myself of this whole messy business. If only it would leave me alone. The story wakes me in the night: my mind working like a nest of ants sifting through the details for a crumb of truth. Most of all, Theseus' betrayal eats at me; and the fact that the world calls that coward a hero: that's the greatest wound of all. Adding even more mystery to the story, there are legends that say Ariadne bore Theseus two sons. Even *I* know that a dead woman can't have babies. So what is the truth?"

"I have no answers to such questions," Demetri said with a frown.

"I understand that, but if you agree to help me learn why Elana's grandfather sold me the beads instead of passing them to you, then perhaps other answers will follow."

Since both Elana and Demetri belonged to secret societies celebrating the lost Minoan culture, they undoubtedly
knew oral traditions that were passed from mother to daughter, and father to son. They very likely performed rituals that
were thousands of years old.

I decided to tempt them even further. I told them about
Jake, about his psychic reading of the beads. I also told them
about my attempts at regression, and my visions of both
Theseus and Ariadne.

"If you help me find the reason Elana's grandfather wanted me to have the beads, if I can discover that one truth,
perhaps it will help me write a believable ending to Ariadne's
story."

"She must go to the Oracle," Elana said with certainty.

"Never!" Demetri shouted. This time he was not just
angry, he was adamant. "Outsiders are never allowed to participate in the rituals."

"It is not for you to say. It is a matter for the Ansasa—
only the Old Mistress can make such a decision."

When their heated discussion switched to Greek, I picked
up the beads and retied them around my neck. Leaning back
in my chair, I relaxed and sipped my tiny cup of Greek coffee, feeling more in control than I had in days. I realized I
was ravenous and ate most of the cheese and bread left from
their *mezes*.

I felt certain that Elana was going to help me find the
way to the truth about Ariadne's ultimate fate. If she did,
there was one more thing I had to decide. Should I brave
the journey to see their *Oracle* alone, or should I ask Jake
to travel the mystery path with me? The picture on his office wall showed him with a tribe of aborigines, and from the

collections in his home I knew he was no stranger to mystical ceremonies. Would he be willing to help me? But...did I
want his company?

Elana and Demetri finally came to an agreement.

"If you want to consult the Oracle, return here tomorrow
afternoon. I will arrange for you to meet the Old Mistress
and ask her permission to attend the ceremony."

ψ

By the time I returned to my hotel, it was past eleven
o'clock. The lobby was deserted except for the desk clerk,
which was unusual. Even the seaside lounge was empty of
late-night guests. When I reached the door to my room, I
purposely fumbled with the key, rattling it in the lock, deliberately making enough noise to frighten away anyone who
might be waiting inside.

The room was cool and damp and flooded with moonlight. The sound of the surf rolled in through the open door
to the balcony.

I left in such a hurry I forgot to close the door, and the
heavy draperies billowed out into the room, pushed by the
rounded shape of the wind.

How could I be so stupid? I did leave the door open, didn't I?

I turned on all the lights and cautiously checked under
the bed, in the bathroom, and behind the shower curtain.
After making certain the room was empty, I locked the doors,
undressed quickly and dropped my clothes where I stood.
Just as I was about to crawl into bed, there was a soft knock
on the door.

"Service," a husky male voice said.

The word was muffled and barely audible. I froze. I

couldn't tell if the knock was on my door, or on the one across the hall.

"You have the wrong room," I shouted at the chained and locked door, straining to hear the tiniest sound.

"ROOM SERVICE," the voice said again in rough English, and this time the knock was louder and it was definitely on my door.

"OPEN!" the voice demanded.

I was not about to open the door.

"Go away. You have the wrong room. I'm calling the manager."

Just as I reached for the phone it rang, jangling shrilly, and I jumped like a startled cat, knocking both the lamp and the phone off the nightstand onto the floor.

Heart ready to burst with fright, I collected the phone and receiver, held my breath, and listened for a sound on the other end of the line. The familiar voice in my ear was such a relief, I let my breath out with a rush and cried, "Ah, Jake, thank God it's you."

"We've been trying to reach you for hours. The desk clerk said you and your husband were not in your room. Are you okay?"

"No. I'm not okay. A man is banging on my door saying he's from room service, and there's no service at this hour."

"I'm in the lobby. I'll be right up. *no excuses!* You're coming back to the villa with me."

CHAPTER TWENTY-THREE

CLIFF HOUSE

I awoke to the sound of the sea crashing against the cliff wall. Groaning with pleasure I stretched full length in Jake's bed. I had managed the first good night's sleep since I had arrived on Crete. Although the bed had been changed the night before, when I buried my nose in the pillow, I could still detect the faint scent of his aftershave.

I wondered where Deupree had slept. There was only one empty guestroom. Perhaps he had lain across my threshold like a gallant knight guarding my door. Dan believed Deupree was a villainous knight in black, but I wasn't sure. His armor was tarnished, but it might shine, if he ever decided to give it a good scrub.

When I thought of Dan, I sighed and wondered where *he* had slept. Did he go to Egypt alone? Did he return home? My feelings toward my husband were a tangled web of anger and hurt, concern and regret, all so painfully knotted I wasn't sure how I was ever going to sort it all out.

Whatever the outcome, it was time to stop analyzing, time to turn off the self-doubt. Right now, the most important thing to decide was whether to include Jake in my search for truth.

Last night, when we drove from the hotel to the villa, I told him about my linguistic mix-up, confusing Dia and Dhia, and he agreed with Elana that the switch in names could be more than an accident.

We even discussed the meaning of the lamp as a symbol

of illumination, or possibly enlightenment. For some per-verse reason, I did not tell him about finding the ring. Nor did I tell him about Elana's suggestion that I speak to the Oracle. This was something I wanted to think about; some-thing I might prefer to handle alone, or maybe not handle at all.

I showered and dressed and found my way to the kitch-en. It felt like early morning to me, but when I finally got around to looking at my watch I discovered that it was shockingly close to noon, and I was supposed to meet Elana at two o'clock in Heraklion. I had to decide soon if I wanted to include Jake in this part of my quest.

The dining table was filled with charts, and ferry and airline schedules. Theo and Jake were busy discussing dif-ferent ways to liberate the guns and open the chest, but their plans were of little interest to me. My immediate goal was to return to Heraklion and learn whether Elana had been able to arrange a meeting with the Old Mistress. I wanted to find out more about consulting the Oracle.

After the "good mornings" and "how did you sleeps" were passed around Theo said, "After your experience in the hotel last night, I think you should stay close to one of us at all times. Seems like that Demetri fellow is a hot-headed individual. You never know what he might have in mind. Cretan men can be unbelievably brave one minute and devious as bazaar thieves the next. If you have offended Demetri's manhood in any way, you are truly in trouble."

Theo's words disturbed me. For some odd reason, it irked me to hear Cretan men described in such a contemp-tuous way. "Aren't you being a little unfair, judging a man before he's been convicted of a crime?"

"The man broke into your room! Isn't that proof of his criminal intentions?"

"I don't know if the intruder was Demetri. Jake *thinks* it was Demetri. The only thing I know for certain is that Demetri is angry and vindictive. After knowing more about the circumstances, I think his anger might be justified, although excessive. Evidently the old antique dealer sold me something that was not his to sell. Besides, if Demetri is such a villain, why didn't he try to take the beads from me by force last night in Elana's shop?"

"He isn't stupid," Jake said scornfully, and joined Theo in his condemnation of Demetri. "What about the man at your hotel door last night? Your unwanted room service? Who could that have been if it wasn't Demetri?"

I couldn't answer his question.

"Theo's right," Jake said. "You stick close to us until this thing is finished."

"I have an appointment to meet with Elana this afternoon."

"No problem," Theo said. "I need to take some things to the *Crystina* before I have her sailed over to Hersonissos. We can go with you to see your shopkeeper."

"I really don't think Elana expects me to come as a group." I was beginning to feel claustrophobic.

Tina jumped up, began grabbing dirty dishes, and making a great clatter in the process. She gave the impression that she was upset about something. She even snapped at Theo, refusing his solicitous offer to help, which was unlike her usual easygoing behavior.

"I'm going for a walk on the beach." Jake and I said the words in unison, which gave them a peculiar echoing sound.

Jake laughed pleasantly, seeming to try a little too much to be *Mister Congeniality.*

"Pretty soon, we're going to be so in tune telepathically, we won't even need words. I haven't decided if you're sending or receiving—probably some of both."

I had no desire to be connected telepathically to him. At this moment I had no desire to even talk to him. I wanted to be left alone to pursue my own needs.

"What is it with you men?" I shouted over my shoulder.

Jake looked innocently confused.

"Oh, don't look at me like that. If we're so telepathically in tune, you know perfectly well what I'm talking about. I don't need a bodyguard, and I'm too old for a chaperon. I'm going to see Elana, alone."

"That may not be a wise thing to do."

"Why not?"

"She may just be leading you to get information."

"Information about what?"

"The guns in the cave."

"I haven't told anyone about the cave. I know the guns are valuable, but you and Theo act so paranoid, anyone would think we'd found the Treasury of Minos."

"You don't have to say anything. You're so easy to read, a child could look at you and know something unusual is happening. You say you didn't tell Elana and Demetri about the stuff we found on Dhia, but the human imagination is a curious thing. It has the tendency to invent the fantastic dream, never common, ordinary reality. You show them an old lamp and Elana and Demetri immediately think it might lead to other things, like gold, or valuable Minoan artifacts."

"Especially since I found the ring," I added with a frown.

"What ring?"

I couldn't quickly think of a credible way to avoid telling him about the ring, and I didn't feel completely okay about keeping it from him anyway.

"Remember, you said you wanted no part of the lamp. When I was washing it last night, I found a gold signet ring embedded inside the oil well. It rekindled Demetri's anger, sort of the proverbial last straw. That's when I told them all my reasons for coming to Dhia. I told them about the book, about Theseus and Ariadne, about you and the regressions. That's when Elana said I should go see the Oracle."

"What Oracle?" Jake threw his hands in the air.

"I'm not exactly sure. She was vague. She acted as if it were some great secret. But it sounds as if I might be able to learn why I have this strong feeling for Dhia. Perhaps, I might find out if the blue beads do have this mysterious power you keep talking about; I might even learn if the lamp and the ring have some special meaning."

"Did you leave the ring with Elana?"

"No. Eventually, I'll take it to the museum, or the Department of Antiquities but, as I told Elana, I'm keeping it for now."

I reached into my pocket and pulled out the heavy circle of gold, capped with an unusually wide, flat crown. I held out my hand with the ring perched like a gold butterfly on my palm.

Jake didn't take the ring, or even touch it. He just held his open palm over mine, and I felt a springy cushion of energy between our two hands. He closed his eyes, intending to concentrate, but even before he could relax his face, he jerked his hand away. He looked hard at me and then turned and without a word walked back toward the stairway up to the villa.

I ran after him. I wanted to know what he felt, but before I could ask, Theo appeared at the top of the steps and called down. "If you want to go to Heraklion with me, I'm leaving here in five minutes."

CHAPTER TWENTY-FOUR

THE OLD MISTRESS

On the trip into town, the two men sat in front and Tina and I sat in the back. It was our first opportunity to have a real conversation. She was a listener, a little reserved, but always friendly.

"Where did you learn so much about sailing?" she asked.

"I can't remember when I didn't know how to sail. My parents had a summer place near a small river in Kentucky. Those were the days when kids played without a lot of supervision, and I did something I would never have allowed my own children to do. The house came with an old wooden skiff that was more raft than boat. I would bail it out, rig it with a tall stick and one of Mom's old bed sheets, and when the wind was blowing at my back, I would talk my best friend into coming with me on an adventure.

"The wind would push us up a straight stretch of the river for about a mile, and then I would fold up our makeshift sail and drift back home with the current. I didn't really learn to sail until I raced competitively on a sailing team in college. That's where I met my husband, Dan. We've always owned a sailboat of one class or another, but my experience with ocean cruising has been on vacations when we chartered motor-sailors in some pretty exotic place."

"You're a lot like Theo. He was brought up on the East Coast, born with a tiller in his hand, as they say, but we're not very well matched when it comes to the sea. If it's reasonably calm, and as long as I stay up on deck, I do pretty well. But when the wind picks up and the waves work up a lather, I'm instantly seasick. Sea bands on my wrists work pretty well, but I'm no help at all when the wind really starts to blow."

We enjoyed the ride, getting to know each other better. I learned that she had a big family and would rather live and work in the states, but Theo thought Italy was best... evidently, I wasn't the only one who made sacrifices to keep the peace.

When we reached Heraklion, I asked Theo to drop me at the Morozini Fountain. As soon as the car stopped, before I could voice even a mild protest, Jake climbed out after me, and Theo quickly sped away.

It was another hot Mediterranean afternoon. The sun had sucked all the moisture from the dreary-looking clumps of marigolds planted in the parched earth that ringed the ancient fountain. Only a narrow thread of water trickled from the gaping mouths of the lion faces that stood guard around the basin.

"I need a lemonade." Without waiting for Jake to reply, I led the way toward a sidewalk *taverna* and collapsed in a chair at a shade-covered table.

"I thought you were in a big hurry to see your friend. Back at the villa, your feathers were in a royal fluff because you had to rush into town."

"Jake, I don't want you to come with me to talk to Elana. I'm going alone. Yesterday, in a fit of pique, Demetri let it slip that there are two secret societies here on Crete: one for men and one for women. I sensed a lot of rivalry, downright animosity, between the two factions. There is a serious male-female power struggle going on here, and I don't want

190 * DORIS KENNEY MARCOTTE

to offer any obstacle that might make Elana change her mind about allowing me to attend the ceremony. I'll ask her if you can join me as an observer, but if she needs to say no, I want her to be able to do so without losing face with you standing right there in front of her."

From Jake's sour look, he was not happy with the situation. I stood up slowly and placed my feet slightly apart. Standing solidly balanced, I made it obvious that I was in no mood to capitulate.

Jake forced a smile and with a sneer said, "Suit yourself. I still don't think it's a good idea for you to go anywhere alone. But, obviously, I can't make you take me with you."

"You know...I don't get it. No matter where I am, whether I'm at home, or here in Crete, someone is always telling me I shouldn't do anything on my own. Believe it or not, I am a very capable person. I raised two children without major mishap, and there's a tough-nosed newspaper editor who's published my articles for years who thinks I have a fair amount of good sense. I have enough muscle to sail a fifty-one-foot yacht with no problem, yet I can't be trusted to take a business trip, or even go into an antique shop without supervision."

"So what am I supposed to do while you go chasing off on your own? I have no particular need to sit here all day waiting for you."

"I didn't ask you to come. However, I do know a lot about waiting. You could say I am a Professional. I have even learned how to *wait* to *wait*. It takes patience, and you need to be creative. I know, pretend you're Greek. A Greek man can sit in the shade and drink coffee all day long without a problem. Better still—buy yourself some worry beads and contemplate your purpose in life."

ψ

Elana was alone in the shop.

"Jake Deupree wants me to ask you if he can attend the ceremony."

"NO! Absolutely not." Elana made a cut with her hand to say the decision was final. "The only men allowed to attend are members of Demetri's order. The Brotherhood serves the Goddess, and they know how to show proper respect. They assist in the rituals, obey the Ansasa, and know their place in our society. They are sworn to follow as tradition dictates."

"I'll go tell Jake. He's waiting for me at the *taverna*."

"Let him wait. You must meet with the Old One to learn if you can go to the Oracle. She is expecting us. Come! It is not far."

She stepped to the beaded curtain and called, "Demetri! Watch the shop while I am away."

Out the front door we went, back the way I had just come. Elana led me by the hand past the *taverna* where Jake was sitting, to the whitewashed house with the beautiful courtyard, the friendly cat, the scarlet geraniums, and the toothless old woman who always smiled at me when I passed.

After speaking Greek to the old lady in a very loud voice, Elana turned to me and said, "She only wears a hearing device for important occasions."

The ear-numbing discussion was brief. I heard the name Demetri twice, and when the loud conversation ended, the old woman once again gave me her toothless smile. She patted me on the arm and said something in Greek that sounded comforting. Using her broom for support, the old grandmother slowly returned to the cool darkness of her shuttered rooms.

"She said you may seek the wisdom of the Oracle the night of the full moon. You are fortunate. Tonight, the moon will be full. I also asked her about your friend Deupree, and she confirmed my position that the only men allowed to attend the ceremony will be Demetri and a few of his friends."

"Tonight? That doesn't give me much time to think. Believe me, I really want to do this but to be truthful, I'm a little afraid. I know why Demetri agreed to help me: he wants me to return the beads. I'm sorry to be blunt, but I'm not sure why you're doing this for me. I have never before enjoyed such uncommonly good treatment. You and the old Ansasa are being so nice and cooperative, it feels a little strange. I worry that I may be intruding where I don't belong. I'm confused. I'm not sure what to do."

"Kate, my grandfather felt, or saw, something in you that sparked some kind of recognition. I feel an attraction as well. We are an ancient people here on our island. We have learned that science and mathematics do not explain all things. Sometimes it is necessary to trust in what you cannot understand to find the truth. Have faith. Return to me tonight at ten o'clock and we will go to a place just outside the city. I will have a costume for you to wear. Bring the beads of lapis lazuli, and the gold signet ring you found inside the lamp. The ceremony does not begin until midnight, but we must give ourselves ample time to prepare. And plan to spend the night here with me. I have an extra bedroom in my apartment upstairs."

"What will…"

"Ask no more questions. I promise you, I will even take

an oath that you will come to no harm. I swear this to you on my dead husband's soul, may he rest in peace.

ψ

"Bullshit! *BULL...SHIT*. They're up to no good! I can feel it!"

Once again, Jake was shaking his arm and rubbing his hand. He paced back and forth across the veranda like an over-imaginative father whose teenaged daughter was about to leave on her very first date.

"Nothing you say will change my mind. I am going!" I said flatly.

"Something's wrong! Trouble! I can feel it!"

Jake made his prediction with a mournful wag of his head and continued to pace.

Watching Jake's theatrics, Tina said, "Well, Jake, my old buddy, my old friend, maybe it's just your time of the month." She threw him a mean grin and flopped down on the couch next to me.

Jake's lip curled. He clenched his fist and looked as if he would love to give Tina a punch in the mouth and I was puzzled. Tina's remark was crude and insensitive—which was so different from her usual behavior. I was puzzled by her sudden change in attitude. All day, she had been sharp and surly with both Theo and Jake, constantly needling them, her eyes hot with unspoken words. Conversely, her conduct toward me was warm and solicitous to the extreme.

Theo was still worrying the salvage problem.

"The portable generator arrives by airfreight from Piraeus this afternoon. We can pick it up at the airport, then drive over to Hersonissos and sleep on the *Crystina* tonight. This will give us the advantage of being ready to leave in the morning before dawn. Since the distance to Dhia is greater than from Venetian Harbor, we will need extra sailing time. And the wind could be right on the nose, which would make it a slogging beat all the way."

"What are you saying?" I asked sharply. Theo's words suddenly registered and I didn't like what I was hearing.

"You haven't been listening, have you? I will repeat. I sent the *Crystina* east to Hersonissos, a small harbor near here. It will be a longer sail but, hopefully, it will fool the crew of the *Sheitan* into thinking we are finished with exploring Dhia. We will go to the *Crystina* this afternoon, spend the night on the boat, and sail to the island early tomorrow morning. We will take the makings to rig a hoist to lift the guns up from the ledge, and a portable generator to power the tools we need to open the chest."

"I can't go anywhere today. I have business tonight in Heraklion."

"Risky business, in my opinion. Every day we delay, the danger increases—every hour even. Not only do we risk discovery, the weather can turn bad at any moment. If you've never experienced a full-blown Meltemi, you should read the description of one in *Zorba the Greek*; then maybe you will have some appreciation for the potential disaster these crazy Greek winds present. That little blow we were in yesterday was only a small breeze compared to the wind in a real Meltemi. A big one can blow forty knots or more."

Theo looked at me with suspicious eyes. "If you're not going to keep your promise to help us sail the treasure out, tell me now, so I can make other plans."

"Treasure?" I forced a dry laugh. "It sounds a bit ludicrous to call a bunch of greasy old guns *treasure*."

Tina glared at Theo vehemently and when he didn't react, she made a strangling noise, jumped up, and stalked out
of the room. The two men ignored her dramatic exit and
continued to pressure me, warning me, scaring me, but before they could convince me to forsake my tryst with Elana
and her secret society, they were interrupted by the cook
calling Theo to the phone. When he returned, his face was
pinched with worry.

"That was a friend at the Port Authority. I asked her to
call me if anything unusual happened concerning the *Sheitan*.
She said their captain just cleared Customs. Evidently, the
boat is leaving Greek waters, which is welcome news. But,
she also said that a man was nosing around early this morning asking questions about the *Crystina*, trying to find out
where she had gone."

"You see, Jake, *that's* the trouble you're sensing. Your bad
vibrations aren't caused by me, they're caused by your precious treasure hunt. I came to Crete for one thing. You came
here for another. At this point in time, your salvage project
is not my most immediate problem. If you can't wait for me
until tomorrow, then I guess you'll have to make the sail to
Dhia without me. You can replace me with some other poor,
gullible fool."

No more talk for me. I sat in the bathroom for a while and
then took another walk on the beach to gather my thoughts
and formulate my own plan of action. After weighing all my
options, I decided that Tina could be the solution to one of
my problems, and I approached her in the kitchen.

"Tina. Come with me to see the Oracle."

"Me? Ohhh, no! I would be scared to death. I don't like

voodoo, or witchcraft, or any of that occult stuff that Jake is into. Anyway, why would you want me to come with you?"

"I trust you. I feel like you are my friend and I could use some good old-fashioned moral support."

"Theo would have a fit."

"I'm not asking Theo. I'm asking you. Please, don't say no. Just think about it."

"Kate, you don't know any real thing about these people. You don't have the slightest idea what they're capable of doing."

"Unfortunately, that's true. It will be an act of faith. However, no matter what the consequences may be, I'm going to do this. I'll be leaving soon to take the bus into town. The trip will take me an hour or more and I'll need to get a bite to eat. I don't want to be late. If you change your mind and decide to go with me, I'll be at the *taverna* where you let me out this afternoon: it's the one nearest the Morozini Fountain. I'll be there until ten o'clock."

"I don't think I have the courage to go with you."

"Whether you come with me or not, I will keep my promise to help you salvage the rifles. I must go with Elana tonight because I truly believe this ceremony is part of what brought me back to Crete. It has to do with a vow I made long before I met the three of you. I *will* help you, but only if you wait until tomorrow. Tonight's ceremony is an opportunity that may never come my way again."

CHAPTER TWENTY-FIVE

DAUGHTERS OF THE VEIL

The sun had set and the cobblestones were beginning to cool. It would have been pleasant to relax and watch the couples walk hand in hand on their nightly promenade, but I was far too distracted. It was nine-thirty, and Tina had still not made an appearance.

"Your food is no good?" the waiter asked.

"No, it's fine. I'm not very hungry. You can bring me a Nescafe."

"Make that two," Tina said as she slid into the seat opposite me.

"You came." I beamed with joy and I relaxed with a sigh of relief.

"I'm here, but don't get excited. I'm not staying; I'm not going with you to the ceremony."

Tina looked miserable. With downcast eyes, she fiddled with the strap on the small purse in her lap. "I was tempted to go with you, but I can't do it. I don't like ceremonies, especially religious ceremonies. Besides, Theo has no tolerance for mysticism. He would be angry if I went with you."

"What about *your* tolerance? I thought that as a professional woman, you, of all people, were your own person. No! Please, forget I said that. I'm sorry. I don't want to cause trouble between you and Theo. This is my problem. I'll be okay."

Tina looked even more miserable.

"I came to tell you something. I've wanted to tell you all

day. Please, understand that Theo and Jake both know what I'm about to say, so I'm not betraying their trust or anything like that."

"What is it? You look like someone died."

"It's about the stuff in the cave on Dhia Island. It's not just a cache of old World War II rifles. Jake didn't tell you the whole truth. You know that piece of wood he chiseled out of the chest? He told you there was a black metal liner under the wood. That wasn't the truth. What he uncovered was solid gold. He and Theo think the chest contains gold bullion. Jake covered the gold with black soot from the burned firewood so you wouldn't be spooked by what he found. The guys think the box is probably lined with gold bars, but they've decided it's not heavy enough to be completely filled with gold. They think that something of even greater value might be stored in the center."

"Gold...GOLD!"

"Shhhh. Yes. That's why Theo and Jake are so concerned. If you make one slip about the cave, or draw further attention to Dhia Island, it may ruin our chance of retrieving it. The guns alone will probably bring each of us several thousand dollars, but gold bars, and whatever else might be inside the chest, could be worth millions."

All signs of enthusiasm and excitement vanished from my face. My stomach clutched into such a knot I wished I hadn't eaten a thing. The shock was so great, I was unable to speak.

"I know how you feel," Tina placed her hand on top of mine. "I wanted the men to tell you sooner, but Jake was afraid you would panic, or have another attack of ethics. Please, listen to me for a minute before you say anything. There's no way to know who the rightful owner might be. Obviously, it wasn't ordinary people. Although the boxes are marked with swastikas, it may not have been left by Germans. All we know for certain is that it has remained there, undisturbed, for at least fifty years. It's possible that we found some long-dead Greek warlord's private treasure trove. I'm sorry if this complicates things for you, but I thought from the very first that you should know what's really at stake. The guys didn't want to scare you because we need you. Theo needs you to help him sail the *Crystina* tomorrow."

Tina squeezed my limp hand, stood up quickly, and walked away.

It was exactly fifteen minutes to ten. Fifteen minutes to make a decision that could change my life, forever.

This was so far from anything I could ever have imagined before I began my quest for truth; it was beyond incredible. This was daydreams and nightmares all rolled into one. I had boasted to Dan and Letty Marie that my quest was going to be an adventure, but this was bizarre, fantastic, unbelievable. I could not find a word powerful enough to describe the emotions charging through my mind and my body.

Choose! That's what Dan told me back at the hotel, but little did he know the magnitude of the choices I would have to consider.

By attending the ceremony, by asking the Oracle about the gold ring, it was true that I would be calling further attention to Dhia. But if I didn't seek the Oracle, I could lose the best perhaps the only chance I would ever have to solve the mystery surrounding Ariadne.

As for salvaging the treasure, if my actions caused us to get caught, I could end up worse than dead. I could spend the rest of my life rotting in a Greek prison.

Truth or treasure. How could I choose?

Maybe it's time to stop worrying about all the what-ifs. I need to stop analyzing and choose what's best for me. Tonight, I will go with Elana to find the truth, and tomorrow I will go with the treasure hunters and help open the chest. That way I won't have to look back and wish I had found the courage to face the unknown, no matter how frightening it might be.

CHAPTER TWENTY-SIX

NIGHT OF THE FULL MOON

E lana bundled me into her car as soon as I arrived. The warm air still held the breath of the sun, and the soft black night was a collage of colored lights. The car sped past houses with brightly lit windows, past hotels overflowing with laughing guests on their way out for an evening of fun.

"Wasn't that my hotel we just passed?"

"Yes."

Elana slowed down and carefully drove into a vacant field crowded with cars. It was a wild place littered with boulders and weeds and a thousand flyaway plastic bags.

"We're so close to the hotel; are we going to the Cave of Elithyia? I remember asking about it the first time I came to Crete. The desk clerk had said the entrance was fenced and locked, and entry was only by permission from the curator at the museum. Are we going to Elithyia?"

Elana did not answer my question. The location would remain secret.

"We must walk from here."

Icicles for fingers and rubber for knees, I had never been more apprehensive. I didn't know what I had gotten myself into, but it was too late to back out now. Just like the Goddess of Snakes, I had grabbed the serpents by their heads, and if I wasn't careful I might feel the venom in their fangs.

Fortunately, the moon was high enough to show the stony ground and the toe-tripping gullies. I expected to see the yawning mouth of a cave, but there was no grand entrance.

Instead, we walked around a thicket of brush and entered a doorway cut directly into the side of a mound of earth.

One small oil lamp sitting in a niche formed in a concrete block wall lit the entryway. I followed Elana, one foot in front of the other, single file, along a passageway that led down a dozen shallow steps cut into the raw earth.

When I made the decision to trust Elana, I turned off all the should-nots and tried to stifle my doubts and fears, mostly. When we reached the bottom of the steps, we entered another narrow corridor, this one cut in stone.

The light was dim. Hanging lanterns filled the air with the chemical odor of burning kerosene. The floor sloped downward at a steep angle and we walked deeper and deeper into the earth. The corridor made a sharp left turn and we entered what appeared to be an older, natural tunnel.

Frescos covered the smooth stone walls. Brilliantly painted images escorted us as we walked along the path. Full-sized images of slim-waisted, bare-chested men carrying urns and skin-shaped sheets of copper marched along beside us. The handsome figures were similar to those uncovered in the Minoan ruins and inside an Egyptian tomb; I wondered if Demetri was their creator.

The corridor appeared to come to a dead end, but once we reached the blank stone wall, a right-angled opening was revealed, and the corridor turned and then turned again. A labyrinth, I thought, losing all sense of direction.

Muffled voices floated along the ceiling and walls, and when the corridor turned for the last time, it opened into a large room furnished with a dozen wooden benches and several crudely built curtained partitions. When Elana and I walked into the room, a group of costumed women were leaving through an opening on the opposite wall.

Pegs on the sides of the partitions held dresses and un-derwear. Women's shoes, all kinds and all sizes, were piled haphazardly on the floor. A wastebasket held empty Fanta cans and crumpled candy wrappers, and the sight of such common, everyday things helped assuage the panic that needed only a nudge to erupt and control my resolve to see this thing through to the end.

I tried to breathe normally instead of taking shallow sips of air. This was an ordinary women's locker room, and the ceremony was a costume party held inside a musty old cave. *Right!* Obviously, it was going to take an enormous amount of effort to rein in my tendency to over-dramatize. Looking back, it was probably one of the most difficult things I have ever tried to do.

Sensing my nervousness, Elana gently squeezed my arm and said, "It is going to be okay. You'll see." She emptied a large soft-sided bag onto one of the benches and laid out an assortment of ruffled skirts and blouses and veils

"The mistresses and matrons go before us to make prep-arations. These are for you. We selected shades of blue to compliment your beads. Everything we do here is accord-ing to ritual and in keeping with the old ways. The blouses are made of chiffon and are worn without undergarments. Some of the women bare their breasts completely, so please do not be shocked when you see them. They dress like the women shown in the frescoes, but most of us prefer a light covering."

"As long as I'm mostly covered, I'll be all right."

Clothing mattered very little to me. I intended to stay in the background, to watch and wait for the opportunity to present my questions to the Oracle.

The air in the room was stagnant, faintly scented with frankincense, perspiration, and the odor of burning olive oil that came from the lamps on the walls.

I entered one of the stalls and changed quickly, pulling on a sleeveless bodice made of tissue-thin gauze. Taking care not to lose my balance and tear the fabric, I stepped into a long, ruffled skirt of pale blue and lowered a second, shorter skirt dyed a deeper shade of blue over the first. The costume seemed familiar: probably because I had written several colorful scenes describing the Minoan clothing in detail. That was undoubtedly the reason for my feeling of déjà vu.

"Have I put this on the right way?"

I hung my street clothes on a peg and set my sandals beneath them on the floor.

"You look perfect."

Elana had changed into a similar tissue-thin bodice and two ruffled skirts. Her outer skirt was dark green, edged with embroidered silver spirals, and her underskirt was bright yellow.

"The Old One has sent a vest and an additional overskirt for you to wear. She also sent a special girdle. You will need me to assist you."

Thank goodness I was slim. The waistband on the heavy overskirt was very tight. Again, the cloth was a deeper blue, a shade of blue as vibrant as my lapis beads, and the embroidery around the hem was worked with fine gold wire which added to its weight. The heat inside the room was suffocating. Without outside ventilation, the air smelled used up and sour.

"I can't breathe. It's so hot. I don't think I can do this."

"Just one minute more and I will find something for you to drink."

The tight-fitting vest had short sleeves and more of the elaborate gold embroidery. It stuck to the damp skin on my arms, but with Elana's help we worked it into place. The neckline plunged below my breasts, making the tiny front fasteners impossible for me to see. By the time Elana had hooked the last one, pulling the tight vest together, my breasts were pushed up to unbelievable heights.

I looked down with amazement at my voluptuously elevated chest. "Oh...my...goodness. I look like a Playboy Bunny. All I need is a little white cottontail on my bum."

Elana giggled nervously, despite her attempt to maintain proper decorum.

"The Old One wants you to wear this gold girdle. It is a great honor. Few have been allowed to wear this treasure."

I was far too distracted to ask, *Why me?* After much tugging and grunting, the girdle closed around my waist with a snap.

"I think I'm going to be sick."

Managing to ignore my rebellious stomach, I helped Elana into her vest, then snapped her into an ornate silver girdle. It wasn't nearly as tight as mine and required much less compression.

"I really don't feel so good." I fanned myself with my hand. "I'm light headed." I sat down on one of the benches with a flop: I was so tightly corseted it was nearly impossible to bend.

"Here. You can drink this. Our facilities are very primitive, but we always keep a pitcher of water at hand."

The liquid was lukewarm and flavored with the faint

taste of almonds.

"Someone must have filled the pitcher with *Soumadha*," she said. "It is more refreshing than plain water. Last, we must do your makeup. I will line your eyes with kohl and then color your lips with a mulberry stain. It is a pity your hair is not long. I could braid it with beads and flowers, but the Old One made a crown of white lilies for you to wear instead. And do not forget your blue beads, yes." She tied the strand around my neck, "And the gold signet ring; wear it on your index finger. Last, the Old One has also given you gold ankle rings to wear. Now. Your costume is complete."

Standing away from me, Elana clapped her hands with pleasure.

"Come! See how excellent you look."

No one would ever recognize me. The costume was breathtaking it was so beautiful. Standing before a long mirror, another scene from my book flashed into my mind.

When Ariadne's mother, Queen Pasiphae, was taken away to mate with the great white bull, her feet were bare and she wore a lily crown. However, she was dressed in a plain white shift.

"I feel faint," I said weakly.

"Drink a little more of the *soumadha*. Once we leave here it will be cooler, more air, not so close. And there will be wine. You will feel better, I promise. Come, we are ready."

CHAPTER TWENTY-SEVEN

MEET THE ORACLE

Before I could protest further, Elana led me out of the room through the rear door. Our bare feet made light slapping sounds against the cool stone floor and I felt gritty dust collecting between my damp toes. The heavy fragrance of frankincense grew stronger, drifting along the corridor, hovering like a cloud of ghostly ectoplasm along the low ceiling and walls.

"The ceremony will be in the throne room."

I could hear the eerie, echoing sound of a flute and a lyre.

The narrow passage finally opened into a cavern lit with thousands of candles stuck into small crevices all around the walls. The tiny flames illuminated a high-domed ceiling and a room filled with women dressed in costumes like Elana's in all the colors of the rainbow. A few bare-chested men stood silently waiting to serve. The female voices were low, but like women everywhere there were giggles and whispers and the room seemed charged with expectation.

Elana led me toward a raised platform and a high-backed chair. Clothed in magnificent splendor, the Old Mistress, the Ansasa, sat on the gilded throne. She smiled broadly as I approached and blessed me with a dazzling display of perfectly formed, snow-white teeth. She looked twenty years younger.

She was a replica of the famous fresco of the Parisian courtesan that was found in the ruins of Knossos Palace. Her twinkling black eyes were lined with a heavy band of kohl, and she wore a Snake Goddess costume, five overskirts, and an apron. Her breasts were bare, nipples and lips rouged red with mulberry stain, and her tiny waist was circled by an intricately designed golden girdle studded with sparkling gemstones.

Dyed Tyrian purple, the color of royalty, her costume was also embroidered with fine gold wire. She wore a gold bee pendant around her neck that was twice the size of the ancient relic so proudly displayed in the Heraklion Museum, and a gold crown studded with flowers sat on her head.

"Come here, child," she said in English.

As Elana propelled me forward she whispered, "She will act as our High Priestess. You do not have to speak louder when you answer her. She is wearing her hearing device and can understand you perfectly. Also, she will speak to you in English, so you will understand."

"This is for you," the old Ansasa said. "Drink! Join us in communion with your sisters and the Holy Mother Earth."

She held two thin-walled goblets in her hands: one for me and one for Elana.

My hands trembled as I accepted the goblet and took a sip of the wine. It tasted very bitter.

Once again, a character from my book whispered in my ears…*Don't drink the wine. The Maenad women are crazy with wine. Don't drink the drugged wine.*

"I can't," I protested.

"Trust, Kate," Elana said. "It is resinated wine. You have drunk our bitter Cretan wine before. Drink with me as your sister."

"I came to see the Oracle."

"We know," the Ansasa said. "But first you must drink

the wine of communion, my child."

My lips quivered. The wine tasted so bitter. I turned to look around me, at the peculiar way the flames from the lamps seemed to leap and dance with life. Fuzzy halos and shooting sparkles of light changed from gold to red, and back to gold again. I blinked my eyes to clear away the mist. My knees felt weak and the girdle squeezed my waist, tighter and tighter.

The heavy beat of a drum joined the flute and the lyre, and together they began to weave a pattern of sensual music. A small group of women, dressed like Elana, began moving in a circle, swaying with the music of the drum and the flute. The women danced with veils, similar to the dance lewd women perform in cabarets.

"Dance with us, Kate," Elana said as she set the goblets aside. "Feel the beat of the drum. Dance to honor the Goddess of Snakes. Celebrate with us in our union with Mother Earth. Dance to the voice of the *oblous* and the drum."

Whether it was the wine, or the heat, or the tight girdle, I felt as buoyant as the bubbles in a glass of champagne. I still felt the solid, cold stone floor beneath my bare feet, but my arms floated as if they were lifted by an invisible wind, and I twirled, and I twirled. At first I danced Elana's dance, matching her step for step, movement for movement, but soon the music carried me to a place of freedom and abandon.

I began to dance my own dance, the undulations of the sea, and the graceful moving limbs of the flowering almond trees. Then the drumbeat led me to perform the dance of the Goddess, the dance of snakes, sinuous arms, gliding over the earth, hips, waist, chest, undulating hips, waist, chest and I moved with the serpentine grace of a standing snake.

After a time the music faded, and there was only the drum, like a heartbeat, the single beat of the drum.

I stood motionless, eyes closed, swaying ever so slightly.

"Let me help you to the throne, my lady," a gruff voice said in my ear.

I looked into a pair of fierce ebony eyes. The eyes belonged to Demetri. But it wasn't Demetri. This man had no mustache; this man's face was shaved clean; even the black hair had been scraped from his chest. His skin was silky smooth and stained a warm reddish brown. A heavy gold double ax swung from a chain around his neck.

"Demetri?" I asked softly.

The young man also wore Tyrian purple, the same as the Ansasa. His wrist cuffs were gold, his neck collar was gold, and his purple kilt was edged in gold. The heavy gold tassel dangling from the front of his Minoan kilt tapped his knees as he walked. He had pulled his long black hair into a braid that he wore pulled over his left ear and shoulder. He was a replica of an ancient Minoan male, and he seemed to be my attendant.

I tried to turn away. "The Oracle. I seek the Oracle."

"Sit here, child."

The old High Priestess stood up and pointed to the gilded throne. Demetri helped me climb the steps to the gold-covered, high-backed chair.

"No. I must find the Oracle."

"You have found the Oracle, my child."

"Where?" I searched the faces of the women crowding around me.

Demetri slowly backed away from me and stood attentively behind the chair.

"My lady," he said, bringing his arm to his chest in a salute. "*You* are the Oracle."

"No, NO! It can't be." I was overwhelmed by fear and confusion and I tried to stand but the Ansasa put a restraining hand on my arm.

Another tall, slim-waisted young man brought a low cushioned stool and placed it near my feet, and Elana came and sat in a squatting position at my side.

"It is true, Kate. You have been chosen to be the Oracle. Grandfather knew you were one of the chosen ones when you first came into the shop. It was a prophecy. The Old Mistress said that was why he sold you the beads. He knew they would bring you back to Kriti."

"But I am not Greek," I protested weakly and coughed, choking on the fumes from a burning bowl of incense and herbs that had been placed on a brazier next to my chair. The pungent vapors took my breath and stung my eyes.

"I must go. I don't want to do this."

"I swear to you, Kate. You will come to no harm."

The urge to resist surged inside me, but my arms and legs would not obey. Only my eyes were free to search. Frantically, I looked for an ally among the dark-eyed faces and I found a pair of gray eyes, a tall male with long plaited hair that was gray at the temples. His chest was also shaved, and his skin was stained nut brown. He had a falcon tattooed on his upper left arm and his eyes looked so familiar

"Deupree?"

I intended to shout, but the words came out as a whisper and the gray eyes were blocked from my line of sight.

Time passed unmeasured.

Questions were asked in Greek and Elana acted as my

interpreter. Without thinking, answers came effortlessly to my lips. Women passed one at a time, taking their place on the stool at my feet to ask their questions and to leave an offering of thanks.

For a time, my head seemed to clear, and I looked anxiously around the room, searching for an altar stone.

"Is this the place where the youth was tied," I asked, my eyes wild with terror.

"No, Kate," Elana whispered. "We have no altar stone. We do not make sacrifice in this place. We only give offerings of first fruits and flowers to Holy Mother Earth. Remember how it was, Kate. Remember how peace-loving it was in the old time."

"I don't want to remember."

More incense and herbs were added to the brazier.

"Breathe deeply, Kate, and the vision will change. Look into the future. Let the past go for now."

The women continued to come. More questions. More answers.

When there were no more seekers, Demetri untied the beads from around my neck and placed them in Elana's hands.

"Kate. Your beads. What is the true meaning held within the blue beads of lapis lazuli?"

"Two circles. Two strands from one. For parted lovers. One to the woman. One to the man."

"But there is only one strand of beads."

"What was lost was found and joined again."

"Were the lovers rejoined?"

"The sword and the crown became one. From where the Meltemi blows. North by west."

"What of the ring?"

"What was lost was found."

"What is the meaning of the ring?"

"What was lost was found."

"Enough," the Old Ansasa said. "No more. Demetri, carry her. She is too weak to walk. Go with Elana and see them safely home."

Demetri brought his arm to his chest in salute.

"May the peace of the Holy Mother go with you, child. You have done well, my daughter."

The old woman kissed me on both cheeks...cheeks that were wet with tears.

CHAPTER TWENTY-EIGHT

WHO OWNS THE BEADS?

City noises, horns, voices, the smell of cinnamon and strong coffee slowly entered my awareness. I was in a strange bed, in a strange room, and my mouth was so dry my lips were sticking together at the corners.

"Ohhhh... *Jeezus*." I sat up. The sheet fell away, and I looked down at my naked body.

"My pajamas. What's going on?"

"Good morning." The muffled words sounded cheerful coming from the other side of the closed bedroom door. "I have coffee," the musical voice sang. "Is it all right to come in?"

The voice sounded like Elana. Of course. Elana. And memory of the night before came rushing back to me, clear and in vivid detail.

"Coffee and sesame puffs with honey. I should be angry with you for last night, but this is an exceptional way to start the morning. My favorite breakfast and I'm hungry enough to eat a donkey." I sighed with pleasure.

"You do not feel ill?"

"No. I feel fine. Whatever you drugged me with last night seems to have disappeared. I don't know what you used, but I don't even feel hung-over. I've never tried smoking pot, or taking LSD, and if you had told me what you were going to do, I would most definitely have refused to participate in your ceremony. Was it the wine?"

"No." Elana looked down, ashamed that she had been

less than truthful. "The drug was in the water in the dressing room. It tastes a lot like *soumadha*. It is an ancient potion, similar to the juice from the poppy, but with no unpleasant side effects. The visions of the Oracle came from the burning incense and herbs in the brazier. The secret composition is similar to the natural vapors once used by the Prophetess at Delphi."

"Things are a little fuzzy, but I think I remember everything that happened. So many people acted like the answers I gave them had great meaning, although it seemed like gibberish to me."

"No, it was not gibberish. Many people were helped. Many truths were found."

"Thank you for asking about the beads and the ring. It's going to take some thought, but I feel the words must have meaning. 'The crown and the sword joined in the northwest.' You know it really was like the Delphic Oracle, cryptic messages and all."

"Do you remember the part when you talked of sacrifice?"

"The memory made me feel sad. I don't know if it was something that really happened to Ariadne, but I wrote that she innocently joined a celebration to the god Dionysos. The Maenads, a group of drunken priestesses, were going to tear a young boy to pieces on a wooden altar in a forest. Ariadne stopped them and nearly died from her wounds. When she participated in the sacrifice, thinking it would bring Theseus back to her, she broke her vows to do no harm. I felt her dishonor. I think it may be why she drove Theseus away."

"Then you are saying that Theseus did not desert Ariadne?"

"I think Ariadne may have deserted Theseus. But I can't prove it. Not yet."

"The Oracle seemed to be saying they were rejoined."

"I know: the sword and the crown in the northwest."

Demetri entered the room and said, "It is a great puzzlement, my lady."

I pulled the sheet further up under my chin. I still couldn't believe how young Demetri looked without his mustache. He was not much older than my Suzie.

"Modesty? You were not so modest last night."

"What do you want, Demetri?" Elana asked irritably.

"I came for my beads."

"I need to keep them a little while longer. But I *will* return them to their rightful owner…as well as the gold signet ring."

"You promised," he said with a weary sigh. "Do you women ever keep your word?"

"Oh my! What time is it? I promised to meet Tina, Jake, and Theo at nine this morning."

"It is eleven o'clock. Mr. Deupree came looking for you about an hour ago. I sent him away. You needed to sleep. He said they would be waiting for you near the fountain."

"Where are my clothes? I must go."

"What about my beads?" Demetri asked irritably.

"Before I leave Crete, even if I don't have all the answers, I swear that I will return the beads."

Demetri rolled his eyes in disgust. "Women!" He ground the word through clamped teeth and left the room.

Quick as I could, I dressed and ran out of Elana's apartment.

Theo's car was parked at the end of the lane, and the three treasure hunters looked as wilted as the flowers around the old lion fountain. They had been waiting for a very long time which made me think of Demetri. He was waiting too, for the beads, and it wasn't fair for me to keep them from him without any explanation.

"Sorry, but I need just a few minutes more. I have one last thing I must do."

I crossed the courtyard ringed with flowers. I tried not to disturb the cat dozing in the shade of a leggy geranium but when I knocked firmly on the door frame she raised her head, stretched languidly, and licked her paw. I couldn't resist peeking through the open door into the darkened room. It was sparsely furnished with a sturdy sofa and chair protected by crocheted doilies on the arms and backs. A faded family portrait of a stern looking man, an unsmiling woman, and one small boy hung over the fireplace.

The odor of garlic frying in olive oil drifted from inside the house, and after a moment, the Old Mistress came shuffling to see who had come to call.

"Welcome, child. Come in out of the heat. Sit here. This is a comfortable chair, more comfortable than this old straight-back chair that is so used to my old bones. I will bring you some cool water. And a sweet. We must drink coffee."

The old woman held up her hand for me to wait while she put in her hearing aid. It was interesting how this woman was not always what she seemed. Sometimes she gave the appearance of being old, toothless, and deaf, but during the ceremony, she was vivacious and full of energy. Now it seemed she could also speak English as well as her native Greek.

"I am truly sorry but I won't have time for coffee. I don't want to interrupt your work. You must be cooking. Something smells delicious."

"Oh, I do not cook. My son cooks. He stuffs the aubergines. I watch and tell him what to do. A man should know his place, don't you think?" She slapped her knee and cackled with glee.

"I have come to ask your advice about the blue beads. I promised to give them to Demetri, but I feel in my heart that I should keep them just a little while longer. You have been so kind and helpful. I wanted you to know that I will return them before I leave Crete."

The old woman's black eyes were filled with compassion. "I trust you," she said and patted my hand affectionately.

Trust. Struggling with my emotions, I could barely speak. Lately, trust was a word I rarely heard in connection with me. According to my husband, I wasn't capable of making a wise decision, or even crossing the street on my own.

"Return the beads to me when you are ready to leave Kriti, and I will give them to their rightful owner."

Before I could answer, Demetri stepped into the room. He looked naked without his beautiful black mustache.

"Have you finished the *aubergines?*" the old woman asked.

"No, Mama."

"Then go back to work." The old woman shooed him back into the kitchen with a wave of both hands.

"Demetri is your son?"

"He is a strong-willed boy. He thinks wisdom is something inherited. One day he will understand that true wisdom can only be earned through study and experience. Perhaps, one day the beads will return to him. But not today. Today the beads still belong to you."

"Thank you. Did Elana tell you about the ring that was hidden inside the lamp I found on Dhia?"

"Yes. May I see it?"

I laid the circle of gold in her pale hand and watched in silence while she examined it carefully. She, too, thought the one distinct mark was meant to be a sword.

"However…swords were never a part of our culture. The old ones did not celebrate war or bloody violence. We danced with bulls and enjoyed boxing matches and wrestling. Many men and women were proficient with the bow and the javelin; a very few were skilled with the sword. We honored the hunt, but the symbols of war were never part of our tradition. This ring does not look like any Minoan artifact I have ever seen."

"There must be some meaning to the symbol."

"Perhaps the words from the Oracle will guide you. Study them. The message they carry comes from within."

"I worry that the authorities will arrest me for having these artifacts. I assure you that I have absolutely no intention of keeping the ring or the lamp."

"Do not be concerned. If you are approached, tell them that you borrowed the ring and the lamp from me. My nephew heads the Antiquities Department in Athens; he would never challenge one of my colleagues."

After a few more pleasant words, and a kiss on both cheeks, we parted.

"Blessings of the Goddess, little one. Go in peace."

CHAPTER TWENTY-NINE

THE RING OF SWORDS

"Theo, please stop the car. I need to buy some flowers from the vendor."

"Why do you need flowers? They won't last ten minutes in this heat."

"I need an offering. The gods won't mind if they're a little wilted."

After we stowed the gear on board the *Crystina,* the day was nearly spent. Supper was sandwiches and beer eaten while the two men huddled over the chart table, going over the plans one more time to make sure there were no flaws. Tina excused herself, saying she wanted some time alone. I took my sad little bouquet up on deck, leaned against the bowsprit, and looked out at the broad expanse of the blue Cretan Sea.

When writing my novel, I had composed many prayers to the gods and goddesses, but for some reason, at that moment, words of adoration and supplication would not come.

The boat swayed gently in the swell. The motion conveyed softness, but the feeling was deceptive. I knew the treachery of Poseidon, the Greek God of the Sea. He was indifferent to the humans who rode the backs of his waves, and in a fit of temper, he would smash a hapless vessel, treating it as a worthless toy. There were many ancient rituals designed to woo the fickle God into guiding a poor sailor and granting safe passage home, but none of them felt right.

I threw the flowers one by one as far as I could out onto

the water. I spread my arms wide and prayed a silent prayer to the powers that be that I would be able to survive whatever tests were sent my way. Then I walked back to my special place before the mast, and sat and watched the sun spread nature's colors across the sky.

Red sky at night, sailor's delight. The old sailor's rhyme sang through my mind as streaks of vermilion, apricot, and gold spread across the horizon, fading after a time to lavender, then to a luminous blue.

The beauty of the sunset should have brought me a feeling of peace, but instead a heavy feeling of longing came over me. Like a rising tide, a dull ache filled my chest and swelled into my throat. I missed Dan. We loved to watch sunsets together, and he would have taken such pleasure in sailing Theo's boat. Never in all the years we'd been married had he been so intolerant, so obstinate, so unforgiving. I couldn't understand why he hated Crete so. He loved travel and sailing. When we first met, his dream was to own a boat like Theo's and cruise the world; but life happens. Reality sets in and dreams are nothing more than smoke on the wind.

ψ

Next morning, although the sky was clear, the *Crystina* was forced to stay in the harbor. Winds pushing forty knots whistled through the rigging, and the boats in the anchorage tugged and heaved on their moorings, quivering to run free.

"Since we're not going to Dhia, I want to go back into Heraklion. Could I borrow the car?" I asked.

Sour looks were exchanged, but no one answered my question.

"Well then, I guess I'll take the bus." I couldn't suppress a small sigh.

"That's not necessary," Jake said. "How long do you think you'll be?"

"I want to go to the Museum and look at the engravings on their seal rings. Do a little research. Perhaps someone there can help me decipher the markings on the crown."

"You won't let up, will you?" Jake said.

"Look. I don't need permission from any of you to do what I came to Crete to do."

Fortunately the *Crystina* was moored stern to the dock and it was easy to leave the boat. It would have been difficult to take the dinghy ashore in such high wind, but I was determined enough to swim if I had no other choice.

"Whoa there, partner. Don't go off in such a huff. I haven't had my daily ration of coffee. I could do with a little snooze in a *taverna*. I'll go with you and wait while *ya do whatever ya have tah do.*"

Jingling keys in hand, Jake led the way to the car. "How do you intend to explain where you got the ring?" he asked.

"I made a rubbing of the design last night. I'm going to say that my mother bought it in an antique shop back in the states...that I'm trying to check its authenticity."

The museum was in temporary quarters, awaiting the completion of a renovation project. Everyone was courteous, but when I finally found someone to look at the rubbing he wasn't from Crete, he wasn't even Greek. He was an American professor on sabbatical from the University of Michigan. He also displayed a definite lack of enthusiasm regarding my request for information.

"It would be much better to see the original, but this

central mark looks more like a sword than a cross. The arrangement of the gouges and holes seem to have no particular significance that I can see, at least none that I can identify. However, I don't think the marks are the result of crude workmanship: the decoration around the rim is far too uniform and very skillfully done. If this is a Minoan ring, it's the largest one I have ever seen. Where did you say it was found?"

"The seller told my mother that it was brought from Crete to America by a Greek immigrant, a story similar to the one about the ivory Snake Goddess in the Boston Museum of Art. There was a story, something about payment for a kind deed, something like that."

"Oh, one of those. The only thing I can suggest is that you go to the National Museum in Athens. Maybe they can help you. Swords are not my specialty. Sorry."

Jake was surprised to see me back so soon. I collapsed in a sullen heap in the chair opposite him, and wore a look of utter despair.

"How did it go?"

"I talked to some clod with no imagination: an American whose specialty is pottery chards. He didn't know diddly about rings. He did say he felt certain the mark was a sword and not a cross."

"Could I see the rubbing?"

"Sure. Why not? Maybe you can interpret its meaning."

Jake carefully unfolded the paper and smoothed it out flat. He turned it, and turned it again, looking at it from several angles.

"Oh, my God!" I covered my mouth with my hand.

"What now?"

"The rubbing! When you turn it like that, it reminds me of a compass rose."

"Did they even have compasses in the time of the ancient Minoans?"

"I don't think so. I just know that suddenly the drawing looks like a chart, a primitive map of some sort. Perhaps the gouges were deliberate, not just flaws in the gold."

"You don't know that. How can you know that?" It was Jake's turn to doubt my intuition.

"I need to take a look at Theo's charts. This feels right, Jake. I think I may be on to something."

"No! No more! Not until we finish with Dhia."

"I know. I *know*! I promised to go with you, didn't I?"

CHAPTER THIRTY

DEAD MAN'S CHEST

It was a good thing the wind returned to normal the next morning. Tempers on board the *Crystina* were whisper thin. All four of us were sick of waiting. Treasure and truth were fast changing from dangling carrots to anchors and chains.

Theo guided the *Crystina* away from the harbor into open water and then he asked me to take the wheel. Yesterday's wind had blown itself out, leaving not even the promise of a breeze. The water was flat as a slick blue plate. We had been motoring for almost an hour. Tina and Theo were below and Jake and I were alone on deck.

"Jake, were you at the women's ceremony the other night in the cave?"

"Who me? I hate caves almost as much as I hate boats."

He passed his hand across his chin, assessing the length of his beard. He scratched his chest through his tee shirt.

"How did you get Demetri to let you take part in the ceremony?"

"That man is a sadistic son of a bitch. I think he just wanted to see if I would shave my arms and chest. I wouldn't be surprised if it was his way of rebelling against the women who were giving him orders."

"It's a good thing you were not discovered. If you had ruined the ceremony for me, I would be on my way home right now instead of keeping my end of our bargain."

"Do you know what a rare privilege it was to be allowed

to attend their ceremony? That was one of the most mystical experiences I've had in years. Who would've thought there were secret societies on Crete that still practice the old religion? I must say you gave an outstanding performance as their Oracle."

"I didn't volunteer. If I had known what Elana intended to do, I would never have gone there in the first place."

"I didn't ask before, I didn't want to pry into your business, but did the words from the Oracle help you in your quest?"

"I'm not sure. I did look in the *Greek Cruising Guide*, but I couldn't find anything there either. Maybe I should go to Athens like the man at the museum suggested. They might be able to offer some insight on the design."

Jake didn't respond. Instead, he stretched out on one of the cockpit cushion, closed his eyes, and pretended to snore.

It was late, nearly eleven o'clock, when we reached Dhia and headed for our usual anchorage. The water was still mirror smooth.

"Why couldn't this haze be fog? We stick out like a cardboard cutout at a turkey shoot. We're entirely too visible." Grim-faced, Jake was rubbing his forearm again.

Trying to lighten Jake's mood I said, "If I knew the name of the goddess in charge of fog and haze, I would make an offering."

This time when we left the *Crystina*, Theo set two anchors, just in case we were delayed again. The unloading went surprisingly well. It took only three trips in the dinghy to take everything and everyone ashore. As captain, Theo was in charge.

"I wish we could leave the guns behind, but I don't think it would be wise. We'll each carry a rifle, and our own water, food, and ammunition in a backpack. That leaves the generator, the tool bag, supports for the hoist, and the gasoline can."

"I have the camera," Tina said.

Although Theo was our leader, I couldn't keep from offering my advice.

"If we sling the heavy stuff on the supports, we can use them as carrying poles on our shoulders. I think Tina and I can manage the tools and the gas can. You and Jake should be able to carry the generator. How much does it weigh? Forty-five pounds or so? Won't be easy, but I bet we could do it."

We did. And it wasn't easy.

Some accommodating goddess had granted Jake's wish for dense, foggy haze. A thick bank of spongy gray clouds had descended upon the island and blessed us with a fine drizzle of rain. The rocky terrain and loose gravel became even more hazardous with a slick coating of wet dust. The trek to the cliff above the cave took us twice as long as before.

The misty rain finally stopped, and the afternoon sun broke through. The air smelled steamy and wet, a fragrance I wanted to capture in a bottle and take home to uncork on a dry summer day.

We spent the afternoon cleaning the rusty anchor bolts, choosing just the right fittings, preparing the hoist, rigging the come-along: detail after boringly tedious detail. Finally, Theo climbed down and waited on the ledge as Jake carefully lowered the generator. They decided it would be prudent to open the chest inside the cave.

"Everything is in place. The question is, do we set to

work now opening the chest, or do we wait and start fresh in the morning?"

"Wait." I said the hateful word with a weary sigh. "Waiting is *not* one of my favorite things."

"I think Kate's right. I don't want to wait, either." Jake periodically gave his arm a shake.

Tina again preferred to stay on top, but in spite of my aversion to the *swastikas*, I wanted to be there when the chest was opened. My second trip down the sloping cliff to the ledge was much less scary. I would never have attempted it without the safety harness, but it was not much of a descent.

"Kate, would you hold the light? If we're lucky, once we drill the lock this thing should pop right open."

The cave magnified the noise of the generator, and combined with the burr of the drill it was turned into an ear-numbing megaphone. The lid didn't exactly pop open when Theo punctured the lock. It parted slowly, opening only an eighth of an inch.

Theo stopped the generator, which was a welcome relief. The buffeting noise had violated the prayerful aura that surrounded the chest.

All breathing stopped as three pairs of hands lifted the lid.

The impact was immediate and overwhelming, accompanied by moans and groans of pleasure.

"Gold bars. That must be platinum. Wonder what's in all those pouches? Hold out your hands, Kate."

Jake untied the cord around one of the stiff leather sacks and tipped the contents into my hands.

"Ohhhh...*Diamonds!*"

Thousands of sparkling stones, every size and shape, spilled from the pouch in a glistening stream.

Theo opened three more pouches filled with sapphires, rubies, and emeralds. All of the stones were cut and polished in every shape imaginable; a few were as large as a small bird's egg. Each one appeared to be unblemished and of the highest quality.

Beneath the quart-sized pouches were stacks of leather jewelers' cases, each one containing dozens of broaches, pendants, necklaces, and rings: exquisite pieces, rare and beautiful, that appeared never to have been worn. A platinum tiara, a sparkling confection set with a thousand diamonds, must surely have been created for a queen.

Tina called down, concerned that the generator had stopped so soon. Her voice was shrill with concern.

"Send up the tiara," I said with a giddy laugh. "Send it up. Hurry!"

Several items were put into an empty knapsack.

"I must take them to her. I must see her face." Theo's eyes were bright and eager with anticipation. He was so elated, I think he could have climbed back up the cliff to Tina without ever touching his hand to the ground.

Rubies, diamonds, and emeralds...oh my. Kneeling beside the chest filled with treasure, I looked across the wealth of a thousand lifetimes into Jake's shining eyes.

"Yeah, I know," he said sadly when he saw my teary eyes. "It would be great to have someone special to share the moment. But you know something? It may be true that money can't buy you love, but it sure as hell can buy just about everything else."

"I thought Tina was like my friend Letty, but she isn't."

"Tina is exceptional, and so is Theo. They know how to love without possessing. That takes a very special talent, one I never mastered."

I poured the diamonds back into their pouch and brushed at my cheeks.

Standing up, looking down at the treasure, I put my hands on my hips and said, "If your intention is to take this stuff back to the *Crystina* today, I think we'd better start hauling it up now." I was rubbing my arm, the mirror image of a worried Psychic Deupree. "Sooner is better than later, don't you think?"

The sun's rapid descent dampened our enthusiasm.

"We can't carry it all. We can take the jewels, and the platinum, maybe a few of the gold bars. We can come back another time, even another year. No need to be too greedy."

By the time everything we wanted to salvage was lifted to the top of the cliff, the moon was on the rise. All of the equipment and tools, except for the supports, had been moved back inside the cave, and signs of our activity were once again brushed from sight. Theo had the foresight to bring extra knapsacks, and by slinging them on the supports, we easily carried everything back to the boat.

There was very little conversation on our trek back across the island. We were carrying the means to change all of our lives and it was a sobering experience.

Earlier, I said I wanted no part in smuggling the guns out of Greece, but the rifles were insignificant compared to the contraband we were carrying. I couldn't keep from thinking about the person who had hidden the treasure. Who was he? Did he have a family? Did he kill the men who helped him hide it in the cave? Who was the rightful owner?

Questions…questions that generated even more questions. Could the treasure have been what drew me to Dhia? Were there ever any answers concerning Ariadne waiting here for me to find? I was no closer to learning the truth about the little Princess than before I came to Crete. And how would I explain sudden wealth to my family and friends? In some ways, I felt like we were robbing the dead.

CHAPTER THIRTY-ONE

BUMPS IN THE NIGHT

The walk back across the island was accomplished with no problems. The last run was made in the dinghy, and the treasure had been carried below. All that remained was to hide the jewels and platinum inside a dozen secret compartments built into the *Crystina*. Until now, they had never been used—Theo had the heart of a pirate, but the conscience of a priest.

"Dom Perignon, my friends. I would like to drink a toast to this spectacular occasion."

We raised our glasses. Theo said, "To Kate and her beads of lapis lazuli."

We took the time to open each leather case before putting it away. We admired rings, necklaces, bracelets, and broaches, each incredible creation more dazzling than the last. As we stowed the treasure, hiding it from spying eyes, we drank French wine, ate Greek pita bread slathered with American peanut butter, and Cretan honey.

"I'm exhausted," Tina said with a yawn.

Theo looked at each of us and smiled; we were four bleary-eyed explorers. "We could do with a short rest. It'll be dawn in a few hours. Good time to leave. We should be able to make an easy sail back to Heraklion. We can be home in time for lunch. Let's try and get some sleep."

ψ

Except for the occasional slap of a wave against the hull,

the night was quiet. For me, tired as I was, sleep would not come. Every muscle in my body ached, but the most painful ache of all was in my heart. I had never experienced such emptiness. It was as if the treasure had cut all ties to my family, separating me from the world I knew and loved.

I wasn't sure I wanted any part of the treasure. The money the jewels and platinum would bring would also bring change. How would it affect my family? Dan had worked all of his life to provide for the children and me; we had a comfortable lifestyle. How would he feel if I brought home a pot full of money? How would he react? If I no longer needed him as my provider, would he still love and protect me? Still more questions… questions with no answers.

As the boat rocked in the surf, the stars framed by the open hatch over my bunk moved back and forth across the opening. The moon flooded the small cabin with pale light.

Sleep still would not come. I stood on the bunk and hauled myself up through the hatch, out onto the deck. The cool wind felt like a chilly breeze on my sun-kissed skin. I needed a warm shirt and I remembered that I had left my sea bag in the cockpit. Feeling around for a sweatshirt, my hand bumped against the statue of the little Goddess of Snakes. Carrying the statue and my oversized shirt, I made my way to my favorite place before the mast. Wrapping up like a moth in a fuzzy cocoon, I hugged my knees to my chest, hoping to find comfort in the gentle rocking of the boat and the soft hum of the wind as it strummed the rigging.

Holding the statue of the Snake Goddess in both hands, I looked intently at the stern eyes and solemn face. I had never thought much about the significance of the snakes, except to respect their bite. Then in a single breath I had an epiphany;

234 ❋ DORIS KENNEY MARCOTTE

I knew the meaning of the snakes. They were the symbols of Power and Control. I closed my eyes and slowly wrapped the fingers of both hands around the body of the little goddess; I felt as if I were holding the snakes in my own hands. Their bodies were pure energy, raw muscle twisting and writhing to break free. When they succumbed at last in defeat, I felt their tails coil around my arms in a victor's embrace. I was in charge of my own destiny for the first time in my life. I had never sought power; I never wanted control for with control came responsibility. I never felt I was wise enough to rule. My role was helper, enabler, first mate, appreciative audience applauding all the actors on the stage.

Amazed by the good solid feel of the snakes in my hands, I felt a healing sense of peace.

Then, in an instant, my reverie was destroyed. Every muscle in my body stiffened with alarm. Narrowing my eyes, straining to see through the dark, I saw movement on shore. Figures were walking across the crest of the hill. Black silhouetted men were visible against the silver-blue of the pre-dawn sky and they were carrying a Zodiac on their shoulders. The only reason for such a portage would be to board the *Crystina*. We were going to be hijacked. They intended to take us by surprise.

Gripped with terror, I slithered back through the hatch and whispered hoarsely, "*Theo! Jake! Tina! Wake up!* We have to leave, *now!*"

The God of Pandemonium ruled the day.

"Anchors! Two bloody anchors out and one of the rodes is chain. When we pull that stuff in, it's so noisy they'll know we're on the move."

I didn't wait for Theo to formulate a plan. I assumed command. "Don't bring it in. Leave it. Open the shackle and dump the chain. The four of us can pull the boat forward on the other anchor line without using the engine. Once we're on top of the hook, we'll fire up the engines, pull it loose from the bottom, and be under way before they know what happened. If the anchor hangs up, we'll cut it free."

"Good plan. Make it happen," Theo said.

The wind was still light, but it was no easy job pulling the *Crystina* forward. All the time, we could see those dark figures moving on shore.

"Get the rifles, Tina, just in case."

"I don't want to shoot anybody," I said, grunting and straining.

"Well, you may not have a choice. And bring the binoculars. Maybe we can see something, even in the dark."

"There's another way," I whispered between grunts.

"What way?"

"Molotov cocktails. I can't throw worth a hoot, but if they come close enough, it could stop them without firing a shot. They might get a little singed, but there's plenty of water to keep them from being burned too badly. And it should scuttle their Zodiac."

"You know how to make a Molotov cocktail?"

"Yes, and don't ask me why. I'll tell you later. Can you continue without Tina and me? I'll need her help."

"Go!"

I prayed that I could find what I needed in the galley.

"Get me some tampons and bring the gauze from the first-aid kit. No lights; a flashlight if you must, but cup your hand over the end. They can't know we're onto them until we're ready."

Tina was glued to the floor.

"Tina? *Move!*"

"No! We should call for help. Call the harbor police. Call a MAYDAY."

"It's too late."

Tina wasn't listening. She reached for the switch just as I covered it with my hand.

"No, Tina. It's too late. Get hold of yourself. I need your help. Get me what I asked…now."

While Tina found gauze and tampons, I rummaged through the galley, looking for thin-walled glass bottles. I found two that suited my purpose.

"Get me a can of alcohol; the stuff you use in the stove."

It took only minutes to assemble the bombs once the components were at hand.

"I'm trying to remember the instructions in the pamphlet. I only read it once. Okay. Wet the gauze and let it hang out like a wick and pray. Pray harder than you've ever prayed in your life because I've never actually made one of these things. I never had the guts to see if it really works."

"I'm so afraid," Tina whispered in a trembling voice.

"Me, too. My hands don't normally shake this way." I closed my eyes and tried to picture the instructions for making the firebombs, hoping that I had remembered all the details.

"Matches? We're ready. Let's go."

Jake and Theo were crouched in the cockpit waiting. "We cleated the rode. We're on top of the hook. If we can't pull it free with the engine, we'll cut it loose."

I held the two firebombs in my arms like precious sleeping babes.

"They're coming," Tina said. She was looking toward

shore with the binoculars. "I can see two assault rifles against the skyline. *Oh, dear God.* They're coming!"

"Well, my ladies. Jake and I will go forward and wait until they're within throwing range. Kate, as soon as you see us light the wicks, start the engine. Both of you stay down inside the cockpit; you will most likely draw their gunfire. Kate, when you see the flames, ease the throttle forward and we will pull in the anchor line as we move. I think there will be enough light for you to see my hand signals. When I drop my arm to my side, put her in reverse. We'll have shipped the anchor, or cut it loose."

Prayer was the order of the day, and no deity's name was taken in vain. I prayed to Jehovah, Jesus and Mary, Poseidon and Aphrodite, that the firebombs would do their work. The wicks flared. I turned the key and the engine caught first try. I heard a single gunshot as I eased the throttle forward.

There was a bright explosion of light and I heard Jake shout, "Gotcha, you son of a bitch." There were more shouts and loud male voices, screaming and swearing in Greek.

I eased the control forward and felt the ship stall, the anchor was reluctant to release its hold on the good earth. I heard Dan's voice inside my head, coaching me, saying, *Not yet, wait for the signal, stay cool, you can do it.* Slowly, the boat inched forward, and when Theo dropped his arm, I put the engine in reverse and carefully backed away from the burning Zodiac. Thankfully, the men were able to retrieve the anchor. We had that precious barbed hook that would secure our safe anchorage at the end of our voyage.

When we came out from around the point, we saw the *Sheitan* wallowing in the surf; it was taking a beating in the surge that rolled in from the open sea.

"It won't be easy for them to get back on board. If they do manage to overtake us, we should be close enough to Heraklion to call the authorities for help."

"Take her out, Kate," Theo yelled. "Open her up all the way."

Remembering the puff of smoke when the *Sheitan's* helmsman blew their engine, I slowly eased forward on the throttle until our speed reached seven knots.

Looking back over his shoulder Theo said, "I want to raise the sails. This is a reaching wind and we might get her up to eight knots, maybe nine, with a little help from the sails. We're not out of the briar patch yet, folks, depending on how good those villains can swim. I want to put as much distance as I can between them and us."

"We can't call for help with the treasure on board."

Jake looked at me as if I had lost my mind. "What treasure?" he asked. "Who said anything about treasure? We went to Dhia to do a little goat hunting and were attacked by hijackers. We even have a bullet hole in the hatch to prove it."

From her seat in the far corner of the cockpit, Tina said, "Speaking of bullet holes. Could someone wrap something around my arm? I'm afraid, my love, that I'm dripping blood on your precious boat."

Excitement turned to alarm. Theo took Tina below, treated her wound the best he could, gave her a pain pill, and then they both returned to the cockpit.

Theo was filled with concern. "It doesn't look like a bullet hole. You must have been cut by a piece of splintered wood. It's an ugly gash. I'm afraid you will have a scar."

"A small reminder of our adventure. I can't bear to think

what would have happened if Kate had not gone out on deck. We could all be dead, right now." Tina shuddered and Theo held her close.

Standing alone at the wheel, I was shaking with chills. The danger was over, and now I could fall apart. Theo moved me aside and took over the wheel. "I'm relieving you of duty, my brave friend. Go below and get some rest."

"I can't do that. You might need me."

"Sorry, partner," Jake said. "You've done your share and more. Get some sleep if you can. You've done enough soldiering for one day."

"Promise to call me, if you need me."

The trip back to Heraklion took less than two hours. If we had spent another fifteen minutes in open water, the wind would have become a problem once again. As it was, we easily motored into the basin behind the breakwater and as we tied the *Crystina* to the mole, the wind once again began to sing in the rigging.

While Jake and I finished tying up the boat, Theo hurried to the Port Authority office, taking the *Crystina's Transit Log* with him. He wanted to clear the boat immediately so it could leave Greek waters as soon as possible. He would send her home to Italy using the professional crew, just as he had every year for the past three years. Nothing different, nothing changed.

To look at the boat, one would never guess that she was hiding millions of dollars in platinum and jewels somewhere in her hull. Nor would anyone guess that she had been involved in an attempted hijacking. Even the stray bullet that dug its way into the hatch cover was barely noticeable.

CHAPTER THIRTY-TWO

THE MAN IN OFF-WHITE

Theo returned from the Port Authority office saying the ship's papers were in order. The *Crystina* was cleared to leave.

Jake once again sat on the edge of the concrete mole dangling his legs over the water.

That night we spent on that ledge on Dhia, I had asked Jake what he would do if we found something really valuable in the chest; he said he always wanted to own a farm. He mentioned a failed marriage as if it were of no consequence, since there were no children. Back in Cincinnati, he told me he inherited the house in Mt. Adams from his great-grand-father, but he had never talked about any other immediate family: no father, mother, brother, or sister. We had spent a lot of time together, but he was still a stranger.

The *Crystina* quivered, eager to cast off her moorings and run with the wind.

Inside, I felt as quivery as Theo's beautiful yacht, and I wondered what it would feel like to run free. The problem was…I didn't want to run free. I liked my life. I just didn't want to be taken for granted; I wanted respect and a modicum of freedom. Somehow I had to find a way to keep the old Kate and embrace something new. Remembering my last conversation with Dan at the hotel, reaching such a goal seemed as unlikely as finding the source of the wind.

Taking a small notebook and pencil from my vest pocket, I wrote down words and thoughts and feelings poured from me, flooding onto half a dozen pages. I closed the book and held it, white-knuckled, in both hands, and pressed it hard against my forehead.

"Holy Mother, if you're out there, please help me. Please, help me find some kind of peace."

ψ

After Theo returned to the boat, the men carried our personal gear to the rental car Jake had left at the marina.

Tina sat with her eyes closed; some of the color had returned to her cheeks.

"Does it hurt?"

"Yes," she said with a grimace. "I'll need to see a doctor. It'll have to be stitched, but the pain pill helped a lot."

"Are we ready to go?" Theo asked. His tone was cordial, but his words were clipped, and he kept looking anxiously at Tina. There was no mention of treasure, and I had the feeling that if I said the word again, all three of them would look at me in amazement and say, "What treasure?"

I still couldn't shake the feeling that what we were doing was wrong. The jewels were stolen property, and when we claimed them as our own, we were hung with the labels of thief and smuggler. If we were caught, the consequences were terrifying.

However, when all the ethical sorting was done, it came down to one question. Should I deprive my family of the security the money from the treasure would bring? What was it Jake said? *Money can't buy love, but it can buy just about everything else.* One day soon I would be a grandmother. I had a grandchild to consider. Grandmother! I had been so caught up in the hunt for treasure the news had barely sunk in...*I* was going to be a grandmother.

But was living a good life only about possessions? Oh, how I wished I could talk to Dan, the old Dan, the Dan I had fallen in love with so many years ago. This was the kind of ethical puzzle we used to discuss for hours on end. Before we were married we talked about everything. Hopes and dreams poured like a river from both of us, but once we were married everything changed. The river very quickly became a little stream, then it became an occasional drip, and for the last few years the stream was nothing but a dry bed filled with rocks and weeds.

Theo helped Tina ashore and walked her to the car.

Jake had waited for me. I was the last to leave the boat and I felt a little light-headed, suddenly apprehensive. I walked on wobbly land-legs along the dock toward the concrete walkway leading up to the car. That's when I saw a man with a scruffy beard, wearing dark glasses and a dingy white suit leaning against the end of the retaining wall. He looked like he was waiting for us.

"Not again," I groaned and covered my eyes. "Are we never going to be free of the *Sheitan*? I don't think I have the strength to endure another confrontation."

Jake put his hand on my arm, held me back, and stepped in front of me. "Don't you worry…I'll take care of this guy."

The man in off-white was about the same size and build as Jake. He walked toward us and stopped barely an arm's length away, removed his sunglasses, and said, "I guess you're Deupree. If you don't mind, I would like to speak to my wife…alone."

My knees nearly buckled. I hadn't recognized my own husband. But no wonder. He looked like an indigent, a vagabond, a down and out bum.

"What happened to you?" I asked with concern.

"I've been waiting here on the dock for days," he said softly. His chin quivered and his red eyes were rimmed with tears.

"I thought you went to Egypt."

"I couldn't go without you. I wanted you to come with me. By the time I got everything straightened out and returned to the hotel, you were gone. No one knew where. Just that you were with Deupree. I came here to see if I could find the sailboat: the one you talked about over the phone. I asked some guys in a white yacht with a US registry if they knew anything about you. They said the boat you were on was called the *Crystina* and it hadn't been seen in the harbor for two days."

"That must have been the *Sheitan*."

"That's right, the *Sheitan*. The Port Authority said the *Crystina* had not cleared customs, so I've been waiting, afraid to go back to the hotel for fear I would miss you."

"I'm surprised you cared. You told me in the beginning, if I came to Crete to not bother coming home."

"For God's sake, Katie. You didn't have to take me literally. You have never, ever pushed back...not until now. You should have known that I didn't mean it. I didn't want you to go. I felt you were going off in the wrong direction, and I didn't know what else to say. I was trying to protect you. That's my job. I just want you to come home. Damn it, Kate!"

He put his hand around the back of my neck and pulled me to him. He hugged me, crushing me against his chest until it hurt. And I hugged him back. He was my home, but for

244 * DORIS KENNEY MARCOTTE

the first time in my life I kept something in reserve. I wasn't ready to fall back into the old *everything's okay* routine. Not this time. Not today.

"I'm still not ready to go home." I said the words and waited for the explosion. He didn't respond immediately. He just sniffed his nose and hugged me some more. When he spoke, his words were muffled against my hair. "Whenever you're ready, we'll go home, together."

ψ

There were no recriminations, no accusations, but, as they say, actions sometimes speak louder than words. When I introduced Dan to Theo and Tina, he shook Theo's hand but, without being too obvious, he didn't shake hands with Jake. Once the jealousy bug has bitten, it's difficult to re-cover from the bite.

When we were back at the hotel, Dan couldn't have been more considerate. He knew I was exhausted and instead of going out to eat he ordered room service, something he had never done before, not for me, not for us. He also asked interested questions about the search. It was painful not telling him about the treasure, but I wouldn't break the promise I had made to my fellow seekers.

After I finished packing, I sat on the side of the bed holding the little stone lamp and the gold ring in my hands.

"It's just not right," I said. "The lamp and the ring belong in the museum although when I went there with the rubbing of the ring they weren't at all interested. They said it was not like any Minoan seal ring they'd ever seen. Evidently they turn down hundreds of donations from people who think their reproductions are the real thing. It was as if they were saying they thought the ring was a fake."

"Then why bother?"

"Maybe you're right. Anyway, swords were never a big part of the Minoan culture."

"Well then, maybe it's not Minoan."

"Not...Minoan." I echoed the words and a rush of insight brought me to my feet. "You're a genius. That's what everyone's been telling me, but it didn't register until now. What's wrong with me? I should have known!"

Within minutes, the guidebooks and museum catalogs were pulled from the luggage and spread out all over the bed.

"I know I brought it. Damn! Why can't I put my hand on something when I really need it?"

"What are you looking for?"

"I found it: The National Museum of Athens' guidebook. I've been looking only at the Minoan collections in all the museums. I should never have had such a narrow focus. If it's not Minoan, then it must be Mycenaean."

"Couldn't you do this on the plane?"

"Yes, I suppose I could, but it won't be necessary. It's here. I have what I came to Crete to find. I had the answer all along. I can't believe it. I found the truth. I know what happened to Ariadne."

Slowly, I untied my strand of bright blue beads and held them in my hand for the last time.

"Now, all that's left is to leave the lamp, the ring, and my beads with the old Ansasa. She will return the beads to their rightful owner, and give the lamp and the ring to the Department of Antiquities."

CHAPTER THIRTY-THREE

BEST FRIENDS FOREVER

Two fat yellow envelopes lay on the passenger seat of my new lapis blue BMW. Following my usual routine, I stopped at Letty's for a quick cup of coffee. I was changing many things in my life, but some things should always remain the same.

"Your coffee tastes different." I took another sip. "What happened to *Designer Coffee of the Month?*"

"Pete likes plain and ordinary and I'm trying to be more sensitive."

"That's good, although I'm going to miss your double mocha latte—not that I'm complaining. You still make the best coffee in town and as always I need coffee. It's been a difficult week."

"Are you still trying to replace the furniture you gave Suzie and Jim?"

"Yes. I didn't realize it would be so difficult, or so expensive. I may have to visit the resale shops to find some decent replacements that don't cost a bucket of money."

"What does Dan say you should do?"

"He said he trusts my judgment to do whatever is best."

"It's about time he appreciated your ability to make wise decisions. You've taken care of him like he's a prince ever since you got married. Has he said anything more about your trip to Crete?"

"Just that he was sorry he wasn't there to help me search. He said he didn't realize how serious I was about finishing my novel until after I had actually left home. It felt good when he complimented me on my determination. You know, the best thing about my quest isn't so much that I found the answers I needed about Ariadne and Theseus, it's that we're actually talking like we used to. It's so satisfying. He's treating me like a companion instead of an appendage."

"I remember when we were roommates in college, you two used to keep me up half the night talking. I had to throw him out so I could get some sleep."

"The conversation is great. He's also deferring to me a lot more and it feels strange. I have never wanted to be captain of our marital ship of state; it's a huge responsibility. I like being first mate. I love being a housewife, but I honestly don't think I could go back to the way it was before my trip to Crete. Independence is addictive but co-independence is doubly so."

"What's in the envelope?"

"The last chapter of the Ariadne story. You've read all the rest."

"Does it have a happy ending? With all the self-examination I've been doing lately, I'm not much into tragedy."

"I think it's a happy ending. It ties up all the loose ends. Speaking of loose ends, how are you and Pete doing with marriage counseling?"

"You know, you've turned into a bit of a smart ass. Pete and I are into role-playing. We are rewriting our scripts, and if it were not so God-awful painful it would be a lot of fun. Remember when you asked me if I missed my old job? I realize that after a few months of retirement, I was bored. Pilates and 10K's are great, but I was using them to burn time. I'm thinking about taking a job as consultant for a local company that produces a magazine for homeowners. It won't be as intense as before, just part-time, but it will let me keep my marketing and creative skills up to speed. And did I tell you, I've taken up gardening. Pete has agreed to take care of my weed-control problem."

"You canceled your WanderWeed contract?"

"They were very accommodating. Pete's doing an amazing job with the yard…much better than the WanderWeed guy, if you know what I mean."

"Whatever you two are doing, I hope you keep it up. In case you haven't noticed, Pete has a perpetual smile on his face."

"The same can be said about your Dan. Although the biggest change I can see is in you. Even the way you walk has changed. If I didn't know you so well, I would think a different person came back from Crete. You seem so confident, so much more self-assured."

"I guess that's what happens when you follow your bliss. Oh, great! Look at the time. I only stopped for a minute. I have an important lunch date that I don't want to miss."

"Anyone I know?"

"Yesterday, Jake Deupree left a message on my answering machine. He didn't leave a number; he just told me to meet him at noon at the Iron Horse Inn. Arrogant as ever, he just assumes I'll be there. And if you say, *Does Dan know?* I swear I'll take a swing at you."

"I won't say it, but only if you promise to tell me everything that happens."

"If I don't stop by on my way home, I'll call you later with all the juicy details."

CHAPTER THIRTY-FOUR

JAKE DEUPREE

For the past six months, I had resisted thinking about Jake because whenever I thought about Jake I thought about treasure, and that was an exercise in speculation that was definitely not productive. Everything that happened on Dhia and Crete was so extraordinary, it was as if it happened to someone else; it felt more like a dream than reality. It was still difficult to believe that a real-life adventure had actually happened to me.

I hadn't told anyone about the treasure chest filled with gold and platinum and jewels, not even Dan. Even if I had, I doubt that he would have believed me. The whole experience was beyond incredible; it was fantasy and myth and *I* could barely believe it actually happened.

But why did Deupree want to meet? I tried to stop going over a list of *maybe this* or *maybe that*, but the biggest maybe of all was *maybe it's about the treasure*.

I hadn't heard from any of my fellow seekers since I left them on Crete. When I helped stow the treasure in the *Crystina's* secret compartments, I released ownership of the cache to Jake and Tina and Theo. I still had mixed feelings about the ethics of removing the treasure from the island. Theo helped a little when he said it was the same as finding a pirates' chest filled with gold and jewels: it was no different than recovering sunken treasure from a Spanish galleon. However, the most serious conundrum of all was that I didn't know how Dan would react to a sudden influx of wealth coming from me; although after he saw the *Crystina* he did say that someday he would like to own a sailing yacht just like it. I told him that miracles can happen. But would he allow me to be his benefactress without feeling diminished, or would his masculine ego get in the way?

But why would Jake want to see me if it wasn't about the treasure? I hated suspense. It's the most insidious kind of waiting. Deliberately casting a spell of mystery, the message Jake left on my recorder hadn't given me a clue.

This time, unlike our first meeting, I dressed with care. My blue beads would have looked nice with my new jade green leather jacket, but the beads were back in Crete where they belonged; I still missed them. Although I had a box full of jewelry, nothing else felt quite the same.

Ψ

The Iron Horse Inn had been serving travelers for well over a hundred years. I found Jake sitting on a stool at the bar, joking and laughing with the bartender, female of course, and I smiled. Some things never change.

"What can I say?" he responded with a silly grin and a helpless shrug of his shoulders.

We looked like a pair of his and her bookends, each of us carrying a yellow manila envelope in our hands.

Lunch was served and the envelopes remained unopened, one on each of the two empty chairs at our table. Jake ordered a bottle of champagne...*interesting*...it seemed he had something he wanted to celebrate. He leaned against the arm of the chair and for the first time since we met, he seemed completely relaxed.

"You go first," he said softly.

I smiled a nervous smile and lightly rested my elbows on the table.

"Well, it's nothing much." I picked up my yellow envelope and gave it to him. "Except for the imminent arrival of my first grandchild, this has been one of the most important things in my life. I thought you might like to read the true ending to the myth of Ariadne and Theseus. This was the reason for my quest. I've added a few characters in order to turn the myth into a novel, but I think it will make sense when you read it. It's just a memento of our adventure."

"It'll be a collector's item when you become a famous author."

"Well, that's still very much in doubt."

"You didn't stay long in Heraklion after your husband came on the scene. Does that mean you found what you were looking for on Dhia?"

"In a roundabout way, I did, although it may never stand the hard reality of an archeologist's pick and brush. At least I appeased my writer's curiosity."

"Was the ring part of the answer?"

"Yes, it focused my attention on swords. It was probably just a coincidence, but who knows. Elana once said that when *the Old Ones* take you by the hand, mysterious things happen. The ring helped me find the gold-handled sword that once belonged to Theseus. I recognized it the moment I saw it, and I know in my heart that it belonged to him."

"That's quite a discovery. Where did you find it? Did you turn it over to the museum?"

"It was already in the Athens National Museum. I believe the sword given to Theseus by his father, King Aegeus, was found in a tomb on Skopelos Island near a bay said to be named after Theseus and Ariadne's son, Staphylos. Since dead women can't have babies, I believe Theseus married Ariadne just as he promised, and after he died his sword was passed to his eldest son. For me, the mystery is solved."

"But why would the storytellers say Theseus abandoned Ariadne on Dia Island? Why would they say she died?"

"You once said I was writing the world's oldest soap opera, and I think that's very close to the truth. I believe Ariadne faked her own death to throw her mother, Minos Pasiphae, off the scent. The old queen mother went crazy with grief after Ariadne helped Theseus kill her half-brother Minotaur. If Pasiphae had found Ariadne, she would have either killed her, or dragged her back to Crete to be punished for betraying her people."

"That makes sense. But why didn't Theseus take Ariadne home to Athens?"

"How could he? Ariadne was the sister of the monster who killed innocent Athenian children; she was their enemy. I believe Ariadne found sanctuary on Skopelos, a small island that's far from both Crete and Athens. It's possible that, for a time, she fooled Theseus into thinking she was dead. Years later, when he discovered the truth, I think he staged his own death and lived the rest of his life in peace with Ariadne. I believe I have proved that the dishonorable charge of abandonment should be removed from Theseus' good name."

Now, it was Jake's turn. He opened his envelope with a flourish and handed me a stack of papers.

"I must give Tina credit; she did most of the work. There are a few places where you need to sign. You'll read in the documents that Theo has acted as your agent, as well as mine. We decided that the best and safest way to transfer the funds is in an upfront deal, paying all taxes, and filing all the necessary papers to establish the two of us as Theo's trading partners."

The sheaf of paperwork was nearly half an inch thick. On top of the stack, Jake slapped a small, black leather checkbook.

"Open it."

With a stomach full of flutters, I slowly raised the cover. The checks were imprinted with a Barclay Bank logo, my name, and my address. The opening balance was $1,500,000.

"That's the first deposit. It may be the smallest. Theo and Tina refuse to accept a four-way split, they're sharing one-third of the proceeds. Some of the pieces of jewelry are so rare they will have to be sold at auction, only one piece at a time, to allay any suspicions. Later, when Theo and I liberate the gold bars and the guns, those proceeds will be added to the shares. I've already told Theo, I will retrieve the rest of the stuff we left in the cave only when the wind is perfect. I want nothing more to do with Meltemis or *mal de mere*."

Words are a pitiful way to communicate. How can sounds adequately express the way a person feels? I could not speak.

"You know, partner, you made one hell of an impression on Theo and Tina. From the way they talk, they both think you're a *Water Walker*. One last piece of information. Now I don't want you to think I've gone soft, but I located a benevolent fund for the children of Crete, and before we divided the cash we gave ten percent of the money to the kids."

I cried. And I laughed. Jake offered me a clean handkerchief, but I thought it was too beautiful to use so I dug a tissue out of my purse.

Jake smiled. His eyes looked gentle and warm as he set a small blue velvet box and a brown suede pouch in front of me on the table.

"What's this?"

He shrugged and made a silly "I don't know" face.

Then laughing softly he said, "The box is from Tina with her love. She says I should tell you that yours is a blue badge of courage, and she made herself a purple heart because she was wounded in action. She insists that they are both Medals of Honor earned in the line of duty."

I opened the box. It held a small broach studded with flashing blue sapphires and a crust of tiny emeralds and diamonds that created an intricate design on the wings of a gold butterfly.

"I think it might fly away if I set it on my hand. It's so beautiful, it's amazing."

I turned the glistening bauble back and forth to admire the sparkling display, laughing as I wiped away the tears.

"The pouch is from a very old friend."

I carefully unknotted the string, poured the contents into my hand, and groaned with pleasure. My hand was filled with beads, blue beads of lapis lazuli, but my smile quickly changed to a frown. The beads were still strung on the thin leather thong, but half of the stones were missing. I looked at Jake quizzically.

"The beads have a story," he said. "Before I left Crete, I went back to the antique shop to say good-bye to Elana; she's a very good-looking widow lady, don't cha know. She was planning to write to you, but decided to use me as a messenger instead. She said that you had asked the old High

Priestess, the Ansasa, to return the blue beads to their rightful owner. Well, it seems the old lady decided the beads really
belong to you, but she believes that they also belong to someone else."

"I don't understand."

Jake pulled a strand of blue beads from his coat pocket. It
was the other half of the blue beads of lapis lazuli. They had
been turned into worry beads that were fastened with a tassel
made of fine gold chain.

"Like you, I didn't understand. So...I went to see the old
lady and we had a long conversation. It seems that when she
wears her false teeth she becomes psychic. Now, isn't that
the wildest thing you ever heard? She thinks it has something to do with a bony ridge inside the roof of her mouth.
Anyway, she agreed to plug in her teeth and let me ask her
some questions."

"You believed her?"

"You don't have to believe her. Just listen. The old lady
goes into a light trance and tells me a bunch of stuff about reincarnation: how groups of people are reincarnated together.
Now, I'm used to all kinds of weirdoes claiming to be clairvoyant, so I decided to check her out. I asked her about some
people I know well, and her responses were so accurate it
was chilling. You might be interested to know that she thinks
you and Theo were once adventuring fools. Seems you were
inseparable, wild, reckless rogues, and a few stories in Greek
history and mythology are devoted to your escapades."

"Did you ask her about Tina and Elana? What about my
husband? What about you?"

"She said Tina was Ariadne's mother, the infamous
Pasiphae, the woman who didn't know how to love. Elana

was Ariadne's maid, and she believes your husband was Ariadne's brother, Minotaur, the adversary of Theseus, the brother that Ariadne betrayed."

"Maybe that explains why Dan hates Crete. Maybe it's a latent memory of a painful past."

"Who knows? However, the biggest revelation came when the old girl said that you and I are the reincarnations of Theseus and Ariadne."

"Really! Actually, I'm not surprised. I had already reached the same conclusion."

"But here's the kicker. She said *you* were the great hero, Theseus. *I* was Princess Ariadne."

Jake laughed and it rolled up from his heart and filled his eyes with a look I had seen a thousand times before. He laughed so hard it was now his turn to wipe the tears from his eyes.

"You know this role reversal is for the birds," he said. "Next time we do this, let's try to get it turned right side around."

He filled our glasses with champagne.

"How about drinking a toast to our past lives, partner."

I thought for a moment.

Then I raised my glass.

"To other times," I said. "To other companions. To past loves and present loves. And to the future. To that some-place in time where anything and everything is possible."

"*Panta yia*…may you always be happy."

"*Epissis*…same to you…my old, old friend."

LaVergne, TN USA
25 January 2011
213906LV00003B/78/P